CTHULHU BLUES

A SPECTRA Files Novel

By
Douglas Wynne

JournalStone

JOURNALSTONE
YOUR LINK TO ARTISTIC TALENT

This is a work of fiction. All of the characters, names, incidents,
organizations, and dialogue in this novel are either the products of the
author's imagination or are used fictitiously.

JournalStone books may be ordered through booksellers or by contacting:

JournalStone

www.journalstone.com

The views expressed in this work are solely those of the authors and do not
necessarily reflect the views of the publisher, and the publisher hereby
disclaims any responsibility for them.

ISBN: 978-1-945373-91-6   (sc)
ISBN: 978-1-945373-92-3   (ebook)

JournalStone rev. date: September 15, 2017

Library of Congress Control Number: 2017948073

Printed in the United States of America

Cover Art & Design: Chuck Killorin
Images: Cover montage contains a derivative of "Octopus vulgaris 02.JPG"
by H. Zell. CC BY-SA 3.0,
http://commons.wikimedia.org/wiki/File:Octopus_vulgaris_02.JPG

Edited by: Vincenzo Bilof

For Jill Sweeney-Bosa

Cthulhu Blues

"The wonders of the music of the future will be of a higher & wider scale and will introduce many sounds that the human ear is now incapable of hearing. Among these new sounds will be the glorious music of angelic chorales. As men hear these they will cease to consider Angels as figments of their imagination."

–Wolfgang Amadeus Mozart

"I trembled at Thy coming, O my God, for Thy messenger was more terrible than the Death-star. On the threshold stood the fulminant figure of Evil, the Horror of emptiness, with his ghastly eyes like poisonous wells. He stood, and the chamber was corrupt; the air stank. He was an old and gnarled fish more hideous than the shells of Abaddon. He enveloped me with his demon tentacles; yea, the eight fears took hold upon me."

–Aleister Crowley, *Liber Cordis Cincti Serpente*

Chapter 1

On the night of the storm, Becca Philips sang in her sleep. Little more than a whisper at first, the song was not detectable by the microphone. Neither was it discernible to the technician from the background noise of air circulating through the vent above the bed, sleet lashing at the windows, or wind lifting the creaking gutters. The words, murmured in a dead language, gained no clarity when they rose above the din of environmental noise to tickle the green lights on the recording software at the monitoring desk where Maria Reid sat watching Becca's vitals at 3:33 A.M.

The cold remains of a coffee in a paper cup at her elbow, Nurse Reid sat alert and attentive at what she had come to think of as the Witching Hour after twelve days of monitoring Becca Philips. The woman's worst recurring nightmares happened like clockwork at 3:33 each morning, or night—or whatever you called the liminal realm in which Maria's shift occurred.

Most nights, the audio recording picked up no more than agitated breathing, and maybe a repeated word or short phrase. But this—a mournful melody bordering on a chant, sung in the guttural syllables of an alien tongue—was something new. Maria felt a tingle run down her spine, like a grain of sleet melting under her smock. She rolled her chair closer to the desk and absently touched the gold cross in the hollow of her throat. She glanced at the monitor for the video camera she'd set up in the corner of the bedroom when Becca had insisted that they hang a curtain over the one-way mirror.

Becca Philips had a fear of mirrors. She claimed it was a recently acquired anxiety, which Maria found odd. Most quirky phobias were holdovers from a childhood or adolescent trauma. The nurse technicians had joked in private that Becca Philips must be a vampire. Janeth, who worked the two nights each week that Maria had off, had pointed out that vampires were nocturnal, but Becca only woke between 3 and 4 A.M. each night, sweating from her clockwork nightmare, even if she did sleep a fair amount in the daytime. And it wasn't like the subject had requested the windows be blacked out—just the mirror. Janeth read too many vampire books to roll with a joke.

All jest aside, Maria knew that sufferers of depression were more likely to sleep in the daytime. Becca Philips came with a diagnosis of severe recurrent depression and seasonal affective disorder. Dr. Ashmead had commented that the diagnosis was from adolescence, even if the mirror phobia wasn't, and that Ms. Philips had been highly functional in recent years, thanks to SSRIs and therapy. The nightmares were also a new development, and it was obvious that they scared Becca, maybe more than the mirror.

Maria had been happy to give the poor girl some relief by installing the wireless camera, which prevented having to move the monitoring equipment into the bedroom. With the wall between them, Maria could cough, sneeze, slurp her coffee, and check her phone without worrying about waking the subject. Just now, though, with the nor'easter raging through the speakers and that creepy melody rising out of the white noise, she caught herself holding her breath, afraid to move, her eyes darting between the grainy night vision video of Becca lying in bed and the flickering green and yellow indicator lights on the audio software.

Becca had rolled onto her back, knees bent and legs tangled in the sheets, her head lolling side to side as she sang. Maria couldn't tell if her eyes were open. She was leaning into the monitor, squinting (as if that would help) when the image stretched sideways like an old TV in proximity to a powerful magnet, then distorted to digital snow and went black.

Maria looked for the little chip of amber light to tell her if the power had gone out on the monitor. Still on.

The track lights over the desk dimmed and swelled. Emergency generators would kick in during a blackout, and the computers had backup battery power supplies to prevent data loss from momentary outages. Not that the machines in this wing of the hospital strictly required it. Though the study subjects slept in a nest of wires—electrodes to measure brain activity, belts to track respiration, and a clip on the finger for blood oxygen—none of them were life-sustaining.

Maria ran her fingers under the video monitor, felt the power button, and clicked it. The amber light winked. The green-hued infrared image struggled to regain coherence, but failed in a scramble of pixels pulsing in rhythm to the sound of the chant emanating from the speakers. Each time the image of the room had almost settled, another syllable from Becca's lips would assail it with a fresh gust of distortion.

Even as she puzzled over the song's effect on her equipment, Maria was aware of its unnerving asymmetric contours—the way the melody hopscotched around an exotic scale, the spaces for a replenishing breath dwindling to nonexistence in the coils of a knot of sound tightening around her brain, making her temples throb.

She smacked the side of the video monitor to no effect. It was hard to think over that nauseating music. Should she call for a doctor? Go into the subject's room and reset the camera?

The prospect of hearing the melody from its source without the distance of speakers suddenly terrified her. She had dated a guy who worked at an auto body shop for a while, and the image that came to mind now was of staring naked eyed at a welder's torch.

A new sound joined the din: a groan that couldn't be issuing from the same throat doing the singing. Another subject from an adjacent room? Maria glanced at the door—not the one that led to Becca's bedroom, but the one that would bring her to an adjacent monitoring room, where another tech (Ryan) monitored another sleeper. Just as she started to rise from her seat, a crash popped the speakers. The audio meter flashed red overload lights.

No time for hesitation now. She had to go in and check on her subject, maybe wake her if she was thrashing in her sleep. Becca didn't have a history of sleepwalking, but then, neither did she have a history of sleep singing. There wasn't much in the room that she could hurt herself with, but there *was* that vase of flowers someone had sent her. If the crash was the vase, Maria was sure she'd have heard it through the wall as well as the speakers, but... *dammit,* she was stalling, like a child afraid of the dark.

The song. It's that song. Why won't she wake up and stop it?

Voices from down the corridor reached the mic in the bedroom and filtered through the speakers. Agitated subjects. Someone—asleep or awake she couldn't say—moaning, "No, *no, no.* You can't *be* here." And an indistinct male voice, low and soothing.

Maria stood and walked toward the bedroom door, her fingers trailing over the surface of her desk, her shoes squeaking on the tiles, the hairs on her arms rising as she approached the solid oak door and the blacked out one-way glass beside it. The eldritch chant seeped from the speakers, tainting the air in the room like a toxin, worming tendrils of sound into her ear canals.

The curtain was suddenly ripped from the window. Maria cried out.

Becca stood at the glass in her hospital gown, clutching the black fabric in her fist, her eyes open but vacant, staring at her own reflection as if in a trance, her mouth moving, pitching the chant up into a region of harmonics that couldn't possibly be the product of a single human voice. There had to be something wrong with the equipment. It couldn't be coming from her throat like that...*could it?*

Maria clutched the steel door handle, her heart racing. She was about to find out.

* * *

Becca was in the Wade House again, following a dragonfly through a labyrinth of corridors until she came to a room she recognized. The empty second floor bedroom where her dog had been attacked by a cat that wasn't a cat but a denizen of another dimension. Or maybe it had once been a cat and now roamed the planes between worlds, alive and not alive, feline and something else. Just as this house was both burned to cinders and somehow still here, its architecture still mutating, its rooms reconfiguring like a Rubik's Cube even now. And what would happen when all the colors lined up? Would the house reappear then in the shelter of the hill at the edge of the woods as if it had never burned? Would the neighbors notice? Or would it remain hard to find?

Would she be lost in its secret spaces forever?

You're dreaming again.

That inner voice was persistent, but she couldn't put her faith in it. Her senses disagreed too much: The cold floorboards under her callused feet, the dust bunnies scudding along the wall where the peeling paper met the trim, the lace of aquamarine light lapping at the edges of the ceiling.

She knew where that light came from: a mirror. A full-length antique mirror in a hinged frame. But that wasn't the whole truth, was it? The watery light entered this world through a mirror, but it came from elsewhere, from a temple on the ocean floor in the South Pacific.

Becca approached the mirror. The dragonfly was gone. Disappeared into the glass? *Was* it glass, or was it water? Would her fingertips break the membrane if she touched it? Would she flood the room, the house? Would she drown? Had the dragonfly drowned?

This was another clue, the voice of her more lucid self told her: If the dragonfly was real and not a mechanical drone, if it could drown in water, if it could pass through a standing wall of water that somehow didn't break, then this *was* a dream, yes? Because none of that made sense.

But when had this house ever made sense? It defied sense down to the last nail and splinter.

Something crashed outside the room, down the hall. A voice cried out in distress, and another made soothing sounds. She cocked her head and listened, but couldn't make out the words. When she turned to face the mirror again, the undulating light had vanished, and the mirror was draped in black cloth.

Now another voice was petitioning her, garbled by water, a murmured invitation to swim.

Becca knew she shouldn't listen, knew she should flee the room, run through the maze of corridors and find the stairs, vault down them to the door, the path, the road.

But something inside her resonated with the unintelligible voice. She couldn't decipher the words, but she knew their meaning, encoded in a muted melody. It told her that it knew her pain, the struggle she had fought for all of her adult life to keep her head above water, to not drown in despair, to not be overwhelmed by the barest of tasks. Getting out of bed in winter. Dressing, feeding herself, and working in the face of crushing futility. It knew the effort it cost her to do these things weighted down as if with pockets full of stones by the losses that had accumulated with each passing year: her mother, her grandmother, her lover, her father. Stones in the pockets of her wet clothes, dragging her down with the water in her boots.

Things did not have to be that way.

She didn't need to keep her head above the waves, muscles aflame with the effort of treading water. She didn't have to fight, the song told her. She wouldn't drown; she would glide over the ocean floor, thriving in her element. If only…

If only she would recognize the voice of the singer.

And then she did. And it was *her* voice.

She reached out, seized the black fabric, and swept it from the mirror.

Someone screamed.

A cyclone of eels revolved in the water below the mirror's surface, coalescing in a pattern resembling a woman turning in a pirouette, trailing scarves of black flesh. A chill coursed through Becca's skin just as warmth ran down the inside of her leg and urine puddled at her feet.

She recognized the monster taking shape before her: Shabbat Cycloth, the Lady of a Thousand Hooks.

Another scream cut the air. Her own voice again, reflecting off the glass, setting the mirror to ripple with the vibration, and cutting the song short.

Becca blinked and looked down the length of her gown, at the wire trailing from her fingertip. A tile floor, a hospital gown. She wasn't in the Wade House. She was at the Psych Center at UMASS Tewksbury, where she had admitted herself for episodes of depression, insomnia, and recurring nightmares. She was in the sleep study wing.

Becca looked at the black cloth clenched in her fist, then slowly raised her gaze to the mirror—not a floor-standing antique in a hinged frame, but a wide pane of one-way glass. Only, it wasn't really a mirror at the moment, as it provided no reflection of her face or the room behind her. It might as well have been a tank at the New England Aquarium, like the ones she had seen when her grandmother brought her there as a girl, years before the aquarium was flooded and shut down in the wake of Hurricane Sonia. She couldn't have been more than eleven when they'd made the trip, but she still vividly remembered standing awestruck at the glass, watching the mako sharks glide by, their rows and rows of teeth mere inches from her face. She felt that same primitive fear now, that same irrational, childish alarm that could not be soothed by the knowledge that the glass protected her, or that the environment she inhabited, that allowed her to breathe, was hostile to the monster on the other side of it.

The form of the goddess rotated before her, unconstrained by mundane laws of time and space. Seconds passed as it whirled in graceful slow-motion, punctuated by a spasm in which the lamprey eels composing it lashed out at the glass too fast for her eyes to track before slowing again.

Had she conjured this with her song? A song she'd never learned, formed from syllables her larynx should not have been capable of producing?

A wave of panic rushed through her as she grasped the implications of what she was seeing and the fact of its lingering beyond the boundary of sleep. The door beside the wide mirror opened and the technician appeared. Curses and footsteps ricocheted off the tiles of the hallway. An orderly came around the corner at a run. Becca turned away from the mirror and the abomination writhing at its edges, swept her outstretched arm across the nightstand, and hurled the vase of blue flowers at the glass.

The mirror shattered and fell to the floor like a sheet of water, dancing on the tiles in a rain of silver shards and twitching fins.

Chapter 2

Jason Brooks had quit gambling in the autumn of 2019, but on the April morning after the nor'easter, he was looking to random chance for his fortune when a call chimed in his earpiece. Brooks ignored the call at first, staring instead at the little window in the black ball he held, where an inverted pyramid was surfacing in blue ink to reveal the message:

OUTLOOK
NOT SO
GOOD

Brooks dropped the Magic 8-Ball back into the cardboard box with the rest of his daughter's bookcase knick-knacks and glanced at his watch for the caller ID: TEWKS PSY. CTR.

"What did you ask it?" Heather said beside him, looking over his shoulder. Despite being doubly distracted by messages in windows, he could hear the false levity in her voice, and it warmed him. She cared about what he hoped to find in his future. Somehow, even after several lunches that had gone pretty well, and in the midst of moving the crap she couldn't bear to part with from her apartment to his house, her curiosity surprised him. Did she secretly hope he'd asked the oracle about his prospects with her mother? She was too wise for that, wasn't she?

Brooks held up a finger and said, "Got a call." He tapped the glass on his wrist and listened to the faint clicking sounds of a switchboard. He was half expecting a fundraising robo-call that had somehow reached him by digital proximity to Nina—his psychiatrist ex-wife—

but then a human voice greeted him by name, in a tone that sounded thin with age.

"Dr. Jack Ashmead calling for Jason Brooks."

"Speaking," Brooks said.

"Mr. Brooks, I'm calling from the Wingate Peaslee Psychiatric Center in Tewksbury, regarding a patient who listed you as her primary contact. Rebecca Rae Philips."

"Sorry, *patient?*" Brooks turned away from Heather and ducked under the three-quarters open garage door onto the icy driveway. "Is she okay?"

"Physically, yes. But she wouldn't have admitted herself if all was well. I don't know how much, if anything, she's shared with you about her condition…but, again, she listed you as an emergency contact. *Are you familiar with Rebecca's psychiatric history?*"

"You mean her depression? Yeah. I thought she was doing better. I thought the medication was working, mostly."

"Mr. Brooks, would you be available to meet with me at the hospital today? It would be better to discuss the matter in person. You could see her, if you like. But she needn't know you're coming unless you decide you want to see her."

"You said 'emergency contact.' What happened?"

A pause. "I really think it would be best if you come in for a discussion."

"Yeah, okay. Look, it's not that I don't care, I'm just confused. I mean…I'm not even family."

"You're the only contact she listed."

"Then who's taking care of Django?"

"Excuse me?"

"Her dog."

Why would she have listed him as a contact and not Neil? He wasn't family either, but he was closer to it. Enough that she called him "uncle."

"Doctor, has she been doing talk therapy with you?"

"Some, yes."

"So she's told you something about me."

"Can you come, Mr. Brooks?"

Brooks looked up the driveway into the garage. Heather wasn't even pretending not to listen to his side of the call.

"She told me that you work for SPECTRA," Ashmead said.

"You know what that is?" Brooks scuffed his work boot against the crust of ice, making it whiten against the black pavement.

"A colleague of mine did a little consulting for your agency. He couldn't talk about it, of course. Neither can Ms. Philips in any detail, which complicates her treatment. She has had episodes consistent with PTSD. Also…there was an incident last night that I believe falls within the range of your investigations."

"Okay," Brooks said. "Where and what time?"

"One-thirty?"

"Fine."

"I'll ping the address to your device."

Brooks tapped his watch to end the call. A second later the screen pulsed with a GPS icon.

"You have to go to work," Heather said. At least she didn't look angry.

"Not exactly work, but yeah. I have to look in on a friend. Sorry, kiddo. There's some wine coolers, bread, and cold cuts in the fridge."

* * *

The trek up Route 128 was an icy mess. The storm had arrived at the tail end of a warm winter. It hadn't piled on snow like some of the late season blizzards Brooks remembered from childhood, but brought enough of a cold front to glaze the tree branches with ice and pull down power lines. Driving north the day after, in what should have been a pretty breezy lunch hour on the highway, he found himself sitting in gridlock while firemen and police ushered cars through a one lane bottle neck around what WBZ reported as a nine-car pileup.

Once he knew the cause of the delay, Brooks switched off the radio and slid a Tool CD into the car stereo. He'd picked up the disc from the used rack at the North Shore Mall Newbury Comics, much to Heather's surprise. The logo on the sticker had caught his eye and reminded him that Becca wore their T-shirts. He'd addressed his daughter's raised eyebrow at the checkout by joking that it was work related research ("I've heard they might be cultists") but really the purchase was driven by curiosity. An effort to get inside Becca's head in some small way.

Or maybe he just missed her.

Sitting in traffic amid the squall of distorted guitar, he wondered what appealed to her about it. He lasted half of one song before turning it off and stewing in silence.

Why turn to crappy music for insight into a friend when he could have just called her?

It was hard to say. Maybe because she wasn't exactly a friend but one of the many lives his had intersected with when it was caught in the SPECTRA crosshairs. He had met Becca as a suspect, actually, during the cult activity of 2019, when the Starry Wisdom Church tried to initiate the apocalypse in Boston. SPECTRA had targeted the young art photographer when certain keywords were sifted from a phone call she'd made in an effort to understand fractal tentacle imagery appearing in her photos of urban ruins. It didn't take Brooks long to figure out that she was innocent—in spite of her family's history of entanglement with the occult—and she soon became a tenacious ally in the effort to understand the phenomena and decode a means of fighting back. It turned out she could be as fierce as her faithful German shepherd mutt when push came to shove.

Two years later, after Becca had left Boston behind for a new life in Brazil, Brooks was sent to pull her back into the fray. The agency enlisted her to explore and document more weird phenomena at a shapeshifting mansion west of Boston, known as the Wade House.

Brooks had helped her track down her father in the midst of that mission, only to see him murdered in a circle of standing stones on the grounds of the estate. They had succeeded in destroying the portals the house concealed and had banished the entities responsible for Luke Philips' death, but in the aftermath, Becca ended her association with SPECTRA. She wasn't a career agent, just someone with a special skill set under contract.

After all they'd been through, Brooks felt more of a bond with Becca than with his ex-wife and estranged daughter, but their shared experiences were horrific, and he could understand her wanting to put them in the past. So he hadn't called. Out of deference to her fragile psychological armor and a reluctance to disturb her equilibrium by dredging up memories of monsters.

But was it really about her fragility? She had shown real grit under pressure during both crises. And the loss of her father, while painful, seemed to have endowed her with some measure of forgiveness and healing with regard to her troubled upbringing.

The time they'd spent together had been a whirlwind, and he wondered now if it all caught up to Becca when events finally settled down. Maybe she'd *needed* someone to talk to; someone who would understand what she was going through. But he wasn't there. The two of them, alone among those exposed to the attacks in Boston, had refused to take Nepenthe afterward—a drug designed to narrow their perception back to the normal human range. Which meant they were the only two people on Earth, as far as he knew, who would notice if trans-dimensional entities tried to claw their way into this world again.

Brooks had seen no signs of that. Had Becca?

The heat in the car felt stifling, but the traffic was moving again. Brooks nudged the window down a crack and kept his eyes on the road as he passed the accident. He turned the stereo on again and tried the next track.

* * *

Tewksbury Psychiatric Center was a modern facility with stainless steel railings, pastel carpets, and an abundance of windows. Nothing like the brick fortress asylum where Becca's grandfather had died. Dr. Ashmead's walnut desktop gleamed in the diffuse light of what was shaping up to be a foggy day as the sun burned off the ice, the centerpiece of an office so uncluttered it made Brooks wonder how the guy got any work done. Not even a computer or coffee cup marred the slab of polished wood. Abstract carvings and glass sculptures adorned the shelves of a bookcase behind the doctor's mesh and leather chair. Dim recessed lighting augmented the gray daylight above a sleek, wave shaped couch that Brooks avoided, opting instead to take a seat in a less comfortable chair that put him at eye level with Ashmead after they shook hands across the desk.

The psychiatrist looked ballpark close to how Brooks imagined him from his voice on the phone: white-haired with drooping jowls and a neatly trimmed mustache, his thin, hunched frame propping up a brown sport coat over a blue checkered plaid shirt without a tie. His grip was gentler than his penetrating blue eyes.

"Thank you for coming," Ashmead began.

Brooks crossed his legs, brushed a bit of lint from his charcoal slacks and folded his hands, keeping the burden of conversation on the man who had summoned him. He noticed the confrontational wrinkle in his own demeanor and chalked it up to the time he'd spent married to a psychiatrist and the residual sense he retained around them that everything was a game or test.

"Your friend Becca has been a tricky case," Ashmead said.

Brooks grinned in spite of himself. "Tough nut to crack, huh?"

"She came to us for help with debilitating anxiety, exacerbated by insomnia and recurring nightmares. Unfortunately, it's been difficult to address the triggers for her anxiety and the content of the nightmares when she insists that she signed an oath of secrecy with your agency in the name of national security."

"That's true," Brooks said.

Ashmead looked relieved. "I appreciate you confirming that. It's the kind of declaration that would ordinarily come from a paranoid narcissist or someone grasping for a defense mechanism, if you'll pardon a term that's become a bit of a cliché."

"In Becca's case, it's not. But I'm afraid *I* can't tell you much, either. About what she's been through."

"I gather you've been through some of it with her?"

"Yes."

"But you were surprised that she listed you as her only contact."

"We haven't really kept in touch."

"Any reason?"

Brooks shrugged, uncomfortable with the feeling that Ashmead was fine-tuning his microscope behind that big empty desk that revealed nothing of the man's personal life and placed no obstacles between them. The doctor laced his fingers and leaned forward, his eyes bright and curious.

"It was a professional relationship, I guess," Brooks said.

"You guess?"

Brooks shifted in his seat. The vinyl squeaked. "Maybe it's like with soldiers who served together. I don't know. Maybe *you'd* know if you've treated vets. They might be the only people who understand what you went through, but that doesn't mean you want them to remind you of it."

Ashmead leaned back and steepled his fingers in front of his pursed lips.

"Anyway, speaking of oaths," Brooks said, "you've been pretty forthcoming about her complaints."

Ashmead nodded, and for a moment his gaze seemed to turn inward as he deliberated. Brooks recognized, from his experience as an interrogator, the moment when the doctor decided he'd toed the line long enough and committed to crossing it.

"I find myself in an odd position," Ashmead said.

"What happened?"

"We've been monitoring Becca's sleep. Charting her nocturnal neural activity and circadian rhythms. I've also insisted that she keep a dream journal, even if she can't share the experiences that might be informing her dreams."

Brooks thought of the dream journals SPECTRA had insisted they keep while staying in the Wade House. He'd written maybe three entries before deciding it was a bullshit task.

Ashmead continued. "She has a recurring nightmare like clockwork every night at the same time."

Brooks didn't have to ask what time. It would be 3:33, the same time he had his.

"In the two weeks she's been here, she hasn't exhibited somnambulism or other parasomnias, so monitoring her has been relatively straightforward."

"You lost me there."

"No sleepwalking or talking. Until last night, when she presented symptoms I would normally associate with a rare condition called RBD. That's REM Behavior Disorder. Patients with RBD act out while dreaming. It can range from unconscious sexual activities to self-abuse to physically attacking a pillow or sleep partner. Becca doesn't fit the demographic for RDB. Almost all of those afflicted are men over the age of fifty; although, there is reason to believe that younger females who take antidepressants may be more prone to it, and she falls into that category."

Brooks leaned forward and straightened his watchband on his wrist. "What did she do?"

"It began with her singing in her sleep, in what may have been a foreign or nonsense language, a glossolalia."

Was Brooks projecting, or had Ashmead's skin gone a shade whiter?

"Did you hear it yourself, this song?"

"No, but we have a recording of it. It's quite chilling, to be frank."

"So...that it? Sleep singing?"

"No. We usually monitor subjects through one-way glass. Becca has a fear of mirrors and insists that we cover hers with a curtain. While singing, she rose from the bed, tore the curtain aside, and threw a vase at the mirror, shattering the glass. All while maintaining REM sleep, according to the machines."

"Jeez. Anyone hurt?"

"No, thankfully. Well, she did step on some of the shards, but the wounds were superficial."

"You said this could be related to her medication?"

"In an effort to remain scientific about it, yes. I have to consider all possible options, and I'm debating the pros and cons of switching her meds. The link between RBD and antidepressants hasn't been proven, but there are studies that suggest it, and Wellbutrin, which affects different brain pathways, may be exempt from those potential side effects. But Becca has been taking Zoloft for years, and this is the first incident of violent sleep behavior."

"Back up. You said you're *trying* to remain scientific? What other point of view is tempting you?"

"Are you familiar with the work of Carl Jung?"

"Yeah. I mean, I haven't read the books, but I have a layman's familiarity."

"I believe his theory of the collective unconscious leaves room for what you might call 'shared psychic phenomena.' He sometimes called it synchronicity. Others might go so far as to label it telepathy. And Freud himself, dubious as many of his theories have turned out to be, said that 'sleep creates favorable conditions for telepathy.'"

Brooks smiled at the quote.

"Does the idea amuse you or make you nervous, Agent Brooks?"

"What do you mean?"

"Your smile. I don't profess to know much about the *Special Physics* SPECTRA investigates, but I'd hoped you might be open to the notion, maybe even willing to confirm whether Becca has exhibited such a talent."

"Sorry to disappoint you, Doc, but no. I've never received mental messages from Becca. Not last night, and not when we worked together."

"I didn't ask if *you* had."

"You want to get to the point?"

"The singing last night caused quite a disturbance on the ward. Patients who had been sleeping woke up terrified, all at the same time. And Becca wasn't the only one to attack her mirror. In sessions today, many patients claimed to have...seen things in the glass. A mass hallucination, if you will. A term I quite dislike; it always feels like a copout."

Brooks opened his mouth to speak and realized how dry it had become. "What exactly did they see?"

"Two other sleep study patients within hearing range of Becca's room saw what I suppose you'd have to call sea monsters. I've spent the morning coaxing drawings and descriptions out of them: A woman made of eels, a slender robed figure with a beard of tentacles... A janitor on the ward claims he saw a bed of flat-faced fish with large eyes and hooked teeth, flickering like lightning in the glossy tile floor he'd just mopped."

"And Becca? What did she see?"

"She won't say. Shattering the mirror woke her up and put an end to the song. It seems to have shattered the illusion for the others as well. As if she was the source. She doesn't remember singing at all."

Brooks cleared his throat. "It can't be the first time you've had a rash of nightmares. Am I right? Maybe the storm got under people's skin. They're here because they're *prone* to nightmares, right?"

"Not all of them. And the janitor wasn't sleeping. Nor does he have a history of mental disturbance."

"Well, all that moaning, screaming, and singing could have agitated his imagination."

Dr. Ashmead's perfectly trimmed mustache twitched, reminding Brooks of a rabbit. "I have to say, I'm disappointed, Agent Brooks." Was there a slight emphasis on the word *agent*? "I had hoped you might be more forthcoming."

"I'd like to see Becca."

"Of course. You understand I want to help her. Even if she can't share certain memories."

Brooks stood and sighed. "Honestly, I don't know why she would come here instead of seeing someone through the agency. No offense, but they already have her records. They know what she's been through."

"Sometimes it's easier to trust strangers who don't have an agenda, as opposed to an employer or a government agency."

Brooks narrowed his eyes at the man. "You had no agenda when you called me?"

"My agenda is only what's best for my patients." Ashmead said. "As it happens, the administrators and I disagree on what that is. I think Becca would be safest to remain in our care. In a more controlled environment than before, of course."

"And what does the management think?"

"That she's a danger to the staff and other patients. That she has already caused too much damage and disturbance for someone barely insured."

"They want to send her home."

"She admitted herself voluntarily. I think they're hoping that SPECTRA will intervene and take care of it now that you're aware. I thought, perhaps, if you confirmed there might be more than mass psychosis at work here, some phenomenon worthy of research…it might sway them. Perhaps a partnership with the agency could be arranged? If they detected even a whiff of potential grant money… I believe I could help her."

"And what does Becca want?"

"She's not talking much today."

"Maybe she'll talk to me."

* * *

Brooks thought the intern had showed him to the wrong room. The woman curled up on top of the neatly made bed matched Becca's basic size and shape, but looked thinner and aged beyond her 26 years—hair stiff and unruly, unblinking eyes as vacant as blue marbles. She wore gray flannel pajama pants with the drawstring removed and a white V-neck T-shirt. Her door, unlocked, was watched by an orderly stationed in a molded plastic chair at the end of the hall. They had moved her from the sleep study wing to a room that was little more than a cell. Brooks swallowed hard and raised a hand to stop his escort from following him in.

"I can find the way back to Dr. Ashmead's office on my own," he told the intern, closing the door on her before she could argue.

"Becca," he said. Her eyelids twitched at the sound of his voice, but her stare remained fixed on the wall, a shade of green that was probably named something like Sea Foam on the swatch; chosen, no doubt, for its soothing hue.

A quick scan of the room revealed no reflective surfaces except for the tall window overlooking the icy parking lot. Brooks thought of a visit he and Becca had paid to the home of one of the Boston event witnesses. Tom Petrie, a mild-mannered IT professional whose exposure to harmonically charged incantations had briefly endowed him with the Extra Dimensional Entity Perception that Brooks and Becca still retained. Tom had been treated with Nepenthe after the crisis, but his child, born the following year, seemed to have inherited the perception, as well as an innate ability to chant incantations from some combination of deep cellular memory and mutant vocal cords. Brooks remembered asking Tom why he and his wife had removed all the mirrors from their home and even taped up the reflective hardware of the kitchen sink. The answer had chilled him: little Noah saw things in mirrors, terrible things that gave him nightmares. The child also produced paintings of these creatures that exceeded the artistic abilities of a normal toddler.

Brooks took a step toward Becca. "Knock knock," he said.

No response, not even a blink.

"Your line is 'Who's there?' And then I say, 'It's your emergency contact, Jason.' Even though I could never get you to call me Jason."

Becca blinked at the wall.

"You in there, *Philips?* Anybody home?" He tapped the corner of the bedframe with his shoe. She closed her eyes and a tear slipped out, darkening the pillowcase.

Brooks sat at the foot of the bed. "So who's taking care of Django while you're in the loony bin?"

Did that grimace contain the ghost of a smile?

"Let me guess: Neil?"

Becca nodded.

"I was surprised when the doc called me instead of him."

"Sorry." Her voice sounded like it hadn't been used in a hundred years.

"Don't be. I'm flattered. I hear you had a rough night."

She swallowed. There was a plastic cup of water on the night table beside the bed. He almost passed it to her, but then decided against it. Too much proximity, any sudden movements, might close that tiny crack he'd wedged open in her armor.

"Doctor Ashmead tells me you sang in your sleep and broke a mirror."

Under the T-shirt, her ribs rose and fell with a deep breath that she didn't waste on words.

"It's okay, we don't have to talk about it. But I'm glad you put my number down. I wish you'd called me when you needed help, before checking in here. That dream…same time, same channel? I have it too, if I don't get hammered."

Brooks laid his hand on the blanket beside Becca's knee. She opened her eyes, grasped his rough fingers in her clammy hand, and squeezed them fiercely.

"Scared," she said, and her lip quivered.

"Me too," he said. "Let's get you out of here."

Chapter 3

Brooks called Heather from the hallway while Becca dressed. "Hey, I need a favor. You mind if a friend of mine borrows some of the clothes you packed up for the move? I'll wash and fold 'em after I pick up her own stuff. And maybe a hairbrush?"

"This the friend you had to go and see so urgently? She's moving in with you?"

"Yeah. No. She's in pretty rough shape and needs a hand is all."

Heather made a sharp sound that might have been a laugh. Brooks scratched the back of his head and looked at the orderly, who had his eyes on his paperback, ears on the conversation. "Just for a little while. She's someone from work. Needs a safe place to clear her head. I'll explain more when I can."

"She's an agent?"

"Not exactly."

"Recovering cultist? Gambler?"

"No and no."

"Dad, what are you getting yourself into?"

"I'll explain when I can. Look, I know it's shitty timing with me trying to help you get off to grad school. I'd say I'll make it up to you, but that sounds like the kind of crap I used to not deliver on. It's just... I'm trying to help someone who is actually a hero, okay? Truly. What happened in Boston when you were living there...it could have been worse. That's all I can say."

Nothing but breathing on the line.

"Heather?"

"Yeah."

"Will you help me?"

"Yeah. A change of clothes and what else? She need a toothbrush and shampoo?"

"Uh-huh."

"I'll pick those up and leave some clothes out. I'll be gone before you get home."

He thought of telling her she didn't have to leave but knew it would be better not to tax Becca with meeting anyone in her current state. Maybe Heather sensed it too, or maybe she was sparing herself. Either way, he was grateful.

* * *

Brooks drove with the windows cracked open in the hope that the cool air might do something to rejuvenate the stranger in the passenger seat. Becca, with the collar of her army jacket turned up, blinked at the brightness of the day. By 4:10, when they left the psych center, most of the ice on the road had melted and a hint of spring wafted off the misty trees lining the grass islands in the highway. To Brooks, it felt like they might be driving out the far side of the last winter storm.

When they turned into the driveway of Brooks' house—a two-story Craftsman in Malden with beige vinyl siding and a built-in garage—Heather's Toyota was already gone, presumably back to her near-empty apartment in Jamaica Plain. Brooks killed the engine and looked at Becca. She stared up at the house but made no move to unbuckle her seatbelt. "You live here?" she asked.

"Yup."

"Alone?"

"Yeah. I moved the family out here after the old house in Revere flooded. Heather was almost out of school by then, so my only criteria was higher ground. When Heather moved out to college, Nina followed and filed for divorce. She bought that brownstone in Brookline, closer to her practice, and I kept this place. It's too big for me but I like mowing the little backyard. Crazy, huh? Anyway, plenty of room for you while we figure out what to do."

Becca bit her lip.

Brooks glanced at the rearview mirror. "Listen," he said, "you sit tight while I run in and hang sheets over the mirrors, okay? Would that make you feel better?"

She nodded.

"Probably an unnecessary precaution," he said. "I mean, you're not gonna start singing the Cthulhu Blues if you're awake, right?"

She let out a little laugh, music to his ears.

"Just in case. Back in a flash."

Brooks hadn't looked for guest bedding since before Nina moved out. In Heather's old room, there was a mirror attached to the dresser on metal tracks. He slid it out and stowed it facedown under the bed. A few closet searches later, he was loaded up with an assortment of short blankets and pillowcases. He tacked two of these up over the bathroom mirrors, above the counter where Heather had left a CVS bag of travel size toiletries.

Back outside, he found Becca sitting on the porch in the whitewashed rocking chair, scratching her arm like she did when she was nervous.

"Come on in," he said. "You hungry?"

* * *

They sat at the dining room table Brooks hadn't used since his marriage ended, between the kitchen with its curtained off sliding glass door and the living room where the flat screen TV was draped with a bed sheet. Brooks watched Becca across a collection of beer bottles and plastic containers from the local Indian restaurant as she cleaned the Tandoori sauce from her plate with the last scrap of naan bread. It was good to see her eating after the weight she'd lost. His worry at not having anything in the fridge suitable for a vegetarian had dissipated when he remembered the menu in a drawer of the little desk where they used to keep the landline phone.

Brooks took a pull on his bottle of Harpoon and set it down beside the rice. "So when did you start having the dream?"

Becca looked up from her plate. "First time was in the Wade House. You?"

"Same. The details have changed some, but I had a dream there about a public pool my ma used to take me and my brother to. In the first dream, I was underwater in that pool. That's when I first saw it. The temple."

"R'lyeh," Becca said.

"Gotta be."

"I remember you told me about it when Tom's kid, Noah, was making bubble bath islands and calling them that."

"That's right."

"I looked into it after. Went back to Arkham and spent a day at Miskatonic combing through my grandmother's collection looking for references to it."

"Find anything interesting?"

"Probably nothing you don't already know."

Brooks shrugged. "SPECTRA's been sifting the web for descriptions of the dream on blogs and social media. There's been a spike in those."

"Do you have it at the same time every night?"

"When I have it, I wake up at three-thirty-three in a cold sweat."

"So it's sporadic for you."

He picked up his empty bottle and shook it like he was ringing a bell. "Drinking before bed helps. But if I have to get up to piss, it can go either way. You'd think that waking up to take a leak would reset my sleep cycle and throw the timing off, only it doesn't. If I have the dream after getting up, it still comes at the same time."

"That's because it's telepathic, right?" Becca ventured. "The dreams all come from the sunken island, from R'lyeh. From the temple of the high priest of the Great Old Ones. That's what the books say, anyway."

"Dead but dreaming," Brooks said.

"Maybe self-medicating isn't the best idea."

Brooks smirked at the bottle. "That's never been my problem."

"You still off gambling?"

"Yes. Not that it's changed much more than my bank balance." He waved a hand at the empty house.

For a moment, the icy water gurgling down the gutter downspout beside the sliding door in the kitchen was the only sound between them.

"Why didn't you go to Nina when you needed help?" Brooks asked.

"How do you know I didn't?"

Brooks scoffed. "After all we've been through, you still think I'm spying on you?"

"No. Sorry. Old habits. It just got too complicated with Nina. I knew too much about her. And the more I got to know you, the weirder it felt. You're not really supposed to be friends with your shrink's spouse. Then there's the little fact that she did work for SPECTRA. They've been pretty good to *my* bank account, but I still can't say I trust them. What are you smiling at?"

"Nothing. I'm glad you consider me a friend, that's all. You trust me. Finally."

"Dude. I wouldn't go *that* far," Becca held her fork like a dart and pointed it toward a container at his elbow. "You gonna eat that last pakora?"

Brooks returned the smile with genuine relief. She was going to be okay. "You have it."

She speared the morsel, took a bite.

"I made up Heather's old room for you. No mirrors. She left some clothes for you that should fit."

"That's kind of her."

"She's a good kid. I'm gonna miss her when she's on the West Coast, but it won't be that different from when she wasn't talking to me. Maybe now she'll call."

Becca pointed the fork at Brooks this time. "You call her."

"Yeah. Anyway, I think we should sleep with the doors open. My room's just down the hall."

"I should probably be sleeping in restraints. You know that, don't you?"

"They don't know the first thing about what you're going through at that psych center."

"Don't you mean what *we're* going through, Mr. Bottle Before Bed?"

"Yeah, well, I'm not singing in my sleep."

"Not yet."

"That was the first time for you, last night? You're sure?"

"I'm not sure of anything. All I know for sure is it's the first time it happened while I was being monitored. And the first time I woke up looking at something I'd conjured."

"*Jesus.*"

"What? You don't think that's what happened?"

Brooks propped his head up on his fingertips, elbow on the table. "No, I do. It's just…to hear you say it…it's fucked up. I think you're better off here for now than in a hospital, but you should think about talking to somebody at the agency. Maybe take that Nepenthe after all."

"You didn't take it after the Wade House, did you?"

Brooks shook his head.

"Why not?"

"Early detection. If something comes through again I want to know about it."

"Exactly. I might take something if it would stop the dreams, but not if it shuts off EDEP."

"Well, maybe we can get you something for dreamless sleep at least. And you're gonna need supervision for more than a few days. You're welcome to stay as long as you like."

"...Thanks." Becca ran a fingernail over the tablecloth.

"But?"

"I don't want to impose on you. With a sleep drug, I could get back to my apartment with Django, where I belong."

"You want to have Neil drop the dog off, he can stay here, too. It's no trouble."

"Really?"

"Of course."

"Okay. Let's give it a night or two first to see what happens. I miss him, but I don't want him sleeping with me if it might not be safe for him."

"It's a deal. I'll set my alarm for 3:15. If you start singing or showing signs of distress, I'll wake you."

"Why don't we both get up at 3:15 and ride out the dream time? I can't believe I didn't think of that before now. I'm not thinking clearly, Brooks. It scares me."

"You're tired. We could do that, but I think I should see it, hear it, for myself. Who knows? Maybe it won't happen again."

"And what do you hope to learn if it does?"

"None of the people at the psych center had EDEP. I do. If I see something even without any mirrors in the room, I'm going to be a lot more concerned with what's happening to you."

Becca wrapped her hand around her throat like a scarf and met his eyes with a glint of fear. "I can feel something different sometimes. When I drink water. And in the shower...in the humid air, it's like it opens up more. Something's changing in me."

"It'll be okay. We'll figure it out, get you help."

"Why would it change now? And why not for you? We were both exposed in '19. And we banished them. Twice. Why are the dreams more active now? They went away after that poisoned house burned down, and it's been *years*. I was getting better. Stronger. And now I'm a wreck again. Why now?"

"I don't know. I wish I did, but I don't."

Becca removed her hand from her throat and placed it on the table. Brooks patted her wrist. She flashed him a sad grin, sighed and said, "Maybe we should talk to Northrup tomorrow. If it happens again tonight."

"Yeah. About that... There have been some changes at the agency."

Becca cocked an eyebrow.

"Northrup is out."

"Out? Like retired?"

"He's had some setbacks. His health isn't good. And then there's the politics."

"Just when I was starting to trust him. What's wrong with his health?"

"I don't know the details. Maybe 'health issues' was just a smoke screen for replacing him with some dignity intact. People talk. I take it with a grain of salt. I got no use for gossip. But I'm feeling the wind blowing from a different direction under the new guy, I can tell you that."

"How do you mean?"

"His name is Warwick McDermott. He worked under Northrup for a while and they locked horns. There are factions within SPECTRA. Also rival schools of thought influencing us from Washington think tanks. Most of them don't know enough about what we do to offer sound advice because of how classified it is. On paper, we barely exist. But with all of the consultants we employ, word gets around anyway. Even your Dr. Ashmead has heard of SPECTRA."

"Not from me. At least, not in any detail."

"I know. But the last two big crises we took on, the ones you were involved in, were too public for comfort. The people who set the agenda, who direct the director, like to remain in the shadows. Field agents like me don't even learn their names. Anyway, the agency has been in a defensive crouch the past few years. Northrup gave assurances that it could never happen again after the Red Equinox, and then it did in Concord.

"The fucked up thing is that McDermott—rather than destroying the books and artifacts we gathered from raids on the Starry Wisdom Church to *ensure* it can't happen again—has ramped up the study of that material to see if we can use it in our defense."

"What makes you so sure that's a bad idea? I mean, what would we have done to stop the Red Equinox without my grandmother's scarab?"

Brooks tilted his head and made a conceding grimace. "For one thing, Hanson worked for *us*, remember? We had a closet cultist on the payroll. Not to mention the one we knew about, Reverend Proctor, who also turned on us. And they weren't even working together. Northrup got burned and he learned from it. He wasn't going to risk it happening again. That's why he wouldn't let the fire trucks through the gate until the Wade House was a heap of ash. He wanted not just the house, but the library, candles, and anything else in there that might be used for evocation to go up in flames with it."

"Do they have anything dangerous?"

"I don't know. They took a lot of books from the church in Boston. There were probably some artifacts, too, like those bronze staffs they used at Bunker Hill. Do you still have the scarab?"

Becca slipped a finger under the collar of her T-shirt and pulled the golden beetle up by its chain, showing it to Brooks before dropping it back under her shirt.

"I'm surprised they haven't come for it."

"Without the gem, it's just jewelry. And they can fuck right off if they think I'd give it to them. Catherine meant for me to have it."

"If they decide they want it, they'll take it."

"Let them try. I have a red belt in Tae Kwon Do."

Brooks laughed. "Seriously?"

"How do you think I've been channeling my anger and frustration for the past three years?"

"Are you going to go for black?"

Her face dropped and she focused on the beer bottle in front of her, rolling it on its edge, idly. "Well…losing your shit kind of gets in the way of your training regimen. I have less depression when I get enough exercise, but things kind of fell apart when the dreams started happening again. So close to the goal too. Sucks."

"You'll get back to it. How about photography? You been working?"

Becca sighed. "PTSD is a pretty good excuse for not achieving the same success as the people I went to school with, but I still feel like a loser."

"Yeah. And I'm sure they all prevented the apocalypse in between shooting for *Vogue* or whatever the fuck."

Becca smiled. "Let's just say work is sporadic. I take it on when I can handle it and try to stretch the checks."

"Sorry. I don't mean to pry. It's just been a while. I've wondered how you've been."

"You had my number. Anyway, it's kinda weird talking with you about normal stuff."

"It is, right? But what else is there besides war stories? And you probably don't want to go there."

"Actually, I do," Becca said, peeling away a strip of the label from the bottle with her thumbnail.

"Go on."

"You said they might come for the scarab. I think they already broke into my dad's cabin and made off with a certain piece of sheet music while we were busy fighting monsters three years ago."

"*The Invisible Symphony.*"

"Luke kept it rolled up, hidden inside a lamp tube. He left me a video message before he died. Said I needed to destroy the score, that it was too dangerous. Especially a choral section that—if it were sung by a mutant choir—could make the breaches that we witnessed look like just a prelude. He said he tried to rewrite sections of the music, but there was no way to realign it."

"What do you mean 'realign it'?"

"I don't know. I'm not a musician. My grandmother studied an ancient cosmology called the Music of the Spheres. She tried to explain it to me one time when I asked about a book she was reading. It had something to do with the idea that the whole universe is vibrating in harmony, and the planets themselves make music by spinning. I know that's not exactly in line with modern physics; maybe it's more of a metaphor. Luke thought that maybe Earth, our dimension, could be aligned with a heavenly one rather than the realm of the Great Old Ones. But I guess he changed his mind toward the end. He'd sworn off tinkering with the symphony and wanted me to destroy it. It was his last wish. But when I went back to the cabin, it was gone."

"And you think SPECTRA took it."

"They probably saw his video before I did. They had access to my phone. He didn't say where the score was hidden, but I knew where he kept it, from when you and I visited him. Only it wasn't there. I think after they came for us in the helicopter, they searched the cabin and found it."

"Makes sense."

"But you don't know. Northrup never mentioned it? You would tell me, right?"

"Of course. But no, I didn't hear anything."

"If anything should be destroyed, it's that score. I want to see it through."

"What are you asking for?"

"Do they store the artifacts in a building you have access to?"

Brooks rubbed the stubble on his chin and frowned. "Yeah. In a vault. But we don't even know if it's there."

"Who else would have taken it?"

Brooks shrugged.

"Are you still in touch with Northrup? Would he know if SPECTRA took it? Maybe he destroyed it himself before he was let go."

"I don't know that he would admit that to me," Brooks said, "but he doesn't have much left to lose."

"If they have it, what kind of vault are we talking about?"

"It's a high security archive. I can't just go waltzing in there, poking around."

"So it's like an evidence locker?"

"A little more sophisticated than that. Some items have special protections, but this would probably be kept with all the other manuscripts and books in a temperature and humidity controlled room. They have a team that works in there in the daytime, studying the books and running tests on the items. Most of what they do is over my head."

"Are you friends with any of them?"

He shook his head. "They're weird. And most of them have a higher security clearance than me. It's not like field agents have drinks with the theoreticians. I could be fired or prosecuted for even talking about what's in there."

She glanced at the electric chandelier hanging over the table. "You think your place is bugged?"

"I know it isn't. I'm just saying."

"I'm not somebody off the street, you know. I've been on the inside."

"As a contractor who's always had an antagonistic relationship with them."

"As the girl who saves their asses when they get in too deep."

"You're something else, you know that?"

"I want you take me to see Northrup."

Brooks scoffed. "He's practically on his death bed and you look like you're ready for yours. That should be a cheerful meeting to sit in on."

"Seriously. If he can convince me they don't have the score locked up, then we won't have to break in and steal it back."

"*Break in.* Christ, Becca, you're in no shape to break into a fridge with a strong magnet on the door. Let's start with getting you a few days rest and recuperation. Meanwhile, I'll do some discrete poking around."

"Okay."

"Why, after three years of not knowing what happened to the score, are you all of the sudden so worried about it?"

"It's the dreams, the singing. If that manuscript is in the wrong hands, and if there are others out there who can sing those chants… then something bad is coming. And there might not be time to stop it."

* * *

Brooks woke to the buzzing of his wristwatch at 3:15 A.M. He groaned, tossed the sheets and blankets aside, and crept past Becca's door to use the bathroom before pulling on a T-shirt and sitting vigil at her bedside.

At 3:33, she stirred, twitched, and groaned in her sleep.

By the yellow glow of a seashell nightlight, he watched the hairs on his forearms rise at the sound of her voice. She kicked at the sheets, then turned her head away from something as if in revulsion, groaned again, and drew a sharp breath. But she did not sing that night, nor did he wake her from her nightmare. He sat and waited, listening for a melody that never came, until the dream he knew all too well passed, and she drifted beyond its turbulence into deeper sleep.

Chapter 4

Tristan Furlong met the man from the antiquarian book and curio shop at the sphinx on the Bay of Maestral. The concrete sculpture, commissioned in 1918 by an eccentric dabbler in the occult as a tribute to his deceased wife, straddles the broken remains of the goldfish pond it once guarded on the grounds of the Villa Atillia, overlooking the street and the bay. Tristan arrived early and paced the green slopes of the garden, but soon grew restless. The landmark held no mystery for him, nothing to contemplate or puzzle over. Just a few years ago, it would have piqued his interest. Back then, he had never visited the old country. Back then, he had been a street busker in Cambridge, Massachusetts, raised by Croatian immigrants who had disowned him when he wasted the opportunity of America on playing music in the street like a beggar, rather than following their footsteps into science or medicine as his elder sister had done. Back then, he had not yet become a vessel for the infinite wisdom of the Black Pharaoh.

Now, unlike the tourists who puzzled over it daily, he could even read the inscription in the sphinx's hair. Alas, like the statue itself, the lines were a sappy tribute to a long dead witch.

Still, he could appreciate that something about Zadar had spoken to the dilettante magician who erected this tribute. Something had always called the Starry Wisdom faithful to this coast. Tristan could sense it stirring in the cool air off the Adriatic Sea even now.

"It's a shame about the vandals."

The man from the shop, Andrija Babic, had come up beside him. "It used to hold a shell in one paw and a dagger in the other, but they were smashed with the pond walls."

Tristan looked sidelong at the stout Italian in the frumpy brown suit. "It's homely," he said. "Why this place? It only makes me wish to see the real thing, to cleanse my mental palette."

Babic shrugged. "Most of my special customers like it. Anyway, it's an easy landmark to find and quiet on a weekday. The villa's a dentist's office now."

Tristan's gaze slid down the man to the leather doctor bag he carried. "You have it?"

"Yes. You're younger than I expected. Not that that's a problem, with references such as yours. Just, most collectors are older."

"Show me."

Babic set the case on the ground, unbuckled the clasps, and withdrew a lacquered wooden box with brass hinges. After a dramatic pause, he lifted the lid to reveal a thorny spiral object nestled in a bed of blue silk. It might have been an oblong conch shell. Its surface, as white as bone, was ornamented with silver edging and small gemstones. The inner chamber gleamed glossy pink, winding away into fleshy depths.

A frisson of excitement passed over Tristan at the sight. "Tell me again what you know of its provenance."

Babic cleared his throat. "In 1604, the Swiss naturalist Conrad Gesner published his bestiary *Historia Animalium*. The Vatican placed it on the prohibited books list because the author was a Protestant. But Gesner had allies. His private library and catalog of clippings are regarded as one of the world's first scientific databases, and he was considered too valuable to shun entirely."

Babic, whose manner had been awkward at first, was loosening up as he hit his stride. He nodded toward the bay. "Just across the water from here, Venetian booksellers petitioned the Church to have his works removed from the blacklist."

Tristan waved his hand. "Enough about books. Tell me about the shell."

"But, you see, the shell is believed to come from Gesner's own collection. His studies and writings also included works on fossils, stones, and gems. His notes indicate that he was undecided on which category this *shankha* properly belonged to."

"Shankha?"

"A Hindu word. It means 'divine conch.' This may be one of the first such ceremonial items to have found its way into a European collection. But only if you believe it originated in the Indian Ocean. My source does not."

"May I?" Tristan tilted his chin toward the open box in Babic's hands. The bookseller offered it up, and Tristan removed the shell from the silk bed, turning it over in his hands.

"Gesner's bestiary was purged of heretical content and reprinted, thanks to his Venetian advocates. In it, among the many creatures now believed to be mythical, is an illustration of what he calls a 'sea devil.' A hybrid of fish and goat. Some scholars suggest that Gesner believed the *shankha* in his collection was one of the horns of this creature, cut from its head when a fisherman found it snared in his net and slayed it. But one of Gesner's assistants kept a journal, which I have read. In it, the boy recounts a story Gesner told him about the shell's origin.

"Now, maybe the old man was pulling his young assistant's leg, but the devotees of the secret church in Zadar give the tale credence. According to the boy, Gesner said a sea devil delivered this shell to a pagan priest at the Palace of Diocletian, just down the coast from here, so that the emperor might use it as an oracle. If that is true, then history works in wondrous ways, indeed, and the shell has now returned home, in a manner of speaking."

"And how was it to be used?"

"Whisper your questions to it, as in a lover's ear, and the sea will answer true."

"Did it answer Diocletian?"

"Who knows? By the time the emperor retired to tend the gardens of his palace, he had already enjoyed his great victories and achieved peace. One wonders what he would ask of an oracle at that late stage of a distinguished life. But the historians say he may have committed suicide, so…perhaps it did."

"Old maids and children believe you can hear the ocean in a conch," Tristan said. "But have you heard any other story of whispering in the *ocean's* ear?"

"No, my friend. Any sailor will tell you Poseidon is deaf to prayers and petitions."

"I was thinking of another god of the deep."

"Well, I suppose that's between you and him. Between you and I, there's still the matter of payment. If you're satisfied."

Tristan closed the lid of the box and latched it. Babic laid it at his feet.

"I'm very meticulous about tracing the line of an artifact," Babic said, straightening his tie. "But I make no promises about results, should you ask it something."

"Understood." Tristan produced an envelope from the breast pocket of his pea coat and passed it to Babic. The little man thumbed through the euro notes inside, licked his lips, and tucked it away with a nod. He turned to go, but hesitated, as if the weight of the cash in his trousers made it difficult for him to move his legs without a final word.

"They say the shell has to be addressed in the proper tongue. You're aware?" Babic swung his doctor bag idly, waiting for a reply that didn't come.

Tristan tucked the box under his arm and started up the path between the pine and olive trees.

"It doesn't alter our deal if you can't pronounce it, you understand? You won't come looking for me," Babic said with a tinge of anxiety in his voice.

Without looking back, Tristan Furlong said, "No worries. I'm quite fluent."

Chapter 5

Becca awoke to the sound of Django whimpering, his cold nose nuzzling at her face. She pushed him away and rolled in the other direction to face the wall. The room was too dark for dawn. Did he really need to go out? Brooks had driven her to Neil's place in Brookline to pick the dog up after stopping by her apartment to grab her things. Django had been ecstatic to see her after almost two weeks apart, and when they arrived at Brooks' house, she had taken him out in the scrappy little back yard to throw a stick around and tire him out.

So why wouldn't he let her sleep?

He paced around the bed trying to reach her face again before finally standing with his front paws on the mattress, whining urgently on the brink of barking.

It was her third night in the house, and according to Brooks she had yet to sing in her sleep. She didn't know what time it was now, but her biological clock told her it was too early for the witching hour alarm. If she didn't shut Django up, he'd wake Brooks in the adjacent room and deprive the poor guy of even more sleep on her account.

Becca propped herself up on her elbows and looked at the dog. "Seriously?"

Django paced an urgent circle, swishing his tail against the bed, then went to the doorway and looked back at her, the whine in his throat percolating to a low growl.

She stood up, tucked her hair behind her ear, and squinted around the room for a shape that might be her jeans. The nightlight did little to illuminate her clutter, and she decided she could handle five minutes of standing outside in the cold in only her boxers and T-shirt while the dog pissed. By the look of him, he needed to go so badly that it wouldn't take longer than that.

"You better not be trying to get me to play ball," she said, and followed him to the hallway. At the sight of her coming, Django turned right, away from the stairs, and perched at the half open door to Brooks' bedroom, where he resumed growling.

Something about that wedge of darkness and the silence beyond it made Becca's stomach squirm. She had the impression that Brooks was not a heavy sleeper, that the sounds of the agitated dog—unfamiliar sounds in his house—should have woken him by now.

She walked to the door, the floorboards creaking softly through the carpet beneath her feet, and pushed it open.

The first thing she saw was the alarm clock display, glowing on the bedside table: 3:13. Next, in the faint spill of green light, she noticed the drawer of the bedside table hanging open. As her eyes adjusted to the darkness, she drew a sharp breath at the sight of Brooks' silhouette, sitting upright at the edge of the bed.

Fear and embarrassment flooded her simultaneously and she took a step backward. "Sorry, I... Sorry we woke you." She threaded her fingers into Django's thick fur, taking him by the scruff and leading him toward the door. But a split second after averting her gaze from the gradually detailed silhouette, her brain made sense of the last thing she'd seen—and her heart froze in her chest.

He was holding a gun in his mouth.

"Brooks?" The name came out as a whisper. The nightlight in the hall failed to reach his eyes with its faint yellow rays, so she couldn't tell if they were open or closed. Was he asleep? She held her index finger up where Django could see it and told him to stay.

Brooks remained motionless at the edge of the bed, the barrel of his service weapon poised in his mouth, jaw slack, hand steady, as Becca approached, slow and silent, taking in the details with mounting horror. His eyes *were* closed, his respiration slow and deep. The gun must have come from the drawer of the nightstand.

Her heart beat harder, faster, with each slow step.

You were supposed to wake sleepwalkers before they could hurt themselves. But if she startled him, he might squeeze the trigger.

Her mouth had gone dry. She parted her lips to say his name again and the crackle they made was loud in her ears.

"Brooks," she whispered.

He gave no indication that he'd heard her.

Was the gun loaded? She had no idea how to eject the magazine, and even if she did, it wouldn't ensure there wasn't a round in the chamber, would it? For the first time since the confrontation at the Wade House, she wished she'd learned something about firearms. She'd been stupid enough to think she was done rubbing elbows with cultists and special agents.

Django growled like the power hum of a poorly grounded machine.

Becca squatted in front of Brooks, afraid that kneeling would make it hard to adapt to whatever might happen when she woke him. She dragged her sweaty hand down her T-shirt, then reached for the gun. Her fingers curled around the cold metal.

Slowly, she pulled the weapon out of his mouth, a string of saliva stretching from his lip to the sight blade. As soon as it was free, she started tilting it away from his face, bending his wrist inward toward his arm, but his fingers tightened on the grip, resisting her.

The alarm clock went off, and with it, the gun.

Django yelped. Dust flurried down from the bullet hole in the ceiling. Brooks jerked awake and tugged the gun away from Becca, his eyes wide and white in the gloom as she fell backward onto the floor. He loomed over her, swaying on his feet, blinking. His bare chest heaved, his breath rasping in his nostrils. Then he turned the gun over in his hand and stared at it, eyes wide and white in the darkness.

"What happened?" he said, turning his wild stare on her.

Django placed himself between them, his hackles up, posturing at Brooks, but not yet committed to barking at him.

"You were asleep," Becca said. She stroked Django's fur down, got to her feet, and found the snooze bar on the beeping alarm clock.

In the silence that followed, she watched Brooks' rigid body slowly relax. He ejected the magazine from the gun and set both pieces down on top of his dresser.

Becca waited until the weapon was out of his hand. Then, as he turned back to her, she embraced him fiercely, all of the fear and potential grief flooding out of her in a string of words whispered into the hollow of his shoulder: "Holy shit, Jason, you almost just shot yourself in front of me. *Fuck.*"

She felt him stiffen again, and then deflate, giving in and stroking her hair. When she'd caught her breath, she broke away from him and beat her fist against his chest. "You keep a fucking loaded gun in your bedside table?"

"I'm an agent, Becca. Enemies don't make appointments. And it's not like I'm gonna find your dog playing with it."

She sat on the bed heavily, and raked her fingers through her hair. "Jesus, Brooks…" She caught her breath. "I always figured if one of us was gonna eat a gun, it would be me."

He sat down beside her and glanced at the clock. "*I'm* supposed to be watching over *you* this time of night. What woke you?"

"Django. He saved your life."

Brooks regarded the dog. It wasn't the first time he'd puzzled over the animal's keen sensitivity. He leaned forward and patted him on the flank and was rewarded with tail wagging and a tongue all over his chin.

"Now I *really* need to rinse my mouth. Nothing like the taste of gun oil and dog breath."

Becca laughed, but it came out more as a shuddering sigh.

"Sorry I scared you," Brooks said.

"Well…I don't think you can take responsibility for it. What were you dreaming?"

He opened his mouth and she could tell he was going to lie, tell her he couldn't remember. But he stopped himself and said, "Not now."

She studied his eyes, then nodded.

"Anyway, the timing can't be a coincidence," Brooks said.

"Right before the alarm."

"Yeah. Maybe…instead of transmitting the same dream at the same time, something decided to come for me early because I've been skipping out on it."

"You think something didn't want you watching over me tonight?"

He grimaced. "The shot would have woken you if the dog didn't. I think it might just want me out of the picture. I'm not as important or useful as you are."

Becca stared at the numbers on the clock: 3:25. "What use am I?" she asked.

"You have the voice now."

* * *

They watched each other sleep in shifts. The gun remained unloaded and stowed in a kitchen drawer downstairs, away from the ammunition. Becca did the second watch before dawn and left Django in the bedroom with Brooks for the last part of it while she ransacked the fridge and found enough eggs, cheese, milk, and cherry tomatoes to make a couple of omelets for breakfast. They were overdue for a shopping trip, but there was enough not-too-stale bread for them to share three pieces of toast. The eggs were past the sell by date, but she dropped each in a glass of water, and none of them floated, a trick her grandmother had taught her. Catherine Philips was a fine cook when she wasn't studying anthropology and the dark arts.

The food was cooked and waiting under a pot lid to keep it warm when Brooks descended the stairs dressed for work with Django at his heels, sniffing the air. The dog sat for Becca and salivated with his head cocked until she gave him a piece of cheese.

"Smells good," Brooks said, retrieving a mug with the SPECTRA logo on it from the cupboard and pouring a cup of black coffee. He peeked at the omelets through the glass lid. "I didn't think you ate eggs."

"I'm vegetarian, not vegan. I do dairy, too."

"How about fish? You eat that? I need to do some shopping."

"If you loan me your car and point me in the right direction, I'll shop. It's the least I can do. But no fish. Our adventures turned me off to it."

Brooks grimaced. "Fair enough."

Becca shoveled the food onto a pair of plates, turned to toss the spatula into the sink, and jumped back, dropping it with a clatter.

Brooks caught her by the shoulders. "What the…"

"Big hairy spider." Becca stared into the stainless steel basin, her hand on her chest. Brooks reached into the sink and plucked the spider up by one leg, then set it on his palm where it skittered over his hand as he rotated it, moving to the sliding glass door. Becca gave him a wide berth. He shook the spider out onto the grass, and turned to her with an amused smirk. "Really? After everything you've seen, you're scared of *spiders*?"

"No… That was a *big* one. Caught me by surprise."

Brooks carried the plates to the table.

Becca followed and took a seat. "Thanks for not killing it."

"No reason to kill something just for being ugly," Brooks said. He took a bite of his omelet and chased it with coffee.

"This is good."

She smiled. "Really?"

"Yeah. I'm amazed you could find anything edible in that fridge, never mind make a hot meal out of it."

"I figure you might need the energy before the day is done." Becca had decided while cooking that she wouldn't bring up what had happened last night. Brooks was not the sort to be at all comfortable with losing control. Still, she felt the need to address the larger problem, and couldn't wait until he finished eating to do it.

Brooks looked at her over the rim of his coffee cup, scrutinizing her like a suspect.

"I want to search those archives for the symphony."

"I can't just take you into work with me and set you loose in a restricted area."

"I know."

"I mean, we still haven't decided if we're even going to ask for help about your voice. If they find out it's changed *and* catch you trying to smuggle that score out... You said you know. So what are you asking me to do?"

"I want to break in after hours."

"Becca." It was the tone he used when Django was sniffing around the trash.

"I'm a good climber. Can you leave a window unlocked?"

Brooks sighed. "I should have left you in the loony bin."

Becca shot him a warning look.

He scoffed. "It's a federal building with cameras all over it. It's home to a senator, the DEA, and Homeland Security. Not to mention our little black ops agency. You don't just leave a window open. Most of them don't open at all."

"Did you look into whether or not it's even there?"

"It's not that simple. Guys I used to be able to count on for discretion don't work there anymore. A lot of heads rolled when the new director came in. I'm lucky I still have a job. I guess I locked horns with Northrup enough times that I'm not considered a loyalist."

"What about him? Did you get in touch like we talked about?"

"I haven't located him yet. I know he's in some kind of hospice, but I don't have contact info. The old phone numbers don't work anymore, and I've heard that he was estranged from his ex-wife and kids, so I'm not sure if I'll be able to reach him through family. There's a secretary looking into it for me. Our group sent him a card that I remember signing, but I don't know if that was at a previous facility. Anyway, she's gonna try to dig it up, but I don't know how much time we have."

"Hospice never means much time."

Brooks gazed into his empty coffee cup and Becca had the feeling he was avoiding her eyes.

"What?"

"Nothing."

"Don't *nothing* me, Brooks."

"Look, I don't know if it's cancer—and let's not forget that he smoked like a chimney—but…the Wade House wasn't exactly OSHA Kosher."

"You think he got it from exposure to the black snow. You think we'll get it, too."

"I don't *know* anything, so I'm not gonna worry until I have to. It's just that we were the only two on the exploration team to make it out alive. In the command hut Northrup had nowhere near as much exposure as we did, but everybody on site must have had *some*. Who knows, maybe what's happening to you is from exposure to the house. It would be sort of a double dose for you after Boston."

"So Northrup maybe has cancer, and I have the voice, and you're wondering what you're going to get?"

He shrugged.

"This is why we need to talk to him. But looking for the symphony can't wait. If it's in the hands of a cultist…if the dreams we're having are being transmitted by someone or something that could make me sing the melody from that score…then I'd be better off with a gun in my mouth."

"Don't say that."

"I want to see it burn, Brooks. Then maybe I'll sleep better."

* * *

Brooks took Becca to work with him after all and marched her right through the front door with a visitor's pass. She sensed him stealing glances at her as they approached the building across the Government Center plaza, watching her size up the John F. Kennedy Federal Building as if for the first time. As if it were one of the abandoned subway stations or asylums she used to photograph with her Urbex buddies. But the complex on Sudbury and Congress was a beast of another order of magnitude. Two monolithic high-rise towers connected by a glass atrium to a four-story building, all of it dressed in unadorned reinforced concrete, gray anodized aluminum, and glass.

Once inside, she gazed up into the brightly lit space, where an enormous American flag hung in what felt like a cathedral of bureaucracy. Brooks waved her through the metal detector, and pinned the temporary ID to her jacket.

In the elevator, they were alone again. Brooks thumbed a button and said, "Nobody knows you've been staying with me. If anyone recognizes you, I'll say I called you in to confirm some details of my follow up report on the Wade House operation. Hell, I even still have some unfinished paperwork from the Boston event. But it would be better if no one from SPECTRA sees you here at all."

"I'm not exactly in disguise, you know." She'd presented a fake ID to security and signed the log as Kristin Dearborn.

"That's okay. You're gonna have a long, boring day in a janitor's closet I know of in a camera blind spot."

"Seriously? I can't hang out in your office?"

"I'll bring you a sandwich at lunchtime and let you out at night."

"You're kidding. Django will be less pent up than me. At least Heather is letting him out. What if I have to pee?"

"There's a sink."

Becca stopped walking and cocked an eyebrow.

"C'mon, you've lived in a hut in the rainforest. You're good at roughing it, right?"

"Glad I brought a paperback. Won't someone notice when I don't sign out?"

"We do interrogations here, remember? Guests of SPECTRA check in for days at a time without leaving."

* * *

Brooks opened the door of the janitor's closet and Becca fell out onto the floor, jolted awake.

"You nod off against the door?" Brooks asked.

She blinked. "What time is it?"

"A little after 10:30. The building's almost empty. For now, anyway."

Becca tried to stand but her leg cramped and she propped herself against the wall, clenching her jaw.

"Give me a minute," she said, massaging her calf through her jeans to get the blood flowing. Brooks craned his neck to look around the nearest corner. Finally, Becca put weight on her leg and snatched her bag from the closet.

"Listen," Brooks said, "we have a tight window of opportunity. There's an equipment transfer scheduled for tonight. They're taking something out of the vault and moving it to a test site. I'm not even supposed to know about it yet, but what it means for us is reduced security. The guards who would normally patrol the archive will be watching the loading dock. We can use that, but we have to get in and out of the vault fast before the moving crew shows up."

Becca nodded.

"Follow me." Brooks said. "And pull your hood up; hide your hair. I can get us to the fire stairs without too many cameras, but I doubt we can avoid all of them."

Every noise they made seemed amplified in the silent halls, their shoes squeaking on the waxed floors, footsteps echoing off the marble walls.

"How did you know a janitor wouldn't find me?"

"The offices down that end are unoccupied. The mop was probably bone dry, right? I don't think anybody's been in there for a month. This way. Quick."

Brooks ushered Becca across an intersection with a wider corridor, flanking her on the left side to block her from the camera view. Once they'd crossed it, he shouldered through a door, guiding her by the elbow into a cavernous stairwell. He trotted down the steps with a hand on the railing, Becca following behind. At the bottom, he turned and held up a finger. Becca hung back while he peeked through a narrow window in the door before opening it and waving for her to follow.

"Basement level," he said. "SPECTRA archives."

They had arrived at what looked like a bank vault door secured with an array of steel gears and rods. Brooks positioned himself in front of a retinal scanner and adjusted the angle of the blue illuminated glass hemisphere to his height. Becca heard a faint chime followed by the heavy clank of the vault door unlocking. Brooks swung it open and led her into a dimly lit corridor. Red digits glowed in the gloom: temperature and humidity figures. The soft sound of dehumidifiers sighed from the corners. Becca could make out the shapes of long rows of glass cases, but their contents remained obscured. The dry air felt charged, whether from static electricity or the presence of eldritch objects, she couldn't say.

"Are you gonna turn the lights on?" Becca asked.

"No. Use your headlamp. If you see the lights come on, snuff it and hide."

Becca found the headlamp in her bag by touch, pulled the strap over her head, and clicked it on to the red night vision mode, bathing the space around her in bloody light. Brooks walked ahead toward a set of glass doors. Becca followed, but found herself dragging her feet, lingering for a glimpse into this glass box, and that one, and that shelf up there in the corner. The unnatural light made it difficult to identify anything—not that she had the knowledge to do so even in the best of conditions—but the shapes were fascinating.

The place felt like a science museum crossed with a carnival freak show. Some of the objects were jewelry—a carved jade amulet of a winged hound, a gold ring with a purple stone. Others were devices—a coffin-shaped box with four hands roaming a brass dial in contrary orbits, an array of components resembling an amateur radio with coils, gauges, and vacuum tubes showing through circular windows cut in sheet metal trimmed with oak. Yet others were vials of powders or jars in which impossible biological specimens floated in brine or alcohol. One of these resembled a lamprey eel that Mark Burns, the marine biologist she'd befriended on the Wade House expedition, had tried to classify before it dissolved in the terrestrial atmosphere. Mark, like most of the people Becca had formed a bond with in her life, was now dead.

Some of the objects were labeled with printed cards (Eye of Ubbo-Sathla, Lamp of Alhazred, Tillinghast Resonator). Others were unidentified. Some were guarded with laser sensors and keypads on their glass cases, while others occupied numbered bays on open shelves.

Brooks glanced at his watch. "We should be okay if we're quick."

"Right," Becca said, distracted by the exotic silhouettes adorning the darkness on all sides.

"Come on," he said, waiting for her in the doorway ahead. Becca swept her hungry gaze over the collection, then forced herself to hurry through the remainder of the section, past brick cylinders, bas relief fragments, and cloudy crystal shards. One of the last items she passed at the end of the row caught her eye and she did a double take: An antique silver spike like a Tibetan *phurba* with a tentacle-wrapped hilt. Was that the ritual dagger used by Reverend John Proctor? She had watched him use it to banish a hostile entity in the Wade House, and later seen it used against him when Dick Hanson, a cultist who had infiltrated SPECTRA, killed Proctor with his own blade. Becca would never forget watching him die with the silver hilt jutting from his neck. But the true power of the weapon had never been its cutting edge. Used in combination with the proper mantras, it had the power to sever the astral threads that connected this world to the other.

Becca stepped through the doorway and joined Brooks in the next room. Here, the glass cases contained fragments of papyrus scrolls and books with rotting bindings and crumbling marbled endpapers. The shelves were lined with intact volumes, a proliferation of cloth and leather spines, many with raised bands, a few with gilt titles.

In a corner stood a steel file cabinet.

"Manuscripts," Brooks said, stepping toward it. "If the score is in the archives, it'll be in here. Second drawer should include sheet music. You sure you can identify the original? They printed a lot of variations on this music when they were trying to unlock that piano."

"I'll know it."

Brooks thumbed the button next to the handle and pulled the drawer open, nodding at Becca to examine the contents.

The first section of files was labeled: Erich Zann. The composer of *The Invisible Symphony.* Becca checked a random page to confirm that it was sheet music. The file folder tabs were difficult to read by the red light. There were a lot of them but no single section contained many pages. She hunched over the cabinet and set her fingers crawling like a spider through the folders. As she'd expected, most of it was photocopies and computer printouts, variations on the original theme with inversions and permutations generated by man and machine. At the back of the section, she found a dog-eared spiral notebook bulging at the edges with random slips of paper. She carefully removed it and recognized the cover at once: Her father's notes on the music, painstakingly compiled over years of experimentation when he'd lived a hermit's life in a cabin in New Hampshire, obsessed with the sonic keys to another world.

"Whatcha got there?" Brooks asked.

"Luke's notebooks. These should have been returned to me."

"What would you do with them? I mean, you want to destroy the original score. Isn't there enough of it in those notebooks to make them dangerous too, in the wrong hands?"

Becca stared at the creases in the cheap cover where the coating had scuffed off. She flipped it over in her hand and looked at the plain cardboard back where Luke had jotted down a couple of phone numbers and left a coffee cup ring. How much of his sweat had this tattered two-dollar notebook absorbed over the years?

"It's a part of him," she said.

Brooks watched her slide it into her shoulder bag. She defied him to protest, her red light bathing his face, but he kept any qualms to himself.

She flipped through the files again, checking every page in the section a second time.

"It's not here."

"Are you sure?"

"Yes, I'm sure. I've been through it twice."

"Check again." Brooks said.

"You check. Maybe I'm blind."

Brooks stepped in as Becca moved away. "What does it look like?"

"It's on older paper. Crumbling. Wider than printer pages. The title's in calligraphy and the composer left an ink thumbprint in the upper right corner."

Brooks clicked his flashlight on. It seemed so bright and white to Becca's eyes after adjusting to the headlamp. She left him to it and wandered back into the artifact room. A moment later, he appeared between the glass doors.

"You're right," he said. "Not there."

"Is there another place it could be?" Becca said. "A safe or something for the most dangerous books and papers? Maybe in the director's office?"

Brooks rubbed his forefinger across his bottom lip, thinking, then said, "No. These are some of the most dangerous books on Earth in here. It makes Miskatonic look like the children's section. I guess it could be in McDermott's private safe, but even if we knew it was, I couldn't get in."

The overhead fixtures clicked to life, flooding the room with white LED strips. The gears and rods of the steel security door they'd entered through turned over.

"Shit," Brooks said. "Hide. *No.* This way."

* * *

The door swung open and a sinewy, dark haired man in a white shirt with the sleeves rolled up knelt beside it. He appeared to be chocking it open with an object Becca couldn't make out from where she crouched behind a shelving unit. When he stood up and looked around the room, she recognized him: Nico Merrit, the agent who had tracked her to her father's cabin three years ago. The agent responsible for bringing Luke to the Wade House, where he was killed. Agent Merrit had worked on the Wade House operation for a while, filling in for Brooks while he recovered from injuries incurred in the twilight realm between worlds. Becca recalled the unspoken power dynamic of that time—the tensions stemming from the sense that Merrit had been sent to observe then-director

Northrup and report back to unnamed superiors about his effectiveness. She wondered now if he had played a role in Northrup's removal.

Merrit walked backward down the artifact corridor, wagging the fingers of his raised hand like a parking attendant while two other men pushed a rolling flight case into the room. "Right here," he said when the case had rolled up in front of the machine with the cables, coils and gauges. "This is it: the resonator. Careful with the tubes. You have bubble wrap in there?"

"Yeah."

"Be generous with it. This thing is the director's baby. If it doesn't work when it gets to Berlin, it's on me."

"Relax," one of the movers said. Becca couldn't see his face, just his black thermal shirt and the cuff of a faded tattoo sleeve poking out. "I used to roadie for Billy Moon. You want to see somebody have a shit fit about vintage gear on the road, look no further. We'll strap it down tight in the truck."

"Is this some kind of museum?" the other grunt asked, looking around.

"Something like that," Merrit said. "Eyes on the prize, friend."

Becca froze as she watched the curious one bend over to get a better look at a set of carved stone figurines lined up on the shelf in front of her face. For a harrowing moment, only the focal point of his gaze kept her from detection. She resisted the impulse to glance at Brooks for guidance, knowing that the motion of her head would only draw the man's eye.

"You guys bust some brine heads?" the mover asked, reaching for a figurine.

Becca felt her heart in her throat, aware that if he removed the statue from its place on the shelf, the empty spot would be filled with her glaring face.

"Don't touch," Merrit said.

"Whatever. Fuckin' squid worshippers make my skin crawl anyway. How is *that* a god? Am I right? More like a fuckin' Chinese lunch special. They should go back where they come from." The guy had a full-on Masshole accent. Becca figured he was the *fahkin'* truck driver.

"Again: Eyes on the task," Merrit said. "Shit in here will give you nightmares, no kidding."

The guy grunted and withdrew his shiny, black whiskered mug from the space between the shelves. Becca exhaled. She turned to Brooks, squatting deep in the corner between the shelf unit and the wall. He nodded, and the two of them waited it out, listening as the movers took the resonator from its glass case, covered it in protective wrap, and transferred it to the flight case.

When they'd rolled the case out of the archives, the computerized locking mechanism of the steel door shuttled back into place. Brooks let out a sigh. He rose from his crouch and Becca heard his knees pop.

"What does that thing do?" she asked.

"It makes entities visible."

"Where are they taking it?"

Brooks shook his head. "I'd like to know."

* * *

They drove back to Malden in the rain. Becca reclined the seat, turned on her side, and said, "Wake me when we get to the house."

"Sorry it wasn't there."

"It's okay."

"I'll find Northrup. Maybe he does know what happened to it."

The rhythm of the windshield wipers and the hum of the road lulled Becca down to sleep's damp shore. "Brooks," she murmured without opening her eyes.

"Yeah?"

"Let's both get up at three and ride out the hour together. Promise."

"Okay."

She shifted, nestling into the car seat, and fell asleep with her hand wrapped around her shoulder bag, feeling the shape of the reverend's ritual dagger through the canvas.

Chapter 6

In the morning Brooks reunited his gun with its magazine and went to work. Becca walked Django around on the wet grass of the scrappy backyard at dawn and then went back to bed. The pair of them had sat up through the three o'clock hour with the TV on in Brooks' bedroom, too tired to talk.

When Becca woke again shortly after 10 A.M., the first thing on her mind was the dagger. Brooks had been behind her in the book and manuscript room when she snatched it on impulse, and she was relieved to find it still in her bag on the chair beside the bed. She didn't think he would search her things while she slept, but couldn't rule out the possibility. He was, after all, essentially a spy, prone to suspicion of all sorts.

Sitting cross-legged on the bed, she turned the weapon over in her hands, examining the details of the carved hilt and inscribed blade by daylight for the first time. She thought of the blood it had absorbed and the light it had shed in the Wade House, and felt a dim pang of guilt.

Last night she didn't know why she had taken it—there'd been no time for rational thought when she'd acted, regretting what her hands had done almost as soon as the dagger disappeared into her bag. Then, Brooks appearing at her back made it impossible for her to return it to the shelf without revealing what she'd done. She hoped he wasn't presently being grilled by the new director about the missing artifact. He had, after all, left a digital record of his presence in the archive, should anyone care to look for it. Having come up empty on the thing they'd actually gone in there to steal, she could have left without giving anyone a reason to check those records. Now she could only hope that either Merrit's visit to the same vault with a moving crew would add uncertainty to the situation, or that the dagger itself wasn't deemed important enough for its absence to be noticed for a while. It *had* been left out on a shelf with no protective glass. And maybe by the time Brooks got home, she would work up the courage to confess the theft.

For now, she found herself entranced by the object's artful design. In retrospect, it was obvious why she wanted it: Her scarab, lacking its fiery gem, also lacked the power to protect her from chthonic forces. Wrapping her fingers around the dagger, she felt empowered in a way she hadn't in years. She rolled the handle between her palms, closed her eyes, and tried to remember the incantation the reverend had chanted while wielding it against the entity that had attacked Django in the guise of a cat. But the memory was too dim, and she soon gave up. The dagger remained cold to the touch even after holding it for longer than it took most metals to absorb body heat. Becca hid it under the mattress at the foot of the bed, then dressed, went downstairs, and drank half a cup of coffee before taking Django for a walk around the neighborhood.

She'd often mused that spring in New England didn't quite exist. It seemed that from March to June someone spun a dial each day for a random effect unconnected to the calendar. It could be anything from snow with arctic gusts of wind to sun with temps in the 70s. On this April day, the dial had landed on the latter, and she had every intention of soaking it up. She packed a book, a bottle of water, and a power bar in her bag, along with a ratty tennis ball for Django to chase, and walked a widening circuit of the surrounding blocks until she happened upon what she was hoping for: a playground with a small sports field where a few nannies and stay-at-home parents were busy with children too young for school.

Becca passed most of the afternoon at the park, throwing the ball for Django, letting kids pet him, and ignoring the novel in her bag. She couldn't quite imagine herself as a mother—the dog was enough—but she liked kids and seldom found herself in their company. It reminded her of Tom's son, Noah, the only other person on Earth she knew of who possessed the same vocal ability gestating in her own larynx. Brooks had kept an eye on Noah while keeping the boy's inborn mutation a secret from SPECTRA out of loyalty to Tom, who had become a friend after the first crisis, and who worried that the agency might take Noah away if they had reason to consider him a threat.

As long as whatever remained of the Starry Wisdom cult didn't know about the child, Becca assumed he was in no danger. When she'd thought about Noah at all in the past few years, the only alarming scenario she'd imagined that put her nerves on edge was the prospect of someone teaching him to sing *The Invisible Symphony*, an evocation lurking in the camouflage of music. A document that, until last night, she had believed was being kept under lock and key in the hands of men ignorant of its secrets and unendowed with the anatomy necessary to perform it.

Now she wasn't so sure.

Watching a boy about Noah's age try to throw a Frisbee that held Django's rapt attention, she was thinking she should ask Brooks for the latest news of the Petrie family when her phone rang in her jacket pocket.

"Hey, Brooks. What's up?"

"I'm cutting out early. Got that address I've been hunting. I'll pick you up in ten."

* * *

The building on High Street in Newburyport where Daniel Northrup would spend his last days looked more like a sprawling colonial boarding house than a hospital. Inside, high ceilings with cracking plaster and dark walnut trim contrasted with modern elevators, wheelchair lifts, and the odd piece of medical equipment. The place had an austere sort of elegance and Becca suspected it wasn't cheap. For an old building, it looked scrubbed clean and smelled faintly of disinfectant.

The nurse at the reception desk in the front parlor greeted them with a quiet, cheerful demeanor and seemed genuinely pleased that Mr. Northrup had visitors. Brooks admitted that they weren't family and gave her their names. She climbed the stairs to the second floor and returned a few minutes later to escort them up to his room—a private unit with striped wallpaper and a window overlooking a scraggly hill tangled with deadfall. They found the former SPECTRA director propped up in a hospital bed with a snow-white pillow under his head. An oxygen tank and mask hung from a hook beside the bed.

Northrup had grown a beard since Becca had last seen him, as if to compensate for the mass his face had lost. She recognized his eyes, sunken deep in their sockets, but not much else. Where his hair had been thick and jet black with frosted temples, it was now all white and thinned. Was it only 3 years ago that he'd seemed so formidable and self-assured?

"I'll be damned," he said. "The dynamic duo." He went from a wet chuckle to a short coughing fit, and held a handkerchief up to his lips. When the coughing subsided, he checked the cloth, as if looking for blood, and said, "To what do I owe the honor?"

Brooks took a wooden chair from an unused desk and placed it beside the bed for Becca. No sooner had he done so than the receptionist nurse reappeared in the doorway with a second chair for him.

"You look like shit, boss," Brooks said with a grin.

Northrup smiled.

"Don't make him laugh," Becca said. Then to Northrup, "How are you doing?"

He scoffed. "I'm dying. What did they used to say? Spoiler alert."

Becca ignored the chair and perched instead at the edge of the bed. She patted Northrup's hand. "I'm sorry."

"It's good to have visitors." He smiled. "But I must admit, it makes me a little nervous seeing the two of you in the same place. Did something happen?"

Brooks shrugged.

"Do you have family checking in on you?" Becca said.

"Not really. My oldest is about your age. We don't see eye to eye on much. After my job put him through college, he decided he didn't approve of it. Last I heard, he was making a lifestyle out of protesting it."

"What, does he belong to People for the Ethical Treatment of Monsters?" Brooks said.

Northrup was seized by another coughing fit and Becca kicked Brooks' leg.

"I told you not to make him laugh."

"It's okay," Northrup said. "He says we're racists persecuting a religious minority, so…" He drummed his fingers on the bed. "I get the feeling we're talking about my kid so we don't have to talk about whatever brought you two here."

Brooks leaned forward, hands clasped between his knees.

"I can take it," Northrup said. "Whatever it is, I probably won't be around long enough to see it."

"I've been having weird dreams," Becca said.

"After what you've been through, I'm not surprised," Northrup said.

"We both are," Brooks said. "The same dream. About the sunken island."

Becca went on to tell him about singing in her sleep and what the song had conjured in the glass. When she'd finished, Northrup looked even more hollowed out, if that were possible.

"You two never took the Nepenthe. That has to be why."

Becca looked at Brooks. He didn't volunteer the information that Noah Petrie also had the voice. Northrup was retired from SPECTRA, but Brooks was still unwilling to betray Tom's confidence. Becca admired his discretion.

"I still can't even sing *regular* music," Brooks said. "But if Becca took the drug now, do you think it would neutralize or reverse the mutation?"

"I don't know," Northrup said. "Might be worth a try."

"I didn't want blinders then and I don't want them now," Becca said. "If something comes through from the other side, I want to know."

"You getting enough sleep?" Northrup asked.

"The dream happens like clockwork," Brooks said. "We set an alarm every night."

Northrup looked from one to the other, but didn't ask them to elaborate on their sleeping arrangements. "I don't know why you came to me with this and not McDermott."

"You don't?" Brooks said.

"You don't trust him. Well...I remember having to work through that with both of you myself."

"It's not the same," Brooks said. "And you don't have to be political anymore."

"My personal feelings probably aren't very objective," Northrup said. "I *was* shown the door. But let's face it, I wouldn't be able to do the job in this condition anyway."

"Did the job make you sick?" Becca asked. "The house?"

Northrup's eyes drifted upward, as if remembering. "Truth is, I don't know. I took certain risks over the years. We knew there could be consequences, dealing with weird physics and forces from outside. But I don't think you need to worry about your own exposure." His face twisted in a wry grin. "It was probably just the Camels. The agency paid for my treatment, but it was too late."

"I've been shut out of certain circles since you've been gone," Brooks said, "but word is McDermott is experimenting with cultist tech to see if it can be used for defense."

Northrup nodded. "That's not the first I've heard of it. You know my stance."

Brooks grinned. "The Frodo Doctrine, you called it. Destroy it all."

Northrup reached for a glass of water on the bedside table. Becca passed it to him and helped steady it while he sucked on the straw. When she'd set it back on the table, she said, "Did you destroy *The Invisible Symphony* before you left? The original?"

Northrup squinted at her. "No. We have your father's notes on it, and some pages Maurice Ramirez left behind, but those are fragmentary. We have reams of permutations the code breakers and Dick Hanson drafted, but not the original manuscript. We never found it. I always thought *you* must have destroyed it. We found the video on your phone of your father asking you to. He said you knew where to find it. I didn't ask you so you wouldn't have to lie. It wasn't there?"

"No. Didn't anyone else at SPECTRA pressure you to track it down? Why didn't they come to question me?"

"When I wrote my report, I said I believed the original had been destroyed by your father. Caleb Wade's weird piano had burned with his house, and there was no one alive who could sing that music anyway. Until now."

"If someone found it, another double agent like Hanson..." Becca had thought this scenario through often, lying awake at night, but to say it aloud chilled her. "If the song I sang in my sleep was from the symphony, if it's being transmitted to me because I'm susceptible to the signal and able to give voice to it... *I* could be a weapon, a key to doors we thought were closed for good."

"I see why you're afraid," Northrup said.

Brooks rubbed his temple. "I'll dig deeper, look at the list of agents who had access to Luke's cabin in New Hampshire."

"Warwick doesn't know what he's playing with in that archive, but there is something that might actually provide some defense," Northrup said. "A book."

"In the archives?" Brooks said.

"No. I tried to get a professor at Miskatonic—the translator— to admit that he had a copy, but he denied it. It's called *The Voice of the Void*. It's the source of the banishing mantras Proctor used in the Wade House. I'm no analyst, and you might want to check with one you can trust, but if you have the voice, you might try to use it to fight back against whatever is controlling you in your sleep."

Becca sighed. "I'm no reverend of the Starry Wisdom, either."

"True," Northrup said. "And even if you were, you'd probably need a ritual dagger, too. Sorry, but it's the only idea I've got."

"We'll look for the book," Brooks said. "Maybe something in it will help to jam the signal until we have some idea of what we're dealing with."

"What was the professor's name?" Becca asked. "The one who translated it?"

"DuQuette. He knew your grandmother. He dedicated it to her."

Chapter 7

The Old Town of Zadar lies across a bridge from the modern city, walled off and crowned with terra cotta tile rooftops. Here the ancient and modern are juxtaposed — Roman ruins and ancient churches stand shoulder to shoulder with modernist concrete block architecture from the post war reconstruction, all of it bleached white in the Adriatic sun, as if the city were carved from bone. Wooden shutters and laundry lines overlook narrow alleys crowded with cafes and jewelers catering to tourists from the cruise ships and the mainland. Art vendors line cobblestone streets worn smooth as ice from centuries of foot traffic. But at the tip of the port city peninsula that Alfred Hitchcock praised for the most beautiful sunsets in the world, a spacious promenade slopes down to the sea and forms the setting for two jewels of architectural art — one in light and one in sound — both in tribute to man's communion with forces of nature.

Shining like a vast sapphire in the white stone waterfront, a 22-meter glass disk of photo-voltage solar modules collects the light of the sun through the day and emits a multicolored light show after dark, when children and lovers dance on the swirling display. The installation is called the Salutation to the Sun. The central large disk represents the sun itself, while smaller glass disks of various sizes represent the planets of the solar system, spaced at relative distances along the waterfront. These planetary disks are ringed with chrome bezels engraved with the names of their respective planets. The sun disk bezel is engraved with all the saints after whom the churches of Zadar have been named, the dates of their feasts, and the declination and altitude of the sun within 23 degrees on each saint's feast day, as well as the length of each day.

The planetary disks leading away from the tip of the peninsula are strewn along the steps of the largest musical instrument in the world, the Sea Organ of Zadar, played unceasingly by the ocean waves since its installation. The tone clusters emitted by the organ correspond to the chords produced by traditional *klapa*—groups of five to eight singers—and are haunting in their unresolved beauty.

Tristan Furlong walked barefoot along the promenade at dawn. In his hand he held the *shanka* shell, in his ears the music of the sea—the lapping of the waves against the white steps, and the airy notes they pushed from subterranean chambers through the ports at his feet.

The waterfront was tranquil at this hour when the tourists were still sleeping in their hotels and cruise ships. Only a few joggers and locals moved along the promenade as he sat down on the top step with the sunrise to his back, the shadow of the city diminishing on the water before him. He put the jeweled shell to his lips and whispered to it, a mantra that swelled from a murmur to a melody. He sang 93 repetitions, imagining the syllables falling like pearls cut loose from a string, swirling down and around the glossy spiral, his petition winding down to the ocean floor, radiating around the globe, stirring the boundary between worlds, and waking the slumbering Priest of the Deep.

When he stopped, his skin buzzed with the oxygenation of his blood. He set the shell down beside him, drawing his feet and hands into the lotus position, straightening his spine, tucking his chin, and focusing his inner gaze on his third eye. Just another euro-hippie meditating on the shore at sunrise to any passersby.

He tuned his ears to the song of the sea through the pipes.

He waited for his answer to emerge from the deep.

The monument to the sun, engraved with the astronomical data for the feasts of Christian saints, was a kind of calendar, but it could not supply the date and hour he needed to confirm for the work he was about to undertake.

Only the Priest of the Deep could do that.

Tristan listened, and the ocean answered his call.

* * *

When he opened his eyes, the waves were gilded. He rose and stretched his muscles, slipped his feet into his sandals and strode through the waking city to the luthier's shop on Ulica Mihovila Klaića. It was too early for business hours, so he rang the bell for the upstairs flat where the man lived above his shop. A boy lifted the sash and looked down.

"Papa is sleeping," the boy said. "The shop is closed. Come back at ten."

"Tell him it's Tristan. I've come for the lyre guitar. I think he'll get up to take my money if it's done."

The boy's head disappeared. A few minutes later a bedraggled Andelo Dragović appeared in the shop window and unlocked the door.

"Dobro jutru," Angelo said without cheer as Tristan stepped into the shop.

Tristan returned the good morning, scanning the counter, eyes hungering for their first glimpse of the instrument he had commissioned. Andelo locked the door behind him. The shop smelled of resinous woods and glue. On the glass countertop, a set of wood chisels and calipers of various sizes were laid out atop a soft leather case. Dark wood shavings littered the floor, while fragments of abalone like fingernail clippings lay scattered on the workbench. A veritable bestiary of guitars and mandolins crowded the walls. Only a few years ago Tristan would have lusted for any of them, but none possessed the elegance of the instrument he had designed under the guidance of Nyarlathotep, who dwelled in the base of his brain.

"Is it ready?" Tristan asked.

"Da, da. I finished late last night. The varnish maybe is not dry yet." Andelo stepped through a curtain. Tristan waited impatiently, gazing at his reflection in the mirror behind the counter. These days, he barely identified with his own face. Only recently had he stopped mistaking it for someone else's.

The luthier reemerged from the back room, holding the instrument in a handkerchief wrapped around the neck.

Tristan took a deep breath, admiring the sweeping contours of the wood, the intricacy of the inlays on the fingerboard, before reaching out to take it. He stayed his hand and formed a question with his eyebrows.

"It's okay. Not too sticky. Take."

He took the guitar by the neck, ran his hand along it, and peered into the crescent shaped sound hole. The design was based on a nine-string French lyre guitar with long hollow horns stretching up around the neck and curving outward at the headstock. He rested the base of the body on the counter and strummed a dissonant chord.

"Strings are still stretching," Andelo said, stepping behind the counter toward the cash register and flipping through a pad of sales slips. "The wood you provided for the bridge...you must tell me what it is. I have never worked with anything so lively."

"A traveler provided it," Tristan said. "A member of my church. He obtained it from a rare tree in a far-off country."

Dragović waved his hand dismissively. "You want to keep your secret, fine. You don't have to be so pretentious."

Tristan tuned the instrument to an open drone chord and strummed again. Harmonics leapt like silver sparks from the soundboard. He closed his eyes and listened to the sustain. It was glorious. He sang a note over the chord, the augmented fourth of the Lydian mode.

When he opened his eyes, the luthier was looking at him eagerly, every inch a child awaiting praise and reward, despite the bristly nose hair and balding pate. "She is a beauty, yes?"

Tristan nodded and smiled. But the smile wasn't for Andelo Dragović. It was for the shadow forming in the mirror behind the old man: The Goat of a Thousand Young stalking the trees of the ancient forest, a shifting conglomeration of eyes, horns, and black smoke approaching, emerging.

"Balance minus deposit comes to seventeen-thousand five hundred kuna."

"Yes," Tristan said. But he was in no hurry to lay the instrument in the case lying open on the counter and reach for his wallet. He strummed another chord and sang another long note to accompany it.

The luthier licked his lips. His salt and pepper nose hairs twitched as if he'd caught a whiff of the musk of Shub Niggurath. "You are satisfied?" he asked.

"Oh yes," Tristan said. "It's important to have an instrument that inspires one, don't you think?"

Dragović nodded. The spiral horns of the beast emerged from the silvered glass, sending a ripple through the surface, as if they had penetrated a vertical pool of still water.

"It helps to feed the muse," Tristan said, watching the myriad hour glass pupils rolling in sour milk eyeballs as the shaggy head reared back.

The luthier jolted suddenly up on his tiptoes, his back arched as if an electrical current had surged through him. The horns impaled him, poking his nightshirt forward in twin points of blood. Tristan laughed. It looked like the old man had grown monstrous breasts. Dragović sucked silent air to power a scream that would never come, his breath a ragged wheeze, his lungs punctured. The goat's head jerked back through the mirror, taking the body with it, the rippling glass solidifying in its wake.

The Dark Young would feast on terrestrial flesh tonight.

Tristan Furlong laid his new axe on its bed of crushed velvet and snapped the case latches shut.

Chapter 8

The morning after he took Becca to the archive, Brooks found a note on his desk summoning him to the director's office. Warwick McDermott had taken over the office previously occupied by Daniel Northrup, but to Brooks that seemed impossible every time he set foot inside it. Sure, the windows were in the same places and the view of Faneuil Hall was the same, but everything else had changed, from the furniture to the anal-retentive care with which the papers, tablets, and writing implements were arranged. The only framed photo showed a younger McDermott in hip waders, river fishing with Dick Cheney. It was signed, "To Theo, a great angler." Brooks had heard the director went by his middle name among friends, but this was the first evidence that he had any.

McDermott was on the phone. He gestured at a chair in front of his desk while wrapping up the call. Brooks sat and focused on the soft, percolating tones of ambient electronic music emanating from a Bose sound system on a shelf that also housed a small collection of occult books. The new director was younger than his predecessor but not by much, judging by the gray hair combed back over his long ears. The music struck Brooks as an odd preference. But, on second thought, it was as antiseptic as the rest of the man's personality.

McDermott set the phone in its cradle and stood. Brooks leaned forward, thinking the boss was going to extend his hand for a shake, but settled back again when McDermott turned to the long dark shelf below the bookcase and poured a refill of pungent Brazilian coffee from a carafe into a delicate china cup. He waved his hand at a second cup, overturned on a linen square, and raised an eyebrow.

"Sure," Brooks said. "Black."

When McDermott had filled the cup and passed it to Brooks, he settled into his office chair, laced his fingers in front of his mauve silk tie, and said, "Becca Philips."

"What about her?" Brooks said.

"You brought her into the archives after-hours. A hidden camera picked you up. What were you looking for?"

Brooks took a sip of coffee. It was the perfect temperature and strength. "A musical score she believed had been seized from her father's cabin."

"*The Invisible Symphony*," McDermott said.

"It was once part of her grandmother's collection."

"Catherine Philips had no claim to the manuscript, but at least she was an academic. Luke Philips, a mere thief, had even less. I'm sure you are aware of the consequences of bringing a civilian without a security clearance into the vault?"

"I thought she still had clearance. She's worked with classified material before."

"You were so confident of her status that you brought her in like a stowaway in the middle of the night."

Brooks kept his silence.

"Why now, Agent Brooks? What is her interest in the score?"

Brooks had thought all morning about what he was willing to offer if it came to this. Now he didn't hesitate. Giving a little might stir things up and send a few rocks tumbling down from on high. They might hit his head, but then, maybe he would learn something about their composition. "She knows someone who was exposed in the Boston event, someone who took Nepenthe and then went on to have a kid. She believes the kid may have a vocal mutation, like the one Daruis Marlowe simulated with the lab-grown larynx."

"Pretend I can't make the connection myself. Why would that make her want to steal *The Invisible Symphony*?"

"Because according to her father, who devoted years to its study, the score contains an apocalyptic choral section that could, if sung with the proper harmonics, shatter the membrane between worlds permanently. Until recently, we thought that was impossible. But if there's one child out there with the voice, there may be more."

McDermott leaned forward. "You're admitting that if you found the score in the vault, you would have helped her steal and destroy it."

"Seems like that would be a lot cleaner than doing something morally questionable to a group of children we may not even be able to find."

McDermott stroked the stem of his coffee cup, but didn't drink. "We haven't been able to find the score, either," he said.

"I didn't know we were looking for it. I figured Northrup might have swept it up after Luke Philips died at the Wade House, and locked it away for safekeeping."

"But you didn't come to me with these concerns when Becca Philips reached out to you."

"She wouldn't tell me anything without my word that I'd keep it confidential. She's worried about what might happen to her friend's child."

"Your word." McDermott ran his tongue across his teeth behind closed lips, accentuating his lantern jaw and prominent chin. He didn't need to say it. Brooks was a covert agent; his word was whatever advanced the SPECTRA agenda.

"We've been through a lot together," Brooks said. "She's served the agency at great personal cost."

"You count her as a friend."

"Yes."

"Who is the child?"

"I don't know. She wouldn't say."

"Careful, Agent Brooks."

"I don't know."

"Find out if it's one of these." McDermott slid a folder across the desktop. Brooks opened the folder. Stapled to the top corner of the first page was a school portrait of a child Noah's age, a boy with hollow eyes. His smile looked like he hadn't broken it in yet. Name: PHINEAS MALIK. Behind the first file were six more, Noah's among them. Brooks' heart rate kicked up at the familiar face. He steadied and deepened his breath, taking care not to show that he was doing so. McDermott watched his body language, a crane stalking the reeds of a riverbank with quiet patience, waiting for a frog to spear.

"You're already looking for the kids," Brooks said.

McDermott nodded. "There have been incidents."

"Incidents?"

"You can read up on the plane to Arizona where the first one lives. See Caroline for your tickets. That's all for now."

* * *

Brooks left his car in the garage for Becca to use while he was away, and arranged for Merrit to pick him up on the morning of their flight. Becca watched from behind a curtain in her second floor bedroom while Brooks put his carry-on bag in the trunk and climbed into the car. Merrit's face behind the windshield was obscured by the glare, but she had the sense that he was scanning the house for signs of her and took a step back from the window. Probably paranoia. Hanging around with spies, she supposed it was contagious.

Brooks had said that he would be gone for at least two days, depending on how things went in Arizona. She made him promise to keep his weapon unloaded overnight and to continue setting the alarm at his motel. This had led to a brief discussion of time zones, a problem that hadn't occurred to either of them before. Brooks believed that the dream would come to him on East Coast time, like a television show airing simultaneously in different parts of the country. "If it's a telepathic signal going out worldwide at the same time every night, I'll adjust for the difference and get up two hours earlier. At least accounting isn't making me share a room with Merrit."

Becca, in turn, had promised to stay at the house, where all of the reflective surfaces were "Cthulhu proof." They'd shared a chuckle about that, and off he'd gone, leaving her feeling lonely the minute he'd left. It was a weird sensation, she realized, and a new one. She was used to living alone with only Django for company.

She had lived in her father's cabin for the past few years, isolated in the White Mountains of New Hampshire, and she was by nature introverted to the extent that crowded places like the supermarket scrambled her brain and set her nerves on edge. And yet, Brooks' company had become a great comfort in a short time.

Nonetheless, there was work to be done while he was away. Her first task, they had agreed, was to warn Tom Petrie that he should expect an official interview with agents Brooks and Merrit within the next three days. She would have to do it in person, as they were now more certain than ever that Tom's phone and email were being monitored by SPECTRA.

The second task on Becca's agenda was one that she hadn't yet shared with Brooks: She would drive to Arkham and search Miskatonic University to see if her grandmother's collection included the book Northrup had mentioned—or any notes pertaining to it.

She took the stolen dagger from under her mattress and tucked it into her shoulder bag with her notebook, pens, and a smartphone with no Internet connection that she carried mainly for snapping photos of documents.

She would tell Brooks about the dagger when he returned, she promised herself. For now, it was a relief that his boss hadn't pressed him on it. At least if it had come up, he could've pleaded ignorance with all honesty. So far, it seemed, its absence hadn't been noted.

She laid a blanket over the backseat of the car for Django, and headed north in the early afternoon. The trip from Malden to Andover was a straight shot up I-93, not much of a detour on the way to Arkham. She kept the GPS off in the car, as a weak precaution against SPECTRA tracking, and recognized the neighborhood when she found it. She'd made no effort to disguise herself but checked each parked car she passed on the street for occupants. All were empty.

Tom's wife, Susan, answered the door, as Becca had expected. On a weekday, Tom would be in the city where he worked as a network admin and Susan would be taking care of Noah. She looked better than she had the first time they'd met. On that occasion, Susan was in a white-hot terror over her child slashing his little hand open to finger-paint the tub with his blood while chanting *R'lyeh* over and over. Today Susan Petrie only looked as tired and exasperated as any full-time mother of a five-year-old answering the door to an unexpected caller.

She looked Becca over, recognition dawning slowly, and possibly only clicking when she noted a quirky, stylized character painted on one of Becca's combat boots. One of Rafael's. The colors were faded despite the clear coat Becca had sprayed on the boots to protect them after Raf's death. She had put enough additional miles on the boots in Brazil and New Hampshire to have almost worn them out, but the characters were the kind of detail that might have imprinted on Susan's memory at a moment of crisis, and lingered long after the face of the woman who wore them had faded.

Susan's eyes widened. She shot a look at Django, sitting on the long bottom step behind Becca, and began to close the door. Slowly, as if in a dream, not knowing how to deal with anyone who might represent the agency when Tom wasn't at home. Or *did* she know what to do? Had the couple made a plan for such an eventuality, and if so, what might that involve? Becca thought of what mothers of all species were willing to do to protect their young when cornered, and suddenly, coming here face-to-face without backup or advance notice seemed profoundly unwise.

"Wait," Becca said. "I have a message. Just a message. From Brooks."

"Why didn't he come himself?" Susan asked through a three-inch crack between the door and frame in which Becca could now see only one of the woman's eyes.

"He's out-of-state. He'll be here sometime in the next few days with another agent. An official visit. This other agent doesn't know that Brooks has stayed in contact with you; at least he *shouldn't* know. But SPECTRA is looking into children like Noah now. They might even be able to help, I don't know. The important thing is that you and Tom have to act like you don't know Brooks."

"But Tom *met* him through SPECTRA, when they rounded up witnesses, when all hell broke loose in Boston."

"Yes, Susan. But Tom hasn't seen Brooks since then, understand? Don't be familiar. Tom hasn't seen Brooks since before Noah was born, and *you've* never met him at all. Okay?"

"Puppy." A child's voice. Noah had appeared and wedged himself in front of his mother. The door opened a little wider as Susan used both hands to pull him back, but he was already reaching through the gap, offering something to Becca. It sparkled blue in his hand.

"I made it myself," Noah said. *"You* have it."

Becca took the object, a cardboard disk the size of a quarter, covered in blue and green glitter and blobs of Elmer's glue.

"Thank you, Noah. Are you sure?"

Susan watched the exchange warily. Noah nodded. "We're doing planet crafts! That's Neptune."

"It's very nice," Becca said, closing her fingers around it.

"What's puppy's name?"

"Django," Becca said.

"Can I pet him?"

"No, sweetie." Susan pulled the boy toward her with a gentle hand on his shoulder and shut the door.

Pulling the car away from the curb, Becca glanced in the rearview mirror. Something black caught her eye, glistening on the verge of visibility, then wriggling out of sight. She hit the brakes and jerked forward over the wheel, felt Django hit the back of her seat.

Looking back at the house, she saw Noah's pale face framed between the parted curtains of a first floor window, eyes vacant, mouth moving as if singing. He withdrew suddenly, the curtain tugged shut by an unseen hand.

Becca waited for her heart to slow, then eased the car onto the road. She wondered if the family would still be here when the agents arrived.

* * *

The dogwood trees were flowering when Becca arrived at Miskatonic University. The day, which had been cold and windy to the south, was mild, almost balmy by the time she reached Arkham. She parked the car, cracked the windows for Django, and walked across the campus, relishing the fragrance of the trees in bloom, letting it soothe her rattled nerves. For a moment, she could almost believe that she was still in her teens, strolling across the quad to visit Catherine at her office in the Anthropology Department.

Becca had intentionally driven the long way around town, avoiding Crane Street and the house where she'd lived with her grandparents after her mother's suicide and her father's departure. She didn't know if the new owners had painted it or changed anything, nor did she want to find out. For now, she would let it remain a place frozen in time, its good and bad memories preserved like insects in amber.

She made her way directly to the ivy-fringed library, where the cool shade of the stacks leeched the heat from her skin and left her feeling more her age.

At the special collections desk, she presented her driver's license and explained that she was not a student but rather a relative of the esteemed Dr. Catherine Philips, and could she please spend some time with her grandmother's papers, manuscripts, and rare works. After a lot of keypunching, the librarian explained that most of the material was boxed up in storage.

Becca replied that she didn't mind looking through it in a storage room. The librarian sighed. Perhaps Becca could return on a different day, after submitting a request to have the collection transferred to a reading room, the severe, thin-lipped woman suggested in a beleaguered tone. She was sorry, she said (though she didn't sound sorry at all to Becca), but it would have been easier to accommodate the request if Becca had made an appointment to view the Philips collection a week or more in advance.

By this time, Becca was feeling fatigued from the stresses of visiting Tom's house, compounded by the emotionally charged memories the trip to Arkham was stirring. For a moment, she had to stop and take stock of herself. Was she really the same person who had stared down cultists and government agents? Who had taken on gods and monsters with little more than her wits? There had been times in the past few years when she'd felt that these experiences had helped her to break through to a new level of self-assurance, but right here and now, sleep deprived and unsure of her goal, it seemed impossible to believe that those actions had been undertaken by the same person who could barely summon the resolve to stand her ground against a bitchy librarian.

She was about to give up the quest for the day and head back to Malden, after maybe finding something to give her blood sugar a lift, when a reedy voice from over her shoulder said, "Did I hear the name Philips?"

Becca turned toward the man emerging from the stacks—old but not frail, bright blue eyes gleaming with mischievous cheer between a neatly trimmed white beard and a mane of thinning hair that still held a trace of gold. His hands, gnarled and liver-spotted, dangled claw-like from the cuffs of his tweed jacket, swinging as he walked.

"Lo and behold," he said, "I hear my old friend's name and this must be her ghost. Is it true, then, that we get to reclaim our prime in the afterlife?"

Annoyed for a second by this puzzling distraction from an objective that was getting harder to attain by the minute, Becca soon found herself smiling as the sense of the words sunk in. "You knew my grandmother?"

"Ah, you must be Rebecca, then." He shook Becca's hand with a surprisingly lively grip and introduced himself. "Anton DuQuette. Catherine was a friend and colleague. We met as students in Dr. Morgan's archaeology class."

"Really," Becca said. "Then this is a lucky meeting. I was hoping to look at my grandmother's collection today, while I have a rare opportunity to visit the college, and the book I was hoping to find is one that you dedicated to her."

Something flickered in DuQuette's eyes, but he didn't ask for the title or miss a beat, only turned his bright, expectant gaze on the librarian. "I'm sure we can accommodate the young Ms. Philip's request, Larissa. Can't we?"

"I was just explaining that it may take a while, Professor. The materials need to be moved from Storage B, the interns are at lunch, and the reading rooms are occupied."

"No worries, then," the old man said, producing a crowded key ring and shaking it like a maraca. He raised his chin and scanned the tables of students. "I'll recruit the requisite muscle myself and have the boxes brought to the faculty conference room."

The librarian opened her mouth, but before she could argue, DuQuette called across the room to a pair of athletic looking boys hunched over notebooks with an open textbook between them. "MacLeod! Nunnally! Come give an old man a hand, will you?"

* * *

After directing the transfer of the boxes to a long oval table in a room with a whiteboard, Professor DuQuette lingered in the doorway.

"You really do resemble her." He smiled sadly. "But if you're looking for a copy of *The Voice of the Void*, I doubt you'll find it here."

"Wouldn't she have kept a rare book that was dedicated to her?"

"It's rare for a reason. My own last copy was destroyed in a house fire. Catherine's, I believe, was stolen from her office by a student. The Starry Wisdom Church has been hellbent on erasing the book from history since the nineties. I'd be very interested to know why you're looking for it now."

Becca considered the man for a moment. Northrup had given her his name, but was it too convenient that he'd showed up and offered help right at the outset of her search?

"Forgive me," Becca said, "but I don't remember you from the funeral."

"I was sorry I couldn't make it. I was abroad at the time."

On impulse, Becca decided to prod for a reaction. "I met one of Catherine's star pupils in Boston. Maybe you knew Maurice Ramirez?"

DuQuette's weathered face turned introspective, as if a shadow passed over it. He swallowed, and when he spoke, there was a deeper sorrow in his voice and eyes. "Maurice made great sacrifices to save a world that failed him."

A ripple of gooseflesh passed over Becca's arms and she drew a deep breath to tamp down the swell of emotion. She nodded and, through tight lips, said, "He did."

"I hear you were with him at the end."

Becca looked past DuQuette at the door, calculating the distance. "Who told you that? It wasn't in any of the papers."

"Frater Ramirez was a member of the Golden Bough, a hermetic order to which I also belong. He broke with the order when he decided we were too cautious and slow to action. Maybe he was right. Even so, I'm afraid he got in too deep and it damaged him. I tried to help. But by the time the Starry Wisdom Church acquired the technology to give voice to the mantras in their dread tomes, he trusted no one."

"*Could* you have helped?"

"Perhaps not. By the time we understood what was happening, the only weapon we knew of to aid in the fight was missing." DuQuette had approached the table while speaking. He rested his hands on a chair back and his gaze fell on Becca's chest. She knew he wasn't imagining her breasts beneath her shirt and rayon scarf.

"Do you still have it?"

She nodded. "But it's only a keepsake now. The gem is gone."

"Gone where?"

"To the other side. Where I hope it's still burning shit down."

DuQuette laughed. "It was probably best that it came to you, after all. Catherine knew that. What Ramirez could have done with it…I'm not sure it would have been enough."

"He knew so much more than me," Becca said. "Maybe she *should* have entrusted it to him."

"You were younger, and saner."

"I don't know about that second one."

"You did well."

"Yeah, well…it was close. Moe didn't live long enough to guide me much. He found out I had the scarab too late. I figured out the mantra for it almost by chance. If Catherine hadn't impressed it on me a long time ago… If I hadn't remembered it at the right time…"

"She impressed it on you for a reason. She knew you were the right person to bear the task, and she gave you the tools to stand in her place when the time came."

"I doubt she was as wise or far-seeing as that. She made mistakes. People paid for them."

DuQuette interlaced his fingers and moved them through a series of small gestures that Becca sensed held some symbolic value to him. "I've taken vows to the order. It would forfeit my life to break them. But I regret that I couldn't guide you then. Perhaps I can now, with caution. If I'd known what you were embarking on, I would have been at Catherine's funeral. I would have reached out."

"Reached out and claimed the scarab?"

"I hope I would have been wiser than that." He tipped his bearded chin at the journal and pen she'd placed on the table beside the box of books and papers. "What did you hope to find in the book?"

"Do your vows allow you to talk about it?"

"To a degree. But it's useless without a certain artifact. A dagger forged of meteoric iron. Church records claim three of these daggers were made and lost throughout history. There's a consensus that the first—from the time of Dionysus—was destroyed, and the most recent was made from a meteor that landed on a farm, not far from here, a century ago. That one may be only a legend. Most scholars believe the meteor dissolved."

"What do you believe?"

"*Solve et coagula,* as the alchemists used to say. Dissolve and recombine. In the right hands, the meteor may indeed have been reconstituted into a powerful weapon."

"I've seen one. It was used by Reverend John Proctor of the Boston Starry Wisdom Church. He used it to banish something that came through from the other side."

"You witnessed this?"

"Yes."

"Proctor did have a reputation for caution where letting the Great Old Ones into our world was concerned. He would have protected such a relic." DuQuette squinted at Becca. "Are you working with him? Is that why you're looking for the *Foní tou Kenoú?*"

"He's dead," Becca said. "The dagger was lost with him."

"I'm sorry to hear that. Rumor was, he'd been recruited by the government to fight an invisible war."

"There's some truth to that."

DuQuette raised an eyebrow.

"What did you call the book?" Becca asked.

"*I Foní tou Kenoú* is the Greek title. But translations have appeared in other lands and languages. It was circulated wider than one would expect for a grimoire that required a rare weapon to be employed. At one point, Catherine had access to a Latin copy of the text: *Vox in Vacuum.* She claimed it went missing from her office along with her notes and the English edition I'd given her. That never sat well with the head librarian, who thought she might have 'removed it from circulation' to her private library. Of course, her private library is here in these boxes now and, I assure you, the book of mantras is not."

"Any idea where it ended up?"

"No. But I've often wondered if she may have passed it to Frater Ramirez."

"Was Catherine a member of the Golden Bough as well?"

"For a time, yes. She left the order shortly after Ramirez did. The way she talked about him, I think she saw him as the most capable among us. He was a talented magician, even after he started losing his mind." DuQuette expelled a sharp nasal laugh. "Maybe more so after. Of course, I see now that *you* were Catherine's true last hope. I have to admit, it's unnerving to find you looking for the book rather than hiding it somewhere. And you tell me the dagger may have passed out of this world, like the Fire of Cairo before it. That would put us in a dire position if we had reason to fear another breach. *Do we,* Ms. Philips?"

"It's possible. Do you think Maurice hid the book somewhere?"

"She would have given it to him if she thought he could track down the dagger and unite it with the book, but from what you've told me, that never happened. So he would have concealed it, kept it safe."

"If you were trying to think like Maurice," Becca said, "where might he hide a book like that for safekeeping?"

"I don't know if *anyone* ever thought like him."

Becca was reminded of how Moe had once hidden a literal key to the adjacent dimension under a horseshoe crab on the shore of that strange world. "So there's no place you can think of? Maybe a place that only members of the order would know about? Or someplace with personal significance to him?"

"I'm afraid the possibilities are endless."

"Why?"

"You must remember that to a mystic like Maurice, every gesture of daily life—never mind an act of such cosmic significance as protecting a book of power—was imbued with potential symbolic associations. The state he functioned in wasn't all that different from that of a schizophrenic. It wouldn't sit right with him to just put the book somewhere safe, he would be compelled to hide it in a place that referenced its nature."

"So someplace that has to do with...voices?"

"Possibly." DuQuette stood up and went to the white board. "Are you familiar with Gematria at all?"

"It's like numerology, right? Where you add up the numeric value of a Greek or Hebrew word or sentence? Catherine was always scribbling calculations on the back of the grocery list."

DuQuette nodded as he uncapped the marker. He wrote two lines on the board:

$$\text{קול של הריק} = 781$$

$$781 = \text{אשפת}$$

"For the sake of example, let's say he had the Hebrew translation of the title in mind when choosing a hiding place."

"But she would have given him the Latin version."

"Yes, but the Latin alphabet doesn't really have numeric equivalents. He *may* have chosen to work his associations in Greek, so already we have no idea if we're even barking up the right tree. But just to illustrate one scenario: He calculates the number of the Hebrew title, which is seven-hundred-eighty-one. Then he chooses another word or phrase, equal to the same value, probably from the Bible. It could be anything, and you can't add up all possibilities for your scavenger hunt. If you get lucky, maybe you find one in a notebook of his that you at least know was on his radar."

Becca felt a tingle in her stomach at the memory of the Hebrew words Maurice had scribbled in chalk all over the ceiling of his makeshift monk's cell in the abandoned textile factory where she'd first encountered him.

"But say he chose this word," DuQuette said, underlining the second line. "It means *dung* or *refuse* and comes from a reference to one of the nine gates of Jerusalem, outside of which there was probably a garbage heap. Which is interesting to us because your scarab—the only other weapon we know of proven to banish these entities—is a dung beetle."

"So what does that mean?"

"My point is that it could mean anything when you try to convert it into the practical actions of a mad man. It could mean he hid the book under a garbage heap. And that's just one possibility."

Becca drummed her fingers against the cover of her notebook.

"You look crestfallen," DuQuette said. "You came here hoping that Catherine might have left you the answers, or at least a clear path to them. But you're not telling me everything. Why are these arcane books and weapons urgently needed now?"

She took a breath and dived in, told him about her recurring dreams, but kept her newfound vocal abilities to herself for the time being. She also neglected to mention the dagger in the bag beside her chair. If the information frightened him, he didn't show it.

"You believe Cthulhu is waking and reaching out in dreams to sensitives like yourself."

"Am I wrong? Has anyone in the order experienced the dreams? Have you?"

"No one in the order would be vulnerable to telepathic dreams."

"And why is that?"

DuQuette took his wallet from the breast pocket of his jacket and removed a card from the fold before tucking it away. He took Becca's pen and wrote on the front of the card where his office hours were listed. But this wasn't more cabalistic calculation; it was a phone number.

"That's my cell," he said. "I trust you'll call me if you need anything. Perhaps when you're ready to be less guarded about your objective." He held up a hand as if to ward off some protest. "I quite understand your reasons for caution."

He flipped the card over and drew a symbol on the blank side: a curved pentagram with an eye in the center, its pupil a pillar of flame. When he'd recapped the pen, he held the card up for her to see.

"Visualize this symbol before sleep. Hold it in your mind's eye. It's a variant of the elder sign, which is graven upon the crypt of Cthulhu. The mark of the Elder Gods who imprisoned the Great Old Ones. Sleep with the glyph under your pillow."

Becca stood up, placed her notebook in her bag, and took the card from him. "Thank you, Professor. You've been more helpful than a box of books, but I should be getting back to my dog."

"Where will you begin your search?"

She shrugged. "Maybe I'll have an idea after a full night's sleep."

But she had one already.

Chapter 9

Brooks listened to an audio book on the flight to Arizona so he wouldn't have to talk to Nico Merrit. They flew into Flagstaff Airport, rented a compact car, and drove forty minutes through Oak Creek Canyon to Sedona. Merrit drove. Brooks rolled his window down to bask in the warm, sage scented breeze and admire the scenery; the contrast of red rock against a cerulean sky dotted with white clouds. It had snowed recently in the valley. Most of it had melted already, but the buttes were capped and dusted with white on their western slopes, creating a surreal juxtaposition of desert with the last throes of a winter he'd hoped they were leaving behind when they flew out of Boston.

The agents checked into separate rooms in the economy Kokopelli Motel, where the VACANCY sign above the parking lot depicted the hump-backed fertility deity playing his flute in silhouette.

The Malik family had relocated to Arizona from Massachusetts with their son, Phineas, three years after the Equinox event. Brooks and Merrit hadn't given them any advance notice of the visit, but satellite and signal surveillance indicated they would be at home on Saturday if there was no deviation from their usual routine.

Brooks spent Friday night in the motel reading the files for the families they were assigned to interview. There wasn't much about Tom's family and Brooks was tempted to indulge a sense of relief reading through the scant information SPECTRA had compiled. An agent could never be sure the powers that be weren't testing him, but maybe his cautious and minimal contact with the family had gone undetected. He only hoped Becca had been able to tip them off without exposing the connection. For all he knew, she was being followed now.

When he caught himself nodding off from jet lag, he tucked his ammo magazine under the mattress, set his alarm, and turned in early to make up for the sleep he knew he would lose later.

From what Brooks could tell, Merrit spent most of the night at a local bar. Walking past his room at 1:30 A.M. while taking in the mild night air during the dreaming hour, Brooks heard him getting laid. But in the morning, Merrit was no worse for wear; clear-eyed, clean shaven, and waiting for Brooks in the continental breakfast lounge.

They passed the Red Planet Diner and an assortment of New Age crystal shops advertising vision quests and "Vortex Tours" until Highway 179 took them over the town line into Oak Creek, winding up into the hills.

Merrit caught Brooks staring at his wallet where he'd stuffed it into the cup holder after filling the gas tank.

"What? Need a loan for a lottery ticket?"

"Just wondering if it's true," Brooks said, "that you carry a newspaper clipping about what happened in Iraq."

Merrit took his eyes off the road long enough to fix Brooks with an icy stare. Looking ahead again, he said, "If you want something to gossip about, why don't you check?"

"You blame me for being curious when we're headed to a house where a child is involved?"

Merrit's jaw clenched. A vein throbbed at his temple.

"Did the *Times* get the facts right?"

"That's classified. Just do your job and I'll do mine."

"Keep your safety on."

"I'm not repeating myself."

The Malik house was a single-story pueblo revival design with a front yard of crushed stone. What it lacked in square footage, it made up for with a stunning view of the Bell Rock butte through the wide living room windows.

A short-haired woman with olive skin answered the doorbell, dressed in yoga pants and a lavender jersey—Demi Malik, judging by the file photo. Merrit held up his ID. Mrs. Malik reluctantly let them in and called for her husband.

Brooks scanned the room. Standard southwestern style decor and a scattering of kid's toys, mostly Legos and art supplies. A few family photos, but no mirrors. Of course, that didn't mean anything in a living room, but he decided to ask to use the bathroom at some point to see if they were absent there as well.

Five-year-old Phineas sat on the living room rug, clutching a gray Lego model that reminded Brooks of an Easter Island head, eyeing the strangers with a look that implied he'd be growling if he were a dog. Brooks found the vibe coming off the pale, hollow-eyed child unsettling. In his limited experience, most kids that age were pretty neutral toward strangers. Maybe Phineas was picking up on Mom's nerves.

Cyrus Malik emerged from what looked like a home office, also dressed in Saturday morning casual: flannel bottoms, a college logo T-shirt, hair mussed up, and hands empty. "What's this?" he said, then composed himself, stepping between his son and the agents in their dark suits. "How can I help you gentlemen?"

"They're SPECTRA," Demi said. "From Boston."

"You came all the way from Boston," Cyrus said, "but you didn't call first?"

"We had other business in the region," Merrit lied. "It's been on the agency's to do list for a while to check in with witnesses of the Equinox terror attack."

"Phineas, go play in your room while Daddy talks with these men. Demi, please make some tea."

"That's okay," Brooks said. "We already had coffee."

"Tea, please," Cyrus repeated and his wife left the room, escorting the boy down the hall.

"This is just a routine follow-up, Mr. Malik," Merrit said, looking around the room with his thumbs hooked in his pockets.

Cyrus gestured at a pair of leather couches at right angles. "Please. Make yourselves comfortable."

"Were sorry to intrude on a Saturday morning," Brooks said.

"We realized on short notice that it was a convenient opportunity for us to check in," Merrit said. "Most of the other families have remained in the greater Boston area."

Cyrus took a seat on a bench facing the couches in front of an upright piano that looked like it was used as much for displaying small sculptures and candle sticks as for music. A storm gray cat sat perched on the lid where a triangle of morning sun warmed the golden wood.

"You last saw us at Government Center for your second shot of Nepenthe in October of that year," Merrit said.

"That's right."

"What prompted the move to Arizona?" Brooks asked.

"Demi was offered a good job with the Sedona-Oak Creek school district. Since I can work from anywhere, it was easy to let her take it. Also, we wanted a change of scenery."

"The weather sure beats Beantown," Brooks said. "Although, it looks like you didn't entirely escape the snow."

Demi returned with a silver tray bearing china teacups and a metal pitcher of milk. She set it on a wood and leather chest that served as a coffee table, and then perched at the edge of a rocking chair. Brooks noticed for the first time that there was no TV in the room. It brought to mind his own widescreen, currently draped with a bed sheet.

Merrit ignored the tea tray. Brooks flashed Demi a tight smile. The aroma of the tea was strange—exotic and not entirely unpleasant. He couldn't place what it reminded him of. Something he'd smelled in a dream? He tried not to stare at the sea-green color in the gold-trimmed cups, and focused on what Merrit was saying.

"Your son was born after the event, correct?"

"Yes," Cyrus said. "The following June."

"In our effort to track you down for this follow-up, we looked at his school records."

Cyrus shifted on the piano bench. "He hardly has any. Do they even keep preschool records?"

"They do," Merrit said. "We were looking for a forwarding address, but I couldn't help noticing that there was a record of disrupting incidents in the classroom. It looks like you pulled him out halfway through the year."

Demi looked as pale as a woman of dark complexion could. Brooks thought *ashen* might be the right word.

"I thought you were here to find out how I've been since the Equinox attack," Cyrus said. "What does that have to do with my son? He wasn't even born yet."

"One of the things we're looking into is whether or not there may have been effects on the offspring of people who were exposed in Boston," Brooks said.

"From the drug you gave him?" Demi asked.

"No," Merrit said. "From the sound waves he was exposed to."

"What kind of effects?" Demi said. "Cancers?"

Brooks couldn't tell if she was genuinely concerned, or if she already knew what they were getting at. If so, she was a convincing actress, at least in service of shielding her child from government scrutiny.

"What happened at the preschool in Massachusetts?" Merrit asked.

The parents looked at each other. An unspoken permission passed from Cyrus to his wife.

"He has nightmares sometimes," Demi said. "It was worse when he first started going to school for a full day. Most likely it was stress, difficulty adjusting to that. I see it a lot in my work with children of that age."

"You're a teacher?" Brooks asked.

"A speech therapist. I often see stress manifested as impairments or developmental delays. Sometimes a child's stress leads to outbursts or nightmares, insufficient sleep…"

"Did Phineas experience any of that, or just the nightmares?" Merrit asked.

"He didn't act out," Cyrus said.

"I think he stopped sleeping enough because he was afraid of having a nightmare," Demi said. "And that resulted in him seeing things in the daytime that scared him."

"Hallucinations?" Brooks said.

"That's a strong word," Demi said. "More like jumping at shadows. Misinterpreting things he saw. I reduced my hours at work, went back to the half-day preschool program, and he did much better."

If she was trying to recontextualize things they'd already learned from the school records, she was doing a good job.

"These shadows…was he seeing them in mirrors?" Merrit asked. "Or other reflective surfaces? Did you move to the desert to get away from water?"

"That's enough," Cyrus said, standing up. "We didn't agree to be interrogated about our son's mental health."

"We're here to help," Brooks said. "To offer support if there's still a problem. Is there?"

"No. There is no problem." Cyrus gestured at the door. "Allow me to see you out."

Brooks stood up. Merrit didn't move. "Phineas is an unusual name," Merrit said. "Where's it from?"

"The Bible," Demi said.

"I don't see why that should have any bearing on anything," Cyrus said.

A keening sound cut the air, high and shimmering. It started as a faint whine, like a dog might make, but twisted as it grew in volume.

Demi went to the hallway that ran the length of the house, the same direction she'd led Phineas when his father sent him to his room.

"What's that?" Brooks said.

Demi wheeled around in the doorframe, unguarded anger blazing in her eyes. "You're upsetting him," she said. "He's sensitive to the tone of your voices. You should go."

"How can he even hear us?" Merrit said, but the parents were ignoring him. Cyrus ushered his wife from the room, his hand on the small of her back. He whispered something in her ear and sent her down the hall.

The noise warbled and wavered, the high legato note descending into a staccato, guttural chant.

Cyrus blocked the hallway, his feet set wide, arms folded over his chest. He wasn't a tall or large man, but he made the most of his stature in the narrow passage.

"Sir, what exactly is your religious affiliation?" Merrit inquired.

"Did you have any contact with members of the Starry Wisdom cult when you lived in Boston?" Brooks said.

"Or since?" Merrit said.

"None. I was a *victim* of the attack. Now you come to my home and threaten my family? When a drug *you* gave me may have impaired my child?"

Brooks held up a placating hand. "Threaten? Slow down. Nobody's threatening anyone."

Cyrus scoffed. "Really. You ask everyone their religion? Or just the immigrants?"

"The Starry Wisdom Church is based in Egypt, where you come from," Merrit said.

"It's active where *you* come from, too. Get out of my house. You want to question me, come back with a warrant and take me in."

The boy's wail faded. Brooks could faintly hear the mother placating him. He knew the family was keeping secrets, but Merrit had made a royal mess of the situation, cornering them with no finesse. Brooks touched Merrit's elbow and said, "C'mon. Let's go."

A cascade of icy notes chimed down the hall. Phineas moaned. Cyrus' head ticked to the side and he glanced over his shoulder at the sound, which evolved into a descending melody, lonely and haunting, forming skeletal chords and curling up into thorny vines of sound, trembling with vibrato. The sound paralyzed Brooks where he stood.

Merrit broke the spell, seizing on Cyrus' distraction, shouldering past him and lunging down the hall before the man could get a grip on him. Brooks followed. As the three men tumbled down the hall, Demi's voice rose over the music and the moaning. "No, Phineas. Don't go. *Don't!*"

Brooks spilled into the boy's bedroom behind Merrit. Phineas was crawling across the floor, his outstretched hand reaching to touch a TV screen from which a pale green light, the color of the untouched tea on the tray they'd left behind, flickered over his awestruck face. His mother, on her hands and knees, tugged at his shirt until she saw the agents in the doorway, her husband unable to stop them. Then she let go, and Brooks realized it wasn't a TV screen but a mirror in a carved oak frame propped up against the wall beside the bed.

Phineas Malik clambered over the frame and through the shimmering glass, vanishing under a swelling wave of nauseating light and music. The glass rippled over the boy's feet and resolved into a reflection of the bedroom. Brooks saw his own face staring back, mouth agape.

Merrit stepped back to a position between the husband and wife. He drew his gun and pointed it at the mirror, but Demi, still on her knees, put her body between the weapon and the glass. Cyrus put his hands up.

"Call HQ," Merrit said to Brooks. "Tell McDermott what happened. Tell them we need local support."

Brooks released his grip on his still holstered gun and tapped the phone icon on his wristwatch. Demi protested that they couldn't be arrested, couldn't leave the house without Phineas. What if he returned to an empty house?

"We'll take the mirror to Boston," Merrit said. "Does he ever come out of a different one?"

"He's never gone through before," Cyrus said. "He just sits in front of it and sings along with the music. Like a normal kid with TV."

"Bullshit!" Merrit shouted. "You knew he'd use it to get away from us."

"My com is going nuts with interference," Brooks said. "I'll try outside."

Merrit stepped aside so Brooks could leave the room, but kept his gun trained on the parents.

Brooks hurried through the house looking at the signal icon on his watch. The screen flickered, and the symbol jumped back and forth between full strength and nothing. He wanted to hear more of the conversation in the child's bedroom, but there would be time for a proper interrogation back in Boston. He wondered if Phineas had ever sung in his sleep.

He stepped out the front door to see if he could connect again some distance from the house and was walking across the gravel yard, adjusting the volume of his ear piece, when something caught his eye—a liquid shimmer like a heat mirage in his peripheral vision. Brooks looked up at the Bell Rock butte. The shapes of hikers moved slowly over its contours. The weather was clear, the sky a pristine blue above rock banded in hues of maroon, ochre, and lavender.

What had stirred the air?

He glanced back at the house, silent and still.

The ripple pulsed across the sky again with a faraway echo of strange chimes. Something flared silver white at the peak of the rock formation, and Brooks could swear he spied the shape of a man with a guitar standing up there. Some New Age pilgrim might carry one on the trail, he knew. But something in his bones told him this was no chakra balancing trail guide providing an ambient soundtrack to vortex tourists.

Brooks had the unsettling sensation that the dark figure was looking directly at him. The air rippled again, and as if the compression of the atmosphere had caused a magnification, the guitarist appeared closer. Blue fire flickered in his hair as he strummed his long-horned instrument.

The ginger hair at the nape of Brooks' neck stood up, and the minstrel vanished in a twist of the air, leaving only the reverberation of the last shimmering chord he'd struck.

Chapter 10

The day after her excursion to Arkham, Becca returned to the abandoned mill on the flooded east bank of the Charles River for the first time since the fall of 2019. She'd considered driving directly to Cambridge after her conversation with Professor DuQuette at Miskatonic, but had been too tired for the clear thinking and puzzle solving the trip would require.

The squat building looked as bleak as ever, even in the spring sunshine. If anything, the harsher highlights glinting off the sheet metal of the peeling ARACHNE TEXTILES sign enhanced its apocalyptic aura. She had found Django in this place when he was a stray, scavenging along the waterfront after Hurricane Sonia, and she wondered how much he remembered of the labyrinthine building that had been his temporary home. He seemed excited to be back, weaving in zig-zags through the maze of rusted machinery and snuffling at the spools and bundles of rotting fabric. Becca indulged the dog's nostalgia, if you could call it such, until they came to a corridor she recognized. She gave a short whistle, and he followed her to a descending metal staircase veering precipitously away from the wall it was barely bolted to. The stairs groaned but didn't give out, and in a moment she was standing at the door to the basement electrical closet Maurice Ramirez had made a nest of.

Milky light filtered down from the floor above through windows opaque with grime. Becca removed the elastic from her ponytail and let her hair fall free. She took the headlamp from her bag, pulled the strap over her head, and clicked it on.

The door was jammed tight to the frame, swollen from the humidity. She pulled hard, yanking it free with a shriek and shudder. Django sniffed at the darkness, then ventured in. Becca pulled the door as wide as possible to let a little light into the cramped room, but it didn't do much to dispel the darkness. She swept the beam of her headlamp over the walls abutting the door to make sure no one was about to jump her, then scanned the room, finding it empty of squatters.

Django pawed and sniffed at a heap of blankets on a cardboard pallet beside the remains of an assortment of candles melted to the floor. Becca wondered if the dog could still detect Maurice's scent lingering in his bedding, but on closer inspection she saw that the blankets were shredded and littered with mouse droppings. Even to her blunt human nose, the room reeked of mold with undertones of urine and old incense. She kicked the blankets around and lifted the cardboard for a glance underneath, but there were no books or journals to be found this time.

Becca took the camera from her bag, set it for flash, and shot a series of photos documenting the Hebrew and Greek words and Arabic numbers chalked across the cave-like plaster ceiling. The sheer complexity of this chicken scratch made her heart sink at the prospect of deciphering even a fraction of it, never mind sifting it for a viable clue to the location of the mantra book. When she finished documenting the ceiling, she took a few more photos of the places where Maurice's notes dribbled down the walls. But as she checked the photos for clarity, she felt the futility of the task weighing on her. This search would be as fruitless as her attempt to find the score in the SPECTRA archives.

Still, it felt like a small accomplishment to finish the set and step out of the room into the relatively cleaner air of the basement corridor where she could breathe deeper. Having captured the data, she considered leaving. It would take forever to puzzle through the translations and calculations, a job best undertaken in front of a big monitor with a legal pad and a cup of tea. But leaving now would also mean having to drive back here again to search for…what? Some physical feature of the place that matched a Hebrew word Maurice had jotted down? It was unlikely that she would know what she was looking for on a second trip any more than she did now. And she lacked the resources to tear the entire mill apart searching for a book. If it was even here.

She scratched at the back of her head and sighed, accepting that any cursory search she was going to conduct would have to be intuitive. With Django at her heels, she wandered the basement, waiting for a feature to catch her eye, and talking aloud to the dog all the while to help her thought process along.

"Air ducts? Maybe. They are kind of high, though…"

Django cocked his head, hanging on her every word.

"For all I know, he buried it at Bunker Hill." Becca sighed. "I think he'd want to keep it close. Close to where he bunked. What do you think, Django? Did Moe hide it close? Are we getting warmer?"

The dog swished his tail.

Toward the end of the hall, she found a grungy bathroom with no water in the toilet. Feeling that it would be an unforgivable omission, she lifted the lid of the toilet tank but found it empty as well. Motion caught her eye in the streaked mirror, like something skittering away at the bottom of a deep pool of silty water. Becca froze and held her breath. She spent a long moment staring at the glass while Django growled, but when nothing stirred, she left the room.

Maurice had talked about "sealing the cracks between worlds" in this place where Darius Marlowe had once experimented with his lab-grown voice box prototypes. Becca had seen with her infrared camera just how thin the membrane between dimensions was in the abandoned mill during that bloody autumn. Was it still? Were fractal tentacles still writhing under the thin veneer of reality here? But she had opened herself to EDEP since the last time she'd been here. If the place was infested with entities from beyond, she would see them with her naked eyes now. Wouldn't she?

She touched the scarab pendant through her shirt, felt the cavity between the pincers where the gem was missing, and pondered the dagger in her bag—equally impotent for all the good it would do her without knowledge of the banishing mantras.

A few yards farther on, she arrived at the final two doors of the basement maintenance corridor. One of these revealed a boiler room with an old iron behemoth sprouting pipes into the ceiling. The other opened on a janitor's closet containing a rope mop and bucket, as well as an assortment of brooms, gallon jugs of cleaning chemicals, and a squat Shop Vac coated in a thick layer of dust.

The corridor ended in darkness and a shallow black puddle of rainwater. Becca considered searching the derelict loom machinery on the level above, but something made her hesitant to leave the basement. It was silly, but she had the idea that if she remained close to where Maurice had slept, she might catch an idea he'd left floating in the air, like a gossamer cobweb snagged in her hair.

She backtracked to where she'd left the door of the janitor's closet ajar, and took the empty mop bucket by the handle. She turned the bucket upside down and set it in the middle of the corridor where she could sit on it and think. It was a less than ideal work space but she made the most of it—syncing the digital camera to her phone so she could view the photos on the larger screen, and then opening her Moleskine notebook to a blank page. She uncapped a felt tipped pen and set the butt end of it on her bottom lip while she pondered the first photo, the fumes of the Sharpie wafting up into her nose facilitating an analytical frame of mind.

Django circled her perch and eventually settled beside her.

The letters Maurice had chalked over the ceiling emanated from a hieroglyph of a scarab beetle at the center of the ceiling—she recognized one of the Hebrew phrases closest to it as the words for "Let there be light," the mantra that had kindled the Fire of Cairo, to vanquish the monsters at the Bunker Hill obelisk and again in the circle of standing stones behind the Wade House. But the scarab wasn't the only graphic element in the cabalistic alphabet soup. There were two other crude illustrations: One was unmistakably the key Maurice had hidden on the Twilight Shore. The other looked close enough to be the tentacle-wrapped ritual dagger.

Becca copied down the three Greek and Hebrew words closest to the dagger, then pocketed the phone and flipped back to the page in her notebook where she had recorded DuQuette's rambling example of the sort of numerological code and associative thinking Maurice might have employed to choose a meaningful hiding place for the book.

Book title:

The Voice of the Void

Greek:
η φωνή του κενού
i foní tou kenoú

Arabic: Sawt Alfaragh

Latin: Vox in Vacuum

Hebrew:
קול של הריק

781 = dung heap
Dung beetle?

She thought about how the Egyptians imagined the god Kephra, in scarab beetle form, rolling the sun across the sky like a ball of dung. But she wasn't looking for the scarab or its gem now. And she hadn't found anything in the toilet tank, if you wanted to stretch the symbol to suit her current environment.

As her mind wandered, she found herself staring at a stain on the wall. It looked like a face with a vaguely reptilian nose. She'd explored enough crumbling buildings in her time, and photographed enough water stains, to know how good the human brain was at seeing patterns and extracting meaning from chaos. At times, she had photographed face-like stains precisely because she wanted to exploit that tendency in the service of art. In light of all that she'd seen in recent years, her skepticism about such ordinary things felt unmoored, as if her exposure to real magic had introduced a corrosive agent to the cement that held the tiles of reality together in the mosaic of her mind so that there would never again be anything she could trust as truly benign or mundane.

And in this place, reality felt thin to begin with.

The walls almost seemed to breathe, and the humid atmosphere of the mill felt heavy with portent. But being here was bringing her no closer to finding a pattern in Maurice's chicken scratch.

The felt tip of the pen tickled her palm and she looked away from the stain to see that she'd unconsciously been drawing on her hand, forming a doodle of a curved pentagram—like the one Anton DuQuette had shown her the previous day. Last night, she'd tucked his card into the pocket at the back of her notebook for safekeeping. She'd been unwilling to risk sleeping through the witching hour to test the symbol's efficacy under her pillow without Brooks in the house for backup. Now she plucked the card from the pocket and examined the details. She filled them in on her hand before putting it back.

Django began to growl, low and constant in the back of his throat, his fur rising in a ridge along his spine, his ears pointing backward. He crouched and bared his teeth, the full array of warning signals manifesting in less than three seconds. Becca followed the focus of his glare to the puddle at the end of the corridor.

She stood and dropped the phone into her jacket pocket. Music reached her ears; faraway and drenched in cavernous reverb, a cascade of chiming notes trickling down the steps of an exotic scale. The puddle rippled from its center with each successive note. Becca's palms went clammy and fear iced down her spine from hairline to tailbone. Django took a step back, growling louder to compete with the volume of the music, dropping into a low crouch from which he could lunge if needed.

Eyes fixed on the water, Becca also took a retreating step, kicking the mop bucket with her heel and breaking the trance she'd drifted into as it clattered away and rolled along the wall. Becca startled, and something—an idea that had until now been teetering at the edge of some high mental shelf—was dislodged and dropped fully formed into her awareness: She saw the cluttered interior of the mop closet from which she'd taken the bucket. The dust-coated Shop Vac. What if Maurice didn't use a mystic code to choose the hiding place for *The Voice of the Void*? What if he'd chosen a pun on the Latin title: *Vox in Vacuum*?

Becca moved toward the closet, her pulse pounding, not daring to look away from the vibrating water. The puddle receded like a tide and slid up the wall, defying gravity. Until now, the chimes had been single notes. Now a chord was struck, and the water parted like a curtain. Becca's will drained away to the sound of Django pissing on the floor beside her.

A scarlet robed figure emerged from the curtain of water, his steep, dark features those of a Nubian king, blue fire flitting in and out of his dusty hair, eyes shining like emeralds. A stringed instrument hovered in front of him. If it was held on by a strap, Becca couldn't see it, but that seemed like a minor offense against the laws of physics in light of everything else she'd observed in the past minute. The instrument resembled a guitar or lute with long horns that curled up around the tuning keys. She recognized the man's face. She had seen it before, at the Christian Science Center reflecting pool in Boston where he had summoned monsters from two feet of water by chanting. This was the Strange Dark One, The Haunter of the Dark in bipedal form, the protean creature Becca's grandmother had referred to as the Black Pharaoh.

He strummed another chord and the entire corridor shimmered in response. Becca felt the bass frequencies roll through her intestines, while the treble stung her eyes like grains of salt or sand. A sibilant moan issued from the thing's mouth, and words formed on a gust of fetid wind: *"Sssing with me, Rebecca."*

Becca whimpered and shook her head. She raised one hand to fend the creature off while digging in her bag for the dagger with the other.

The pharaoh's features morphed into those of a black panther, hissing in rage and pain. Django took heart and barked a flurry of threats.

Becca, now holding the dagger in her right hand, realized the reaction had been provoked by her left. She turned it inward and saw the sweat-smudged black glyph she had distractedly inked on her skin.

She had not summoned this entity with her voice. Could she banish it with a mere symbol? If the membrane here was thin enough to be malleable, could *she* wield some control as well?

Becca raised her boot and stamped her foot where the puddle had been before it climbed the wall. As she did so, she thrust her hand forward, palm out, all of the muscle memory required to break wood at the dojo snapping into focus and reinforcing the projection of her will toward the dread minstrel. An invisible shockwave coursed down her arm, and a string broke on the guitar. It whipped through the air like a living limb, writhing and lashing out to sting her face, leaving a trail of phosphorescence in its wake.

The pharaoh retreated into the folds of dirty water and Becca caught a glimpse of other denizens of that realm gathering at the hem of his robe: black fur, horns, and clicking mandibles. A wave of musk flooded her sinuses, making her gag and retch. She forced herself to step forward, holding her hand out as a ward in front of her.

The parted water slapped together and splashed to the floor, spraying her clothes and face.

Becca turned on her heel and yanked the closet door open. She dragged the vacuum out by the handle, sending clattering mops and brooms to the hallway floor, then crouched and fumbled with the latches, her fingers trembling with adrenaline and anticipation. When the lid came off, her heart sank at the sight of dust, dirt, and a tangled ball of textile thread clogging the half-full drum. She thrust her hand into the mess, rooting around in desperation until she felt it: something too bulky to have passed through the vacuum hose. She pulled it out and wiped it off—a Ziploc freezer bag containing a tattered, leather-bound book.

"Django. Let's go."

The dog looked up from sniffing at the filthy puddle on the floor. His fur still standing on end in anticipation of a fight, he eagerly trotted after her, up the stairs and out of the building.

Chapter 11

Tom Petrie could smell the ozone in the air as the largest air insulated Van De Graaff generator in the world cycled up. He looked down the row of seats, past Noah, at Ian, the most anxious of the children in Tom's group. Ian had his hands cupped over his ears, but at least he'd quit uttering that high-pitched whine. Gathering his coat in his lap, Tom prepared himself to usher the kid out of the theater if the finale got too intense for him. It wasn't Tom's first time seeing the lightning show at the Boston Museum of Science, but for a lot of these kids, it was. When Tom thought about the content of the show, he mostly remembered the cool facts the kids would learn, like how a car is the safest place to be in a lightning storm—but not because of the rubber tires. Seeing the lecturer press her hand to the bars of the metal cage while zapping it with 2,000,000 volts from the 40 foot tall orb-topped pillars was wonderfully terrifying until she explained that the reason she was safe was because electricity traveled over the outer surface of the cage to seek the ground, and couldn't pass through the bars to cook her hand.

What he'd forgotten, when proposing the museum to Mrs. Yardley for the last field trip of the year, was how loudly the generator crackled every time it discharged a bolt. That, and how the atmosphere in the theater felt electrified enough to raise the hair on your arms. Glancing down the row in the other direction, he saw Mrs. Yardley giving him a wide-eyed look that said: *Is this almost over?*

Tom nodded in a way he hoped was reassuring, and returned a grin that probably only made him look like an idiot. As the parent of a child with "issues," Tom made sure that either he or Susan could accompany Noah on any field trips the class took. It had been a delicate process informing the teacher and school nurse of Noah's triggers. As perplexed as it left them, Tom had opted to keep it simple, describing his son's condition as a rare phobia of mirrors and reflective surfaces. In the classroom, this didn't present a problem unless Noah had to use the bathroom, and at the age of five it was still possible to have the teacher accompany him to usher him past the dreaded thing. Nonetheless, Tom knew Noah sometimes tried to avoid having to go to the bathroom at school, a strategy that had resulted in several accidents and the need to pack a change of clothes in his backpack.

At least the Montessori school presented a contained environment with not many variables. Field trips were another matter. It was tempting to exempt Noah from them, but it pained Tom and Susan to think that their son couldn't share the same range of experiences as his classmates just because he might see something that spooked him. He would have to adapt to the larger world a little at a time, and so Tom tried to steer things when he could. He also tried to emphasize a rational scientific view of the world for his son. He thought that might be Noah's best defense against fear in the years to come.

Tom didn't understand everything that had happened to him in Boston in the autumn of 2019, nor did he understand the effects of the event inherited by Noah, but that didn't mean the mystery had to be evil or unsettling. That was what he told himself often, and again as he watched the cage rise between the poles of the generator, realizing—perhaps too late—that he had chosen this exhibit more for himself than for the children. It was just another attempt to convince himself that if the forces tormenting his son could be understood, if their causes, conditions, and rules could be known, then maybe they could be endured safely. Maybe they didn't have to be a cause for terror, as lightning had been for primitive man.

Beside him, Noah covered his ears, but his eyes remained wide with delight as the final volley of violet-white lightning bolts flashed around the room, striking their prearranged targets in quick succession.

Tom put his hand on Noah's knobby knee and gave it a gentle squeeze. So maybe he *was* a helicopter parent, hovering around his boy, ready to intervene at the first sign of distress. It wasn't for nothing. Experience had shown how quickly things could spiral out of control without supervision. Hell, even *with* supervision. Like the time Noah cut his hand open with his mother's razor in the bathtub while lost in one of his reveries, chanting about a sunken island. Nothing like that had happened in a while, but Noah *had* recently started singing in his sleep—a sound so unsettling that Tom and Susan spent a good part of each night lying awake in anticipation of the chilling melody.

Helicopter parent. The phrase rolled around like a stray marble circling Tom's skull until it bumped up against something he'd tucked away in the shadows. He didn't remember much about the so-called Red Equinox, but now, as the lightning flashed around the dark theater, he heard rotors, and his mind flashed back to an image of a tall, dark man striding slowly through the Christian Science plaza, between the church and the marble lip of the reflecting pool. Why now? His breath shortened and sweat prickled in his armpits. That man had sprouted ribbons of black ink from his shoulder blades, writhing around him like tendrils in water. A lightning storm in miniature had licked at his temples like a crown of fire.

Tom came back to the theater with a jolt, his back arching in his seat as if the final lightning strike had found him. The house lights came up. The audience clapped, stirred in their seats, and began to chatter.

Mrs. Yardley composed herself and glanced around at the children. "Well, that was very educational," she said with an air of relief. "Gather your things, children, and stay with your chaperones. We'll make our way to the exhibit halls now before lunch."

"You okay, Ian?" Tom asked the straw-haired boy beside him.

The kid nodded.

"What did *you* think, Noah?"

"Wicked cool!"

Tom laughed and tousled his son's hair, which earned him a withering look. "That's my little buddy. Boston to the core. Let's go. Follow Mrs. Yardley's group."

"Can we go to the butterfly garden?" a girl named Maeve asked, pointing at the sign for it off to the right.

"No, honey, that's not on our list. Costs extra," Tom said. He did a quick head count and had to call Ian back from wandering to the stairwell.

"But I want to see the T. Rex, Mr. Petrie," Ian whined, leaving his rattled nerves behind him in the theater. It was amazing how resilient kids could be.

"Later, maybe. If we all go together. Come on, this way. Don't you want to learn about the science of playgrounds?"

"No."

"It'll be fun. You can burn some of that energy you just collected."

"What?"

"You know, pretend the lightning exhibit charged you up with energy you can use to lift weights and run fast. They have a thing that measures how fast you can run. Like on The Flash."

"The what?"

"It's an old TV show. About parallel worlds and... Never mind. Let's go."

The Science in the Park exhibit was already bustling with older kids from another field trip. Adding the kindergarteners increased the pandemonium exponentially—the shrieks, sneaker squeaks, and chatter echoing around the vast hall. Tom's group fractured as soon as they entered the area, each of his kids choosing a different activity with classmates from one of the other chaperones' groups. At least the open area made it easy to scan the room and keep an eye on them all with no partitions in the way.

Noah headed to the bicycle wheel, Maeve to the seesaw, and Sophie to the running track. Ian waited for an older boy to tire of the weights and levers, but soon shuffled back over to Tom.

"I have to pee."

"Okay." Tom scanned the larger exhibit hall and found the Blue Wing restroom signs across the stairwell. Mrs. Yardley was too far away to shout at over the noise, but Tom caught the eye of another chaperone with a raised hand. "Lisa." He pointed at the shuffling boy beside him. "I'm taking Ian to the boys' room." She made the OK sign, and Tom led Ian through the currents of rainy day patrons toward the men's room, thinking about the criminal background check form he'd had to fill out to be a school chaperone. He supposed it was, in part, for scenarios like this one.

Walking back a moment later to the playground exhibit, hands still damp despite the jet-powered dryer, Tom felt a flutter in his stomach. A second later, his right eyelid started to twitch. He recognized his own stress reactions before fully tuning in to what his ears had detected: an exotic, slightly dissonant melody gliding along beneath the chatter of the children, like a water snake weaving through a forest of little legs at a riverbank.

He froze and put a hand on Ian's shoulder, stopping him in place.

"What are we stopping for?"

"*Shhh.*" Tom held up a finger and cocked his ear.

Was that Noah's voice? Was it the melody he sang in his sleep? Or was Tom so sleep deprived and paranoid that he was hearing it in random noise now, like seeing Jesus in a piece of burnt toast?

Chimes trickled through the crowd off to his right, mimicking the melody he thought he'd heard. Some kind of sound exhibit? His heart rate had gone up to the register it would be in if the restroom trip had required a jog up a staircase. He snapped out of listening mode and picked up his pace, pushing the boy along in front of him, and scanning the field trip children from a distance. His eyes flitted frantically, searching for a glimpse of Noah, eyelid twitching all the while.

It seemed to take forever to guide Ian through the crowd milling around the 4D theater, then past some kind of lighthouse, and finally back to the green painted room with the seesaw. Maeve was still riding it. Sophie had joined her on the opposite end. The bicycle wheel was spinning unattended on the residual momentum of whoever had just abandoned the activity.

If Noah was still in the area, Tom didn't see him.

Mrs. Yardley was trying to organize the kids into something like a line at the running track with the digital speedometer. Tom sidled through and touched her arm. "Have you seen Noah?"

Her eyebrows went up, but not as much as he knew they would have if he'd asked about a kid that wasn't his own.

"I thought you took him to the bathroom. Lisa said—"

"That was Ian. Noah's not here."

"Maybe he went after you. I'll keep an eye on your kids. Backtrack to the bathroom and look for him."

"Ian, stay with Mrs. Yardley."

Tom power-walked back to the main concourse, weaving through the throng and trying not to let his escalating panic make him frantic. He knew if that happened, his sense and senses would be diminished, his chances of spotting his son in the crowd lessened. But knowing the pitfall didn't mean he could avoid it.

"Breathe," he muttered under his breath, craning his neck to see past taller men. "How far could he go?" And why the hell would Noah's teacher think he'd brought his son into a public bathroom? Those places were all mirrors. Didn't she get it by now?

"Breathe, Tom. Don't put your anger on her." *And now I'm talking to myself like a nut job. Susan's gonna kill me. She knew this was a bad idea. Too many variables.*

The crowd milling around the 4D theater was even thicker than it had been just moments ago. Had to be a show letting out. He was considering going the long way around the stairs when something caught his eye and made him do a double take.

The lighthouse between the playground exhibit and the theater hadn't really registered with him the first time he'd passed it. Now he tuned in to the structure: a blue and white striped octagonal tower with an illuminated glass section at the top, filled with dozens of prismatic mirrored cubes. A large sign emanated from the glass, like a ray of light.

LIGHT HOUSE
Beaming, Bouncing, and Bending Light

Beyond the sign, all manner of prism, projection, and mirror activities awaited. Taking them in, Tom felt as if he'd stepped into a plunging elevator.

Off to the right, the bespectacled face of an Indian boy smiled and bobbed from side to side, refracted at myriad angles from a wall of mirrors. A few feet farther on, a girl and her bearded father watched their own reflections warp and bulge in an array of convex mirrors mounted on the wall. Tom stood under the sign, listening for Noah's voice, or even for those tuneless chimes, but he heard nothing of the sort—only the sound of agitated children's voices, some kind of commotion deeper into the exhibit, and a placating adult tone.

He turned and looked at the restrooms, hoping to see Noah emerging from the men's room or drinking from the water fountain on his tiptoes. He knew his son wouldn't go into a public bathroom. They had limited his fluid intake this morning and Tom had made him pee one more time before leaving the school so he wouldn't need to go here. But next to that hall of mirrors, the bathroom seemed relatively harmless.

Tom's twitchy gaze ricocheted around the hall. He took quick inventory of the staircase, thinking maybe Noah had gone down to look at the dinosaur skeleton like Ian had wanted to, and then his eyes locked on something that made the whole scene feel like a bad dream:

Jason Brooks was jogging up the stairs with another man—another SPECTRA agent, judging by the plain black suit—and they were scanning the crowd, too.

Were they also looking for Noah?

Tom felt a wave of relief capped with a foam of dread at this possibility. Brooks made eye contact with him and quickened his pace up the stairs.

"Mr. Petrie?" Brooks said.

"What are you doing here?" Tom said. Brooks flicked his eyes at his partner and Tom processed the fact that Brooks had addressed him by his last name. They were supposed to interview him at his house tomorrow. That was what Becca had told Susan. But Tom wasn't supposed to know that.

Brooks started again. "Mr. Petrie, I'm Agent Jason Brooks, and this is Agent Merrit. We're with SPECTRA. We met briefly some years ago, when you witnessed the event in Boston."

Tom looked away, still scanning for Noah. "How did you find me here?"

"Your wife said you'd be here," Merrit said, "with your son. Where is he?"

"Missing. He's missing," Tom said. He could feel his face crumbling inward as he gave voice to the horrible word.

Now Agent Merrit was staring into the Light House exhibit, too. Tom thought he looked apprehensive. "Shit, Jason," he said. "Look at this place."

Brooks *was* looking at it, the color draining from his face. "Is he in there?"

"I don't know," Tom said. "He has a thing about mirrors. Freaks out around them, but sometimes he's drawn to them."

Brooks touched his jacket, where a gun might be concealed in a shoulder holster, then blinked and strode into the exhibit. There were too many people around to go brandishing a weapon, but Brooks had once watched monsters pour out of the biggest mirror in Boston, the John Hancock Building, and obviously wasn't ruling it out.

Tom followed Brooks past the mosaic of mirrors, the convex mirrors, and the station where couples blended their facial features with optics. He followed Brooks past the tables of prisms and the photoreceptive wall where children projected their shadows, leaving fading impressions. Tom drifted like a phantom or a sleepwalker after Brooks, while Agent Merrit shadowed him.

The voices of children grew louder as they turned a corner and entered a room that housed what looked like a forest of slim white trees with green painted leaves, all connected by stylized roots and branches. A girl rose from a crouch where she'd been peering into a space between the trees, and Tom saw at least a dozen of the same girl rise with her, each glimpsed from a slightly different angle. The spaces between the trees were mirrors, of course. The girl waved her arm and a multitude of arms waved back at her, each smaller than the one before it as they marched off to infinity. She looked like Shiva, the many-limbed god of destruction. She knocked her little fist on the glass. An infinity of fists knocked back simultaneously.

Seeing the reflected men behind her, she turned to face them and said, "How do you make it do the trick?"

"The trick?" Brooks said.

"Make it play the music again," a chubby boy in a baseball cap said.

"What music?" Tom asked him.

"It starts with the music, and then you see the man with the weird guitar and the goats."

"It plays a movie," the girl said. "But only one kid could make it play."

"He's done it before," the boy said.

"He must have," the girl said. "He knew the song. He sang it and stepped right through the glass without breaking it."

"It's not the song, dummy," the boy said. "There has to be a button that lets you in."

Tom just stared at him.

The girl was pressing her palms against an army of her doppelgangers again, feeling each pane of glass like a mime. "It's an optical illusion," she said. "One of these isn't a mirror, it's a doorway."

Chapter 12

"Looks familiar," Brooks said. "What is it?" He waited for Becca to throw the dirty tennis ball across the yard for Django, then handed the scrap of paper back to her. She had copied the symbol from the back of DuQuette's office hours card so she wouldn't be handing his contact info over with it, having decided that she would tell Brooks about him only if she could confirm that the dagger and book provided some viable defense after all.

"It's called the elder sign. I found it going through my grandmother's papers at Miskatonic. It's supposed to provide some defense against the Old Ones. Even in dreams."

"How?"

"I want to sleep with it under my pillow, see what happens. Or doesn't."

"Okay. But I'm still watching over you."

"Of course."

"That it? A doodle? Nothing else we can use?"

Becca scratched her arm and ticked her head no, took the ball from Django again. Brooks looked up at the dusky sky. He had shadows under his eyes.

"How is Tom holding up?" Becca asked. "Have you talked to him since Noah's disappearance?" Brooks had filled Becca in on the broad strokes of his trips to Arizona and Boston. A third child on the list, a girl, had vanished into a puddle in her backyard after her mother heard ethereal music through the kitchen window. The agency's assumption was that if three children had crossed over within a day, there were likely others that they didn't know about. They even had their own acronym. COVs: Children of the Voice.

Brooks shrugged. "He looked shell-shocked when we dropped him off at home. Same as he looked five years ago after watching the monsters tear through reality like tissue paper."

"It's the Black Pharaoh again," Becca said. "He's using music to lure them."

"You think he has the symphony?"

"Why else would he need them?"

"But why take them across to the other side?" Brooks said. "Can they rupture the membrane by singing over there?"

"I don't know. As usual, we're caught in a game we don't know the rules for."

Brooks glanced at his watch. "We should turn in early tonight. I'm still jet lagged and I have to leave for New Hampshire at the crack of dawn. I'd like to minimize the impact of the three o'clock vigil."

"Maybe it'll be the last time, if this symbol works."

"I don't know why it would, but what the fuck do I know? Apparently magic works. I just can't seem to take that for granted yet unless it's being used to kill me."

Becca threw the ball and wiped the dirt-infused dog slime off her hand onto the thigh of her jeans. "Do you really think that family from Arizona are cultists? That they *wanted* their son to go through?"

"It was that or hand him over to us. What would you do?"

"That's not an answer. You said Merrit thinks they're closet cultists. Do you?"

"Maybe. Probably."

"Do you think they know anything that could help us get Noah back?"

"Ask me again tomorrow night."

Becca cocked an eyebrow.

"We've been working on the father since we got him back to Government Center. Tomorrow, we're going to give the mother a *demonstration of power* and see if it inspires a change of attitude."

"What does that mean?"

"McDermott is holding his cards close. You'll know when I do."

* * *

Becca slept through the night. At daybreak, Brooks drove alone to the granite quarry west of Manchester, NH. He showed his ID at the security checkpoint, received a blank yellow card he was told to keep on his person, and continued on a dirt road for what felt like a longer ride on the inside of the perimeter fence than it had taken him to reach the site from Malden. For this, his first trip to SPECTRAs only aboveground test site on the East Coast, he'd consulted a printout for directions, which he handed over to the guard in the booth on arrival. The guard fed the paper into a shredder—standard protocol for a location that was off-limits to satellite photography and that still showed outdated imagery when anyone pulled it up on Google Earth.

If you did punch the site coordinates in, you would find an image of the quarry—a stepped granite crater with black water at the bottom—but not the security features, Quonset huts, trailers, and observation towers that had been constructed since 2010. And if you decided it looked like a nice place to take a swim on a hot summer day, you would be politely turned away by men in uniform brandishing assault rifles. Of course, that contributed to local legends, curious teens, and a small graveyard of video drones that had been knocked out of the sky by unknown means as soon as they crossed the perimeter.

Brooks joined the other agents milling into a hut the size of a small aircraft hangar for the briefing. Once inside, he scanned the crowd and found a few familiar faces, but Nico Merrit was not among them. Director McDermott stood off to the side of the riser where a podium had been equipped with a microphone. When everyone had taken seats or assumed parade rest standing positions, a wide man in green fatigues with a pewter buzz cut stepped onto the platform with a sheet of paper in his hand. He set his notes down on the podium and adjusted the microphone height, sending a series of percussive thuds through the speakers.

"Gentlemen. Ladies. My name is General Bartlett, and I will be overseeing the military component of today's experiment. It is my understanding that SPECTRA engineers stationed on the floating platform in the quarry pit will activate a device at precisely thirteen hundred hours. This event, if successful, will...*generate*—for lack of a better term—a life form expected to be hostile. Further, it is understood that the creature may be resilient to, or even unaffected by, conventional weapons.

"A second team of SPECTRA engineers, stationed on Red Overlook, will engage the creature with a second device—an experimental weapon. Should this weapon fail, my men will engage with conventional tactics from sniper positions and towers surrounding the pit.

"Every agent present has received a colored card upon entry. Please examine them now."

Suit coats ruffled as the cards were produced. Brooks waved his yellow card like he was waiting for a Polaroid to develop.

"The color of your card corresponds to your observation deck assignment. All SPECTRA agents attending as witnesses will watch from either Blue or Yellow Deck. Do not leave your platform. This is imperative, ladies and gentlemen. If we end up shooting fish in a barrel, you will be out of the line of fire on your overlook decks. But should you stray from your assigned locations, I will be unable to guarantee your safety.

"Furthermore, if we do engage with conventional weapons, do *not* join the fight with you own sidearm. This orchestra does not need your kazoo. Are we clear?"

A murmur of assent passed through the hut.

"All right, then. Let's take our positions."

* * *

From Yellow Deck, the quarry pit reminded Brooks of the ruins of an ancient city, the granite carved in stepped layers, streaked with black oil. At the bottom, sheltered from the wind, dark water stirred by a light breeze reflected the silver sun like faceted onyx. The only color down there was the conspicuous Red Deck where two engineers in Kevlar body armor were checking the gauges on the Tillinghast Resonator Merrit had removed from the archive below the JFK building.

Across the way, Brooks could see Blue Deck filling up with agents, while the platform he had been assigned to remained sparsely populated, as if it were the VIP seating. A black Town Car pulled up at 12:50. Nico Merrit climbed out of the passenger side with a blue card poking out of his jacket pocket, while the driver opened the backdoor for Demi Malik, Phineas' mother. She was dressed in a SPECTRA polo shirt and khaki slacks. The agents hadn't given her time to pack a bag before leaving Arizona. Brooks wasn't familiar with her resting expression, but he thought she looked defiant. Merrit escorted her to Blue Deck like a press-ganged prom date.

"Our guest of honor," McDermott said. Brooks was slightly startled to find the director standing at his side.

Brooks turned to the man. He was even harder to read than usual in expensive, if awkward, sunglasses. Was that a hint of a smile between the lantern jaw and the black lenses?

"What if she's just a parent whose kid was abducted by a cult?" Brooks said.

"Please. The child's name is Phineas. Some scholars say that means *mouth of the serpent* in Hebrew. They've been grooming him for the apocalypse since the day he was born."

Brooks nodded at the resonator. "Is this an experiment or a show?"

"Both."

"The general didn't sound too confident."

"That's because he's out of his depth."

Brooks looked at the weapon manned by the second pair of engineers on the platform between the observation decks. He couldn't tell what it was made of—maybe some kind of carbon fiber. It sprouted from a tripod of sinewy legs, as if it had grown out of the ground, making it hard to sort form from function. Vents and tubes swooped, curved, and connected the components with the sort of sexual flair favored by hot rod car designers. There was an intricacy to the texture of the weapon that suggested it was carved or molded with embedded symbols; something like a hybrid of braille and cuneiform. One of the engineers swiveled the barrel of the thing and sighted it with a scope on the water below. The other busied himself adjusting a pair of long silicone gloves with flipper shaped fingers.

Brooks nodded at the device. "Those mitts don't look like they're made for precision sniping."

"They cost more than most aircraft," McDermott said. "We've fitted them with cryogenic DNA samples preserved from a certain Antarctic excavation. The operator's body heat will thaw and activate the samples for long enough to test the weapon before they degrade."

Brooks stared into the director's dark lenses. "Alien tech?"

"The cannon, we reverse engineered, but the DNA...well, if the donor was alien, then so are we, Agent Brooks. The Elder Gods were here long before us."

McDermott took a step toward the railing, but Brooks grabbed his elbow and leaned close enough to be heard in a stage whisper. "Am I more exposed than the others here? I'm the only one with the perception."

McDermott gazed at Blue Deck, where Demi Malik was anxiously contemplating the dark water below. "I'm not so sure about that," he said. "You might see it first. She, if her son's songs have opened her eyes, might see it with you. But once the resonator is warmed up, we're all in the same boat."

Brooks noticed he'd been holding his breath. He let it out.

"Do tell me when you see it coming," McDermott said.

* * *

Becca had read somewhere that the seasons were shifting, a theory borne out in her own experience in New England. Every year of her adult life, it seemed winter had started and ended later. There were still the exceptions that proved the rule—the Halloween snow flurry or balmy week in March, but by and large she found the cold weather holding off until January and then hanging on well into April. Fall felt extended. Spring had ceased to exist. Sometime shortly after the last blizzard, a cosmic switch would flip and temperatures would spike into the 80s and 90s without so much as a how do you do. Winter, it seemed, had become unmoored from the clock change. March was a double-headed lion that had eaten the lamb. For a girl with seasonal affective disorder, it was a bitch to say the least.

On the April morning the day after Brooks' return, the Route 1 corridor north of Boston was soaked with cold rain, darkening the windows of the room where she lay curled in bed with Django, and making it easy for her to sleep in for the first time since she'd taken refuge in the house. When she woke at 10:40, the first thing she did was grope for the scrap of paper under her pillow and curled her fingers around it gratefully. She'd slept through the night without the dream, without singing or sleepwalking. She knew Brooks had sat for the usual watch, but he hadn't needed to wake her.

She smoothed out the paper and looked at the curling pentagram with the flaming eye at its center. The lines were blurry from where she'd clutched it in her sweating fist. She could have kissed it. Instead, she placed it back under the pillow and slipped out of bed, scratching her bird's nest of stiff hair. She stomped to the bathroom and brushed her teeth in front of the mirror Brooks had covered with a pillowcase held on by duct tape.

Becca showered and fixed breakfast for herself and the dog. After they'd eaten, she drank tea at the dining room table and spent the rainy morning studying *The Voice of the Void*, her eyes lingering on any page marked by Maurice's pencil, her mind returning often to that white pillowcase shrouding the bathroom mirror.

She had slept a full night without confronting monsters in her sleep and couldn't believe what she was about to do in that bathroom while Brooks was in New Hampshire.

* * *

"Is that what I think it is?"

Brooks stood beside McDermott at the railing as an electric winch lowered a blackened wooden door with an ornate silver doorknob into the pit. The wood was badly burned, reduced to charcoal in places. Mounted in an equally scorched frame, the combination appeared to have been reconstructed and reinforced with new nails, their heads shining in the daylight.

McDermott nodded as the door passed them by. When it had previously been above them, Brooks noticed sigils and names in an arcane alphabet graven in the wood and filled with white candle wax. Now, as the door passed below their level, he saw that its outer side was adorned in the same fashion.

"You salvaged it from the Wade House," Brooks said. "What's written on it?"

"An evocation from the *Necronomicon*. Words of power that no living man or woman—I won't say *child*—has the ability to speak. But I believe the medium makes up for the method in this case. Think of it as an invitation sent on the finest vellum."

"Who are we inviting to their slaughter?"

"A minor deity. A guardian of the gate."

Brooks felt his flesh crawl beneath his shirt and tie. He had seen the creature before, watched it murder Becca's father in a circle of standing stones.

The winch clicked out the inches. The door's descent slowed until it just touched the surface of the water some three yards out from the red platform. Ripples spread from the rectangle, fragmenting the reflection of the cloud-veiled sun, a burnished silver coin sparking on a grinding wheel.

Through the steel cables, Brooks saw Demi Malik clutching the railing of the blue platform, Nico Merrit speaking into her short, wind-tossed hair. Brooks wondered if he was telling her that the cannon they were about to demonstrate could just as easily be trained on her son if she didn't start helping.

Motion drew Brooks' gaze back to the door resting on the water below—green fireflies swarming—no, sniper scope lasers skittering over the charred wood, coalescing on the target's point of entry.

* * *

Clutching the dagger in her right hand, Becca reached out with her left and ripped the pillowcase from the mirror, like gauze from an infected wound.

She knew the words and melody, the fragment of the summoning song she'd dreamed in the hospital, and she knew *what* it would summon if she sang it. The phrase had looped in her head even in waking hours these past few weeks, an earworm of the vilest kind. All she had to do was give it voice and the Lady of a Thousand Hooks would rise from the silvered glass.

She regarded her hollow-eyed reflection. A single night's sleep hadn't been enough to restore her. A sheen of sweat shone on her face and chest, where the impotent scarab beetle hung above the rim of her black tank top.

Heart pounding, she closed her eyes and recalled the banishing mantra from *The Voice of the Void*, her lips moving, portioning the silent breath, rehearsing without uttering the words.

She knew she could conjure, but could she banish? That was what she intended to test. But what if she failed? What would be the price of granting the dark goddess entry?

She fumbled for the little leather book on the marble sink top, flipped it open to her bookmark—DuQuette's card—and ran her finger over the mantra again, confirming her memorization, then turned the page and looked again at the diagram, the glyph she was to carve in the air with the ritual dagger, one stroke for each syllable.

Django whined from the other side of the bathroom door.

If all she accomplished here was her own death in the act of smashing a genie's bottle, who would know what she had set loose into the world? She couldn't expect the dog to explain her intentions when Brooks found her flayed body in his bathtub.

Django, as if reading her thoughts, scratched at the door and expelled a short, sharp bark.

Becca closed the book and it slipped out of her clammy hand. When it hit the floor, the business card fell out—Professor DuQuette's name and office hours blazing up at her like a beacon in blue ink.

She snatched up the book and card, tucked the dagger into her belt, and left the room, closing the door behind her. In a moment, she was sitting at the edge of her bed, heart thundering, cell phone to her ear, waiting for voicemail to pick up and trying to steady her breathing in case he actually answered.

"Anton DuQuette speaking. Hello?"

"It's Becca Philips."

"Becca. Of course. How are you? Has my prescription for sleep been efficacious?"

It took her a second to process what he meant. "Yes, thank you. And I found what I was looking for."

"Did you indeed? Where did our friend stash it, if you don't mind my asking? Did it involve a puzzle? I love a good puzzle."

"Sort of, yes. But I'd prefer to tell you in person, if that's possible."

"Certainly. Will you be up this way again soon? I'd love to have a look. Perhaps I can be of assistance with pronunciations, not that it makes much difference, I suppose. The book is of strictly academic interest without the fabled weapon I speculated about."

Becca bit her thumbnail. "What if it wasn't a fable?"

A beat of silence on the line.

"Were they together? No, don't answer that. When can we meet? I'll cancel my afternoon class if you can come today."

"I don't have a car," Becca said.

"Then I'll come to you."

This was all happening fast, but she could still hang up and he wouldn't know where to find her. His enthusiasm was palpable, intense enough to trigger her warning lights. "You said you belonged to a secret society with Maurice and Catherine."

"I agree with you that this is a conversation best conducted in person." His tone carried an edge of fear.

"I want to meet *alone*. With none of your brothers. I want to test what I've found but I need backup. And it can't wait. Children's lives may depend on it."

"Slow down, Becca. It's not that simple. You can't test a banishing without an evocation. It's dangerous business."

"You knew about my necklace."

"Yes."

"But Catherine kept it from the order. She didn't leave it to you. So how do I know she trusted you?"

He took the time to gather his thoughts before answering, sensing how close she was to hanging up if he failed the test. "I believe Catherine hoped you would find me, or I you. She would have wanted me to help you. I failed her, and I'm sorry for that. But now I have a second chance."

"You knew the mantra to awaken the light?"

"Of course."

"What about the gem? Did you know where it was hidden? Do you know where I found it?"

"It was hidden at a place with a history of transit between worlds."

"Don't talk in riddles. Name it."

Silence unspooled between them and Becca wondered if, his bluff called, he'd hung up. She checked the display: the call timer was still ticking.

"Here's a riddle that answers your question, but just between us," DuQuette said. "In case any little birds are listening. What's white when dirty?"

Becca had heard this one before, from Catherine in fact. But he'd left off the second half. The way Catherine had told it was: What's white when dirty and black when clean? Answer: a chalkboard. But with only the first half of the clue, it could just as well be a birdbath spattered with guano.

"Meet me there," Becca said. "One o'clock."

* * *

Brooks couldn't hear the hum of the resonator powering up from his position on the platform, but he could feel it in his teeth and testicles. Beside him, McDermott tapped his wristwatch and spoke into his earpiece. Brooks couldn't hear what he said, but in response, one of the engineers on the red platform with the resonator—a man wearing body armor and a flotation vest— walked onto a plank suspended over the door. He knelt, reached out a gloved hand, and turned the silver doorknob, around which a steel cable was looped. When he'd returned to the relative safety of the steel grate deck, the engineer gave a hand signal to the winch operator in the crane.

Brooks sensed the agents and soldiers around him drawing a collective breath. All bodies, whether in fatigues or suits, were as still as a photograph as the cable pulled on the doorknob and the door came loose from the charred frame.

It was as if opening the door had completed an electrical circuit. Suddenly, the black water was illuminated from within, revealing a swarm of alien organisms ranging from the amoeboid to the insectile, to more complex variations of marine life, twitching and undulating in a wash of violet light.

The green lasers tracked some of the larger specimens, but the snipers held their fire.

Brooks watched, entranced. The languid motion of the organisms in the water was almost soothing to behold. Then, as suddenly as they had appeared, they scattered, coalescing around the outer rim of the pool, clearing the way for something vast to rise in the center.

The door obscured the creature as it surfaced, but Brooks saw enough to recognize the form: A tail that belonged to neither scorpion nor manta ray but some hybrid of the two, scarred crustacean armor, an array of clawed arms.

Lung Crawthok had answered the director's invitation.

McDermott gazed up at the crane operator and gave a signal through his com. The winch motor engaged, causing the door to open with a creak amplified by the stepped walls of the granite crater.

The creature's face emerged from the violet murk, taking on detail as it approached the glassy surface of the water. Now Brooks could see the fang-tipped triangular flaps of flayed skin, like flower petals framing rows of horselike teeth, and the humanoid arms and legs folding inward. The creature rolled in a somersault, the tip of its tail slicing the water as it completed a revolution and breached the surface, erupting from the doorframe in a spray of white water. The armored engineers surrounding the resonator scampered backward, nearly knocking each other into the water, clutching at the railings as the creature dropped to the platform, twirling its bronze harpoon-tipped staff.

When the god touched down, the steel grate tilted under the water, sending one of the three engineers flailing for purchase and landing with a splash beside the door. The creatures waiting at the circumference of the pool swarmed in, latched on, and pulled him under despite his flotation vest. He was gone before he could utter a sputtering cry for help, his dismemberment a shadow show of violet light and bleeding silhouette.

Muzzles flashed from the towers above, but Brooks couldn't tell if anyone had scored a hit. Stray rounds plunked into the water and sparked off the metal platform. For a second, he thought the snipers were terrible shots. Then he realized he was only seeing the ricochets—and that they were *all* ricochets. The red platform engineers cowered, covering their faces with their Kevlar plated arms. One was bleeding from his boot, another from his abdomen. The general must've given a signal because the firing stopped all at once, as suddenly as it had begun.

A bowel-shaking pulse radiated through the quarry on a wave of stone dust, raking the surface of the water like helicopter rotors, forcing the remaining pair of engineers to let go of their wounds and seize the railings, lest they follow their companion into the feeding bowl.

Brooks shielded his eyes and looked up into the glare of the sun over the rim of the pit. No, that wasn't the sun; it was the tripod cannon firing a crackling ball of pink fire that seemed to defy all states of matter as it oozed from the metal maw of the weapon and rolled across the intervening space to splash light across the monster's pinchers and torso.

On impact, Lung Crawthok staggered backward a half step, then lunged forward, driving the flue of his harpoon through a cowering engineer, impaling him through the belly. The blood was lost on the red metal but for the hot spray that splashed across the last engineer's helmet visor. He screamed as the creature raised his wriggling comrade into the air.

Brooks felt his own gut lurch in sympathy watching the creature embrace its victim in a cage of claws, the man's head disappearing into petals of flesh, his decapitated body tossed into the water for the lesser denizens of the deep dimension to feast on.

The third engineer scrambled up a rope ladder toward a place where the granite steps would offer him options for escape. Another pulse from the plasma cannon pounded the quarry like a drum. The rolling pink orb was darker this time, shot through with shafts of cerulean blue. This one burst against the creature's head, causing it to teeter for a moment in which Brooks thought it would fall backward through the door. Instead, it let out a piercing shriek, sending Brooks to his knees with everyone around him.

Only McDermott remained at the railing, grinning into the pit like a man having the time of his life.

Brooks pulled himself up and clapped a hand on the director's shoulder. "That cannon isn't up to the job!" he shouted.

"It's powering up. The next shot will take it down."

The general raised a hand to stay the M5 rifles…but was that a rocket launcher poised on the shoulder of the soldier positioned beside him on the green deck?

The monster clambered over the resonator, stabbed its foreclaws into cracks in the granite, and skittered up the rock wall with a speed that defied its weight and mass. The last engineer had almost reached the top of the rope ladder when a serrated claw that had to be three feet long cut him clean in half. Brooks turned his head, but not fast enough to miss the sight of white spinal vertebrae poking out of the meat of the man's bottom half as it tumbled over the rock face and splashed into the water.

Another pulse shook the quarry, another plasma ball rolled through the air. It knocked the creature off the quarry wall, fracturing its armor with runnels of corrosive light, but the monster's flailing tail kept it from falling backward through the doorway. It landed on the red platform and dropped to one knee.

Brooks could hear people retching, could smell the acid of their vomit on the air, but he couldn't take his eyes off the gaping horizontal door and the monster teetering at its threshold. It was impossible to reconcile the size of the creature with the portal it had come through. But then, he remembered, there was never anything rational about the geometry of the Wade House.

Something blazed past his face with a *whoosh*, not a slow plasma blast, but a rocket. A cloud of orange fire bloomed in the bottom of the quarry and the observation decks rocked.

When the smoke cleared, the resonator was scattered in fragments of copper and glass, and the water had gone dark. The creature was unharmed. It launched into the air, vaulted up the quarry wall, passing between the cables and platforms, its blazing emerald eyes pinned on Brooks.

McDermott turned away from the railing. Was that fear on his pale face? Violet light seeped out from under the lenses of his dark shades.

"Do you still see it?" McDermott asked.

Brooks nodded. "It sees me, too. It's coming."

McDermott shoved Brooks in the chest, pushing him away from the railing. The other agents on the deck gave them a wide berth. Without the resonator, they couldn't see the monster, nor could it see them. The director pressed a finger to his ear and gave a command. Across the chasm, the cannon operator swiveled the weapon in his gloved hands and trained it on McDermott.

McDermott held his arm up in an L beside his head, index finger pointing at the sky.

Brooks felt the urge to draw his gun, but what good would it do if all those armor piercing rounds had failed? The only thing his 9mm could do was end McDermott's suffering if Lung Crawthok took him. But no, the creature couldn't touch the director while they inhabited different dimensions. Only Brooks had a foot in each world. Or were those shades McDermott wore some kind of personal resonator prototype?

McDermott pulled them off his face as Lung Crawthok vaulted over the railing. Ghost claws passed through his body, failing to connect with living tissue.

McDermott swept his arm down, signaling the gunner.

A violet light flared behind man and beast and McDermott hit the deck. The monster shuddered and sizzled as deep purple plasma washed over it—face flaps twitching and teeth chittering, its throat issuing a gurgle of what Brooks prayed was more pain than rage. He held his breath, watching as the creature toppled backward off the platform and down through the open doorway with a splash.

Chapter 13

To Becca's relief, Allston Asylum remained perched atop the hill overlooking Commonwealth Avenue. She'd feared that it might have met the wrecking ball since her last visit, or that SPECTRA might have cordoned it off with an electrified fence, like the Wade House.

She had the carpod drop her off at the bottom of Brainerd Road so she could walk up the hill with Django on a leash, thinking it would be harder for anyone to trail her on foot without being conspicuous. A panoramic view of the city emerged as they ascended: Dark clouds hovered over the skyscrapers, but the rain had passed, leaving shining drops on the parked cars and mailboxes, the day already warm enough to make her sweat from the exertion. Her bag bumped at her hip with each step, heavy with the book, dagger and camera. She didn't know what she might need that last for, but experience had shown it was usually better to have it.

At the summit, she checked her phone and found she was ten minutes early. Scanning the street, she saw no sign of the professor in any of the parked cars, but she had no intention of lingering in plain sight. If he knew the place, then he could find her in the courtyard. Maybe he was already there.

Apart from the new graffiti, she could almost believe that not a day had passed since she'd last walked across the overgrown field and stepped over the fallen door into the rambling brick building. Inside, she unclipped Django's leash and let him roam. He sniffed at the corners for animal droppings, and marked the wall.

She let the dog set their course through the building, indulging his urge to explore, before focusing on what she'd come here for. She hurried to keep up with him, her boots crunching the flakes of peeled paint that covered the cracked tile floors like autumn leaves, telling herself that it was simply good reconnaissance to scout out the location first and to trust the ferreting out of any hidden inhabitants to Django's sharper senses. But after following his aimless trail for a while, she realized that every moment spent roaming the outer corridors of this place was a moment spent avoiding the inevitable confrontation with the tragic memory that waited at the center.

She stopped at a blank patch of wall beside a winding staircase, and ran her fingertips over the water stained paint. Was this the place where she had explained infrared photography and ultraviolet light to Rafael? Django glanced back at her and whined.

"Wait," she said, rummaging in her bag for her headlamp. Without putting the elastic strap over her head, she clicked the light to the UV setting and scanned it over the wall, feeling a flutter in her stomach when her old invisible graffiti glowed ghostly white in the purple haze: RAF & BECCA WERE HERE.

She clicked the light off, dropped it in her bag, and followed Django, sniffling almost as much as he was now, as tears welled up and threatened to spill over.

Professor DuQuette was not waiting for her in the courtyard. The birdbath—a mosaic of colored glass and concrete, cradling a bed of slimy leaves at the bottom of two inches of stagnant water— looked just as it had on the day she'd found Reverend Proctor kneeling before it, making his prayers and prostrations.

Had the dagger she now carried in her canvas bag been concealed beneath his black frock at that first meeting? He'd seemed, at the time, a man far more interested in summoning than banishing.

Becca walked a slow circle around the fountain, her memories layered on top of one another like a triple-exposed photograph. Looking back at the building through a rosebush overtaken by vines, she saw the shattered window of the day room where she and Catherine had visited her grandfather, Peter, when the madness had its hooks in him. Somewhere in that room was a fragmentary mural on a wall that Rafael had painted—waterfalls and butterflies pouring out of cracks in the plaster.

Becca contemplated the dead leaves in the birdbath. Surely they'd fallen since she'd last been here, but she couldn't shake the feeling that they were mocking Rafael's death, pretending that nothing violent had happened here, that a transfigured Darius Marlowe had not emerged from the basin to wrap his tentacles around her lover's face and drown him in filth.

And now she *was* crying, and realizing what a horrible place she'd chosen to try and find the strength for what she intended to do. Darius was also dead; she'd sent him to his death down the central shaft of the Bunker Hill obelisk. She couldn't conjure him or kill him twice. This might be a place where worlds rubbed up against each other, where the membrane was thin, and that might lend her experiment a nudge in both directions, but it was also a place that drained her emotionally.

She'd been pacing in tight circles, growing dizzy without noticing. Now she stopped and swayed. She knelt and touched the ground where Rafael's body, now scattered in ash and washed down a river in Brazil, had lain in the dusty weeds, drawing its last breath. Kneeling on the damp earth, she was overcome with a compulsion to lay where he had, and curling her body around the base of the birdbath, she gave in to it.

* * *

Someone shook Becca's shoulder and she opened her eyes with a start. Django licked her face.

"Rebecca. Are you all right?" DuQuette said.

She rolled away from the birdbath and propped herself up with a splayed hand.

"Sorry…"

"It's all right. Here: water. Have a sip."

A clear plastic bottle appeared in front of her, crinkled from reuse, but full. She sat up, took it, and drank. It was wonderfully cold. She reached out and ran her finger over the divot in the concrete where Rafael had pried the ruby free of the glass mosaic it had been camouflaged in, where her grandfather had used a piece of chewing gum to adhere a magical gem to the birdbath decades ago. For a second, she could almost believe that this had all been a delusional spiral into madness, that maybe the bottom had dropped out on her baseline depression in 2019 and she'd fallen down the rabbit hole into high-def paranoid schizophrenia. Seeing covert government agents in Boston cops, or magicians in homeless vagabonds and college professors. Maybe the asylum was still operational and *she* was a patient, weaving apocalyptic fantasias from whole cloth.

The notion was almost a comfort. But no. It was all too real. She had slipped through a secret door that her family cracked open long ago and found herself with each passing year more immersed in an alternate world where everyone corroborated the impossible.

Rafael had died here, but he had pried the stone free with his Bowie knife first. The same knife she had used to fend off Darius Marlowe at the top of the obelisk. But ultimately, no ordinary knife could protect you from such creatures. Only the one in her bag could do that.

"Your brave friend," DuQuette said, "didn't die in vain."

"You know about that?" Was DuQuette telepathic, or did he get his information from mundane channels?

"Some of it, yes."

"The Starry Wisdom infiltrated SPECTRA. Does the Golden Bough have spies and moles, too?"

"We have eyes and ears. But there aren't enough of us for that sort of thing. We gather more intelligence from visions seen in meditation with a scrying bowl. Fragments, usually, but together we can sometimes piece together the narrative."

She studied his eyes beneath their bushy white brows. He was dressed in corduroy pants, a pale blue shirt, and the same tweed jacket as when she'd first met him.

"Catherine never mentioned she was in a secret society."

He smiled as if to say, *That's because it's secret.*

"But then, there were a lot of things she didn't tell me."

"There was much that she didn't understand until it was too late."

"You say Rafael didn't die in vain, but the gem is gone now."

"The blade and book may be enough to stop what's coming."

Becca reached into her bag and withdrew the silver dagger. "How did you know I have it? Was that a vision in water, too?"

"Just a hunch. But I'm relieved to see it."

"Did you know I would come to the university? You weren't in the stacks that day by coincidence, were you?"

"I had hoped you would come. And you should know by now that there are no coincidences."

"Doesn't that suggest a higher power? Higher than these gods of chaos and malice?"

"That's a mystery," he said, gazing at the square of sky beyond the brick building surrounding them.

"*That's* a cop out. Doesn't white magic suggest a god behind it on our side?"

"I doubt it's that simple, Becca. I don't think the gods of chaos are any more *evil* than cancer cells. Maybe God is the whole of creation—darkness and light, chaos and order, dissonance and harmony, each dependent on the other for its existence and meaning. The Gnostics had a name for such a god: Abraxas. The Chinese call it Tao. But in the *Bhagavad Gita*, Krishna tells Arjuna that just because death and decay will claim us all inevitably in an infinite vicious cycle, that doesn't mean there's nothing to fight for. I chose to fight for light, harmony, and love a long time ago. What do you choose?"

Becca chuckled. He sounded like Catherine. "Revenge is usually enough to get me through the day."

"Try love."

"Okay," she said, removing the book from her bag. "Teach me how to slay these motherfuckers with love."

DuQuette took the book and led her to a bench beside a fallen tree. He dusted the dead leaves and dirt off the seat with a handkerchief, gestured for her to sit, and then settled beside her, leafing through the slim volume with a delicate touch. The wind picked up in the courtyard and trilled the pages between his fingers.

"I almost sang to a mirror this morning," Becca said, "to see if I could wound or banish what came out."

DuQuette stared at her for a moment. She wasn't sure what he was searching for in her eyes. "It's good that we ended up here," he said, looking around. "This is a good place for such an experiment."

"A thin place," she said.

"That's right."

"Doesn't that just make it easier for them to come through?"

"And easier for you to learn how to push back. There is ebb and flow here. It has a resonant history."

"For the church," Becca said. "Their Saint Jeremy brought something through here."

DuQuette nodded. "A partial manifestation. He was born with half a voice. But that's not the only history that resonates in this courtyard. There's *your* part. Your courage, your friend's sacrifice, your love. Those are currents that wouldn't fuel your effort in front of a bathroom mirror. But in front of that basin of water…you might harness powerful forces."

Becca stared at the birdbath.

"Do you know the song of summoning?"

She nodded. The thought of singing it voluntarily terrified her. "I wish I didn't."

"You hear it in your sleep."

"Yes."

He pointed to a line in the book. "The banishing. Only you can pronounce the syllables properly. Try it."

Becca spoke the strange words. They sounded weak, like an electric guitar plucked without amplification.

DuQuette sounded out the mantra for her. "I can't vibrate them the way you can, but you can hear the difference in the vowels, yes?"

She nodded. "But how do you *know*? The book is so old. You can't have heard it spoken."

"There are similarities to formulas that survived in Greek and Egyptian. I can only draw on sources like the *Papyrus of Abaris*, and I may have it wrong…but it's an educated guess, a chance we have to take."

Becca spoke the words again, this time shifting her voice into that strange new register where it sounded like she was harmonizing with herself.

"I think you're ready," DuQuette said.

Becca took Django's leash from her bag, looped it around a leg of the rusting bench, and clipped it onto his collar.

DuQuette approached the birdbath. From his jacket pockets, he produced two stoppered bottles. He uncorked the first and sprinkled some white powder from it in a wide circle around the base of the birdbath.

"What's that?" Becca asked. She stood a few steps back, holding the book and dagger in her hands.

"Natron. For purification and protection. Hurry, step inside the circle before it's complete."

Becca stepped up to the basin as DuQuette completed the circle behind her. In her cargo pants, flannel shirt and tank top, she felt like anything but a magician. The only thing ceremonial about her attire was the golden scarab dangling inert from her neck.

"Here." He handed her the second bottle, already uncorked. It smelled of honey, cinnamon, and myrrh. "Consecrated oil," he said in response to her unspoken question. "Pour it into the basin. All of it."

Becca did as he said, handed the empty bottle back, and watched the oil twisting in the stagnant water. She lowered her eyelids and deepened her breath, centering herself, searching for the deep point of stillness at the core of her mind.

She sensed DuQuette stepping back, treading quietly, having done all he could to advise and set her on the path. If the tools and instructions failed her now, she doubted he would be able to do much more than watch.

Becca sang the dream song. It came quick and easy, rushing through her like a river finding its course when the dam has broken, her consciousness swept along on its current with vertiginous momentum. This song had been rattling around in her nerves for weeks, maybe years, straining at the bonds of her dreams. Now let loose, it overwhelmed her. Her voice was not her own; it came from a place deeper than her physiology. It was the voice of ancestors who had slithered across beaches, walked across continents long lost to the volcanic tides of epochs.

It was beautiful and terrible, and in submission to its command, the dark pool opened like a great eye. Beads of water and oil spiraled out on a horizontal plane, rotating like planets around the basin. Ribbons of green-black flesh wound out of the portal to form a twisting monolith glittering with needle teeth, alternating between slow cohesion and sudden synchronized turns, swooping and diving like a flock of starlings or a school of minnows.

Becca knew its name, had been scrutinized by its icy gaze before. And as if sensing her recognition, it reconciled into its true form, the dancing goddess of the gate, Shabbat Cycloth. She sensed pleasure quivering through the cloud of lamprey creatures as they coalesced into the shape of a hand, an arm, and reached down to confer a blessing upon she who had summoned them, summoned *it*.

Becca brought the dagger up in a flashing arc, intoning the mantra as she severed the limb: *ASKEI KAI TASKEI!*

Violet blood and black light poured out in the wake of the blade, the cold metal humming in her hand. This was a different song, a symphony of silver trembling in her bones.

The goddess recoiled, scattered, then reconstituted in a sudden strike, lacerating Becca's chest and cheek as she reared back on her heels. Instinctively, Becca changed her grip on the weapon and jabbed with the blade jutting out the bottom of her fist. It was a blind, impulsive strike, but it connected with flesh, releasing another spray of unearthly blood and light, accompanied by a wail from the heart of the cyclone.

Somewhere far away, Django was barking.

The creature lashed out again, stinging her exposed biceps, but as she pivoted away, she realized too late that it was a feint to draw her unguarded side toward a fast-forming vortex of eels. They wrapped around her arm, fastening it in a burning trap. Becca cried out in pain. It was like getting snared in ribbons of kelp laced with cactus needles.

"Strike again!" DuQuette's voice sounded distant, as if it reached her through water. Becca gave in to the creature's pull, springing forward and using the energy of the tugging ribbons wrapped around her arm to drive the dagger into the heart of the thing. *"ARDAMATHA!"* she cried, harmonics ringing in her ears.

A flash of light knocked her back as if a bomb had detonated. She landed on her ass on the muddy ground outside the circle, as the portal closed on what looked like a black star the size of a human heart, going supernova. The afterimage burned inside her closed eyelids, and she felt a rain of gelatinous scraps against the arm with which she shielded her face. But when she opened her eyes, there were no remains to be seen on the birdbath or the ground.

Chapter 14

Becca paced the courtyard, her sweaty hair sticking to her face. DuQuette had tried to get her to sit on the bench again and drink some more water, but she was too excited for that, flush with adrenaline and victory. She still clutched the silver dagger, and kept glancing back at the birdbath, as if she expected something else to emerge from it. She almost wanted something else to come through so she could do it again. Maybe the consort of the cosmic bitch she'd just annihilated, that harpoon wielding crab god.

"Did you see it?" she said to DuQuette. "I finished her. There can't be anything left." She whirled and stared at him. He looked awed, stunned.

"Long years of practice have granted me a little sight. But not what you can see... Not until just now. Your song burned the scales from my eyes."

"So you saw that. She couldn't reconstitute in her own world, could she? I know she's made of scraps to begin with, but I *devastated* her."

"I can't be sure," DuQuette said, "but yes, it looked like you did. I would caution you though..."

"Against what?"

"Overconfidence. It must be exhilarating to be a conduit for the light, to feel the song coursing through your heart, hand, and blade. But you're one person, Becca, and they are legion. And right now you look like you want to go marching into their world."

"I have to. They've abducted children. My *friend's* child. They must have the symphony. The Black Pharaoh is probably training those kids to sing it as we speak. He's *weaponizing* them." Becca broke eye contact with her newfound mentor, knowing how fierce she must look to him, how fanatical. She slowed her breathing and waited for her heart rate to follow.

"Think it through, Becca. What would you do? You have power now, yes. But do you have knowledge? Where would you even begin to try and find the children?" He offered her the water bottle again. She accepted it and drank.

"I don't know," she said. "This is a thin place, right? So I find a puddle and sing my way through it, maybe go through the birdbath."

"And find yourself where?"

She opened her mouth, but no words came out.

"You have no idea," DuQuette said. "There are many dark paths between our world and theirs. Nyarlathotep lured the children with music, but where did he lead them? How would you find your way?"

"He tried to lure me, too. But I wasn't ready."

"And now that you are and you've proven your power by attacking a minor deity, you may not find a welcoming committee when you step blindly through."

Becca sighed. "Maybe you're right. Maybe I need to talk to Brooks."

"Your agent friend? Can you trust him?"

"Absolutely."

"And yet you've kept secrets from him. The blade, the book."

"I wanted to know that it worked. If I told him I took the dagger, and if his superiors asked him about it, interrogated him because they found it missing from the archive... If he didn't know I took it, he wouldn't be lying, risking his job and betraying his oath to the government."

"You say you trust this man, but I'm not sure you do."

Becca contemplated the dagger in her hand. "I've had to be careful. Leadership and loyalties shift like sand dunes at an agency like SPECTRA. I've worked for them before. If I went to them now, they might offer support, maybe even tell me something I don't know. But they also might take this away and lock me up, use what

I've learned in a way that could put those kids in danger. I can't be responsible for that."

DuQuette nodded. "There's a third way, Becca, between diving blindly into another world, or running back to SPECTRA."

"Tell me."

"We scry. We seek a vision in the water, to find the children."

"You can do that?"

"Together we can. You have a link to one of them. What was his name?"

"Noah."

DuQuette stepped up to the birdbath. "Can you visualize him clearly?"

"Sort of," Becca said. "I've only met him a couple of times. Brooks kept their secret, that Noah had the voice. He's probably regretting that now. Maybe SPECTRA *could* have prevented his abduction."

"Well, it's too late now." DuQuette poured three more drops of the golden oil into the basin. Becca was surprised to see the same dirty rainwater and decaying leaves as before, as if a dark goddess hadn't exploded out of it mere moments ago. "You'll have to do your best with the last memory you have of him."

"It was just the other day," she said. "I went to their house to warn them that SPECTRA knew about Noah." The memory of the boy's face as he handed her the glittering paper planet made her voice waver. She exhaled heavily. "He was so happy to see me, like he knew we had something in common. He gave me a little craft he made."

DuQuette looked up from the basin. "Do you still have it?"

Becca went to the bench where Django was panting, unclipped him from the leash, and dug the little paper disk from the pocket of her bag that she'd tucked it into. "Here." She offered it to DuQuette. "It's supposed to be the planet Neptune."

"Interesting." He took it from her and examined it, turning the disk this way and that, the flecks of blue and green glitter shining even in the overcast sunlight.

"What are you looking for?" Becca asked.

"I suppose finding a hair of his stuck to it would be too much to hope for, but the fact that he made it with his own hands should more than suffice for a magical link. His fingerprints are likely in the glue. Assuming his mother didn't make it for him."

Becca shrugged. "He's pretty advanced for his age."

"May I?" DuQuette gestured at the dirty water.

She nodded and the old mage tossed the disk into the water. It floated for a moment, then tipped under the surface and glided down to join the leaves, like a coin cast into a wishing well.

Becca reached into the bag again and took out her camera, the one she'd modified to shoot in infrared, the same one that had once captured images of entities from the other side lurking at the threshold of reality. She had an idea that it might capture a fleeting glimpse of the other side now, if she was lucky.

DuQuette muttered something under his breath, gesturing over the basin, his fingers folding through a series of intricate mudras. The water glowed and wavered. Becca tensed and considered trading the camera for the dagger again. What if she had only wounded the monster? What if the portal opened to let it through again? But she wasn't singing the evocation, wasn't calling it forth, and whatever spell DuQuette was weaving seemed to be having a different effect.

"Picture Noah," DuQuette said. "Hold him in your mind's eye."

Becca closed her eyes and did her best. When she opened them again, an image had formed in the water, like a photo etched on a silver plate.

A town at the edge of a river or sea. An old town, maybe somewhere in Europe. White buildings, sandstone cathedrals, and narrow alleyways. And then the image was in motion; pedestrians blurring by on cobblestone paths as her point of view rose and glided over the tiled rooftops with the pigeons, swooped under the power cables between the buildings, and soared beyond a long pavilion, out over the gilded waves. She blinked and lost the sense of immersion, saw the scene bounded by the rim of the birdbath again, wavering on the surface of a puddle.

"There were people on the street," she said. "Did you see them? They went by in a blur. But I didn't see Noah."

"It's an earthly city," DuQuette said. "Do you recognize it?"

"No." She raised her camera and clicked a few shots of the receding waterfront city, hoping to capture something distinctive—a landmark building, or a sign in some language that would narrow their search. "Can we control the view?"

"It doesn't work like that," DuQuette said. "Absorb whatever you can. There's interference. Perhaps a glamour of concealment has been cast on the children. I don't think I can hold it much longer."

Becca didn't know if the camera was capturing anything but dead leaves in shallow water. She held it at her throat, looking over it at the dimming apparition while holding the shutter button down. The image wavered and unraveled. She saw a white ship docked at the end of the pavilion, and then it was gone, leaving a blue planet the size of a silver dollar glittering in the murk.

"I saw a ship," she said.

DuQuette nodded. "A cruise ship. Maybe the children are on it."

Becca was already clicking through the photos on the camera LCD.

"Did you get anything?" DuQuette asked, leaning in.

"Probably not enough to identify the city if neither of us know it. What do I do? Post them on the Internet and ask if anyone recognizes the place?" She was thumbing through them fast, her disappointment escalating to frustration on the way to panic.

"Wait. Go back one," DuQuette said.

They had come to the end of the series with the white ship in the corner of the frame, the majority of each shot showing only an amorphous body of water.

"Can you zoom in on the stern of the cruise ship?"

Becca clicked a button. The photograph was magnified until she could read the grainy words, the name of the vessel: THE AEGEAN STAR.

"You got it. We can search for that cruise ship and find out what port it's docked at right now."

The idea gave her hope. If it really was a glimpse of where in the world Noah and the others were, it gave them a place to start. Still, she would have felt better if she'd seen his face. "You don't think cultists transported the kids out of the country on a cruise ship, do you? Wouldn't that be hard to get away with?"

"I doubt they did. If it looked like Canada or the Caribbean, I wouldn't rule it out. But the city looked European. Maybe the Mediterranean. And they couldn't have made it that far by sea, not so soon. I believe they traveled the byways between our world and theirs, the Twilight Shore, where time and space are stretched and compressed. For those who know the way, it's the shortest distance between any two points on Earth. Like folding paper and piercing it with a needle. Speaking of which, you're bleeding."

Becca touched her cheek and collarbone where Shabbat Cycloth had slashed her. Her fingers came away bloody. She turned her arm and found a spiral of ruby red pinpricks.

"Does it hurt?" DuQuette asked.

"Only a little, but I bet they'll sting like a bitch tomorrow if they're like most animal bites."

"At least it missed your neck. You need to clean those up with some disinfectant. Where are you staying?"

"Agent Brooks' house."

DuQuette had seemed unflappable in the face of monsters and miracles, but now his eyes grew wide. "Oh my. Are you two…"

"*No.* No, we're not."

"Well, it might not be the best place to go until you know your next move. Unless you want their help. I mean, they must keep tabs on their agents. Your chances of being found obviously go up if you're with him."

"I know. But they do have resources. It might be time to ask for help, I don't know."

"I suspect you're the one with the most resources now. And if they knew you had the gift, the voice… No, I don't think it would be wise to reveal that."

"I told the former director," Becca said.

"You did?" DuQuette looked positively alarmed now. He cast a glance around the courtyard, as if he expected men with automatic weapons to come crashing through the broken windows of the asylum and rappelling down from the roof. And why not? Becca had witnessed almost that very scene the last time she was here.

"I trust him. They forced him out. He's dying. I thought he would know what happened to the symphony, but he swore SPECTRA never had it. I checked the archive myself. All I found was my father's notes."

"Your father's notes?"

"He studied the symphony for years, trying to decode what he called an inversion of the melody. He had this theory that most of the insanity in the world came from proximity to the dimension of the Great Old Ones. Like hell was always brushing up against us. He thought if Zann's symphony could open the way between worlds permanently, then maybe an inversion of it could align us with a *heavenly* realm, or shatter the connection altogether."

DuQuette took the paper planet out of the basin and shook the water off it. She noticed his hand trembling as he folded it in his handkerchief. He had a faraway look on his face as he muttered something under his breath.

"What's that?"

"We were working in parallel, your father and I," DuQuette said. "You'll forgive me, but until we met, I believed Luke had sold or destroyed the music just to spite Catherine. I never imagined he'd devoted his life to the study of it."

"It got to the point where it was all he cared about," Becca said. "But what do you mean, working in parallel? You're a musician?"

"Violin. Catherine and I experimented with inversions of the choral section at Miskatonic in the nineties. I still have the notes and eight-track recordings. I felt we were getting close, but then Luke absconded with the score. We never dared to make an exact transcription or recording of the original. We felt that one copy in the world was dangerous enough. I wish I could compare his notes to my own." He looked zoned out again for a moment, then he met Becca's eyes and said, "Do you know how many Children of the Voice they've identified?"

"No. Why?"

"The choral section requires eight voices. If they don't have enough children, they might need you as well."

"They tried to take me once. Maybe they'll try again. If we can't identify that city, if I can't get there another way...letting them take me might be the only way to find Noah and the others."

DuQuette touched Becca's arm and nodded at one of the passages through the asylum. "I'm feeling more than a little exposed here. And we should find you some antibiotic ointment to treat those cuts. The car is this way."

Chapter 15

Warwick McDermott stood in front of a trio of LCD screens, addressing an assembly of agents in one of the smaller huts on the quarry property. "Stratford. Where are we at with Cyrus Malik?"

In the second row, Irene Stratford cleared her throat. "No developments. Every time we dial up the intensity of interrogation, he lapses into gibberish prayers." Agitated murmurs spread through the room and she clarified: "That's not to say that he has the voice like his son. But it's possible that meditation and chanting practices have given him some ability to control his pain level, or maybe withdraw from this world into the other just enough that we can't break him."

"Does he ask about his wife?" Nico Merrit asked Stratford. "Does he think we're doing the same stuff to her?"

"No. All we get out of him when he isn't chanting is threats of a lawsuit with the ACLU."

Someone chuckled.

The screens behind McDermott were split between satellite video of the quarry and infrared stills of the creature. The Wade House door had been removed and loaded onto a truck. "We need to keep pressure on the mother about what will happen to the boy if we find him without her help," McDermott said. "A more difficult threat to sell now that we've failed a demonstration of overwhelming force against one of their gods, even in controlled conditions."

"That was controlled?" Brooks whispered. Agent Stratford swatted his leg with the back of her hand in reproach.

"The plasma cannon isn't drawing enough power from the other side," the director continued. "Our engineers in Boston are revamping the gloves to try and scale that up with more Elder DNA on the contacts. In the meanwhile…well, we weakened the creature and sent it back. Three of our best gave their lives to prove that we have some hope of fighting back."

Nodding at Bill Klinger in the front row, McDermott said, "Status of the search for Children of the Voice who haven't walked through a mirror yet."

"None found. All confirmed cases happened on the same day."

A young agent whom Brooks had seen around but didn't know by name approached the director with a tablet in his hand and spoke something in his ear.

McDermott nodded, then finished with Klinger: "Don't stop looking. If we find a COV, I want a drone ready to follow them through any portal for a look around."

"Got it," Klinger said.

McDermott pointed at the young agent with the tablet and said, "Patch it through."

The center screen behind the lectern switched over to a video feed of a technician at HQ.

"What do you have?" McDermott asked.

"One of the motion detector cameras we have monitoring cultist hotspots picked up activity," the technician said, typing on an off-screen keyboard as he spoke, glancing between the two monitors. "It's Allston Asylum. Appears to be Becca Philips and an older gentleman we haven't identified yet."

Brooks felt his stomach clench.

"I wouldn't have flagged it as urgent, but it gets weird fast. It's an incursion, and it looks like Philips caused it intentionally."

McDermott scanned the assembly, his gaze fixing on Brooks.

"Should I roll the feed?" the tech on the monitor asked.

"Please," McDermott said.

Brooks watched the scene unfold in ghostly infrared shot from a high angle, a camera tucked under an eave near the roof overlooking the courtyard. He watched the old man prepare the birdbath by pouring an unidentifiable substance in it. Brooks was pretty sure he'd never seen the guy before, but he didn't raise his face toward the camera, so it was hard to tell. Was he coercing Becca? Was he a cultist? He watched with growing unease as Becca, holding a dagger that resembled the one John Proctor had carried on the Wade House expedition, stepped up to the basin and started singing. There was no audio, but Brooks could imagine the sound. The song itself seemed to cause electromagnetic interference, scrambling the camera's image. Twice the picture returned enough to show the water rising from the basin in a slow-moving cyclone. Brooks caught sight of what looked like eels thrashing in the twisting water. The scar on his left thigh twitched.

Then the feed went black and the pasty face of the young tech filled the screen again.

"That's it?" McDermott asked the monitor. "Do we know what manifested?"

"The guys downstairs think it's Shabat Cycloth."

"So she evoked it," McDermott said. "Summoned it at a Starry Wisdom sacred site."

Brooks tapped his foot, edging forward on his folding chair, wanting to stand up and interject, but not knowing where to begin or what to say.

"Does the video come back later? Do we know if the entity escaped the courtyard?" McDermott asked.

"Unconfirmed. We do have more video, but there's no sign of the creature. It's like nothing happened. Philips and her companion are just staring at the birdbath. She takes some pictures of it and they leave. Do you want to see it?"

"Send it to my tablet. Where is Philips now?"

"We're trying to establish that."

"*Trying?*"

"We have satellite photos of a vehicle parked in front of the asylum at the time of the video. We couldn't get a drone over it in time to follow, so we're cleaning up an image of the license plate. They can't be out of the city yet."

"Get the BPD on it," McDermott said. "But I don't want them apprehended. Not yet. I want to know where they're going. I want them tracked by drone. Let me know when they're locked in."

"Yes sir."

"Do we have facial recognition on her companion?"

"Also in progress."

"Work fast," McDermott said. He clicked the call off with his remote and spoke to the room. "Let's move. Local team will deal with the remains. Stratford, notify next of kin. I want everyone else at HQ by sixteen-hundred hours."

Brooks gave Stratford a sympathetic look, but the sound of his own name jerked his attention back to McDermott. "Brooks. Report to hut B14."

* * *

Polygraph Transcript

Interview of Agent Jason Brooks Conducted by Agent Clive Holden for Dir. Warwick McDermott on April 29th, 2025, at Manchester, NH, Satellite SPECTRA Facility. Length 21 minutes, 32 seconds.

13:40:28 p.m.

CH: Is your name Jason Brooks?

JB: Yes.

CH: Are you currently employed by SPECTRA?

JB: Yes.

CH: Do you live at 51 Lawrence Street in Malden, Massachusetts?

JB: Yes.

CH: Are you a Yankees fan?

JB: Fuck no.

CH: Do you have a gambling problem?

JB: No. I mean yes. I don't gamble anymore. I go to GA meetings. This is all in my personnel file.

CH: Understood. I'm just establishing a baseline. Are you a member of the Starry Wisdom Church?

JB: No.

CH: Have you ever been a member of the Starry Wisdom Church?

JB: No.

CH: Are you in contact with Becca Philips?

JB: Define contact.

CH: Have you seen Ms. Philips in the last 48 hours?

JB: Yes.

CH: Where did you see her?

JB: At my house.

CH: Why was she at your house?

JB: We have something in common. We were both exposed to the harmonics in the Boston attacks and chose not to take Nepenthe. We've kept in touch.

CH: And why did she visit your house?

JB: She needed someone to talk to.

CH: What about?

JB: She's had a complication, a health issue related to her exposure. Her voice is changing.

CH: Changing how?

JB: Like the kids who were born with it.

CH: Has your own voice changed since the events of 2019?

JB: No.

CH: Did Becca Philips intend to report the change in her voice to the agency?

JB: That's what we talked about. She's afraid that if she reports it, she may be detained and subjected to experimentation. For the record, I couldn't honestly try to convince her that wouldn't happen.

CH: Are you romantically involved with Becca Philips?

JB: No.

CH: Did she spend the night at your house?

JB: None of your fucking business.

CH: Have you ever had sexual relations with Becca Philips?

JB: No.

CH: Agent Brooks, I'm being asked to emphasize the importance of this question. It may seem like prying to you, and of no legitimate interest to the agency, but I can assure you that such an assumption could not be more wrong. All of the Children of the Voice were born to couples in which only one parent was exposed to the harmonics. We don't know what the consequences would be if two exposed parents—both of whom retained extra dimensional perception and one of whom is the only adult known to have *developed* the voice—were to reproduce. Nor can we assume what Becca Philips' intentions may be in that area, especially considering her mental health and family history. So I would urge you to give the question careful consideration before answering.

JB: I've never had sex with Becca Philips.

CH: Have you wanted to?

JB: Now you're getting personal, Bucko.

CH: A desire can affect your polygraph readings, even if you've never acted on it.

JB: I'm a straight man. She's a fine-looking woman.

CH: Did you grant Becca Philips access to the artifact and document archive at the JFK building on the night of April 23rd?

JB: Yes.

CH: For what purpose?

JB: She thought SPECTRA had taken *The Invisible Symphony* from her father's house and she wanted to destroy it.

CH: In light of her actions today, do you still believe that she wanted to destroy it?

JB: Yes. It was her father's last request, so, yes.

CH: Why, after three years, did she become interested in finding the symphony now?

JB: She was having intense dreams. Something was calling her, trying to use her voice. She thought if it was happening to her, it might be happening to others. And she knew that if the symphony ended up in the wrong hands, anyone who had the voice might be coerced into singing it.

CH: And you shared her concerns?

JB: Yes.

CH: Why didn't you bring them to the director?

JB: Too much paperwork.

CH: This isn't a joke, Agent Brooks. Your answers will have consequences for yourself and others. Why didn't you inform the director of Ms. Philips' mutation and your shared concerns about the symphony?

JB: Seriously, destroying secret government property with scientific and historic value…that's no small thing to get approval for, especially in light of the current director's position on using eldritch tech in service to the cause. And like I said, I was trying to protect a friend from, I don't know…dissection?

CH: But you didn't find the symphony because SPECTRA never found it either. Have you or Philips located it since?

JB: No. I haven't. I don't know about Becca.

CH: Are you aware that she stole an artifact from the archive under your supervision?

JB: What artifact?

CH: The silver dagger she was seen brandishing in the video recorded today in Allston. Was that the real reason you gave her access to the archive? To steal the ritual dagger she is now armed with?

JB: No. I didn't know. Are you sure it's one from the archive?

CH: Have you been in contact with Daniel Northrup recently?

JB: No.

CH: To your knowledge, has Becca Philips been in contact with Daniel Northrup?

JB: No.

CH: Do you know the identity of the man she's traveling with? Is he Starry Wisdom?

JB: I've never seen him before.

Chapter 16

Daniel Northrup lay awake, staring at the ceiling, when the nurse came in to tell him he had a visitor. "His name is Warwick McDermott. Are you up for a visitor?"

He thumbed the button to raise his bed to the upright position, and tugged the oxygen mask down. "Send him in."

McDermott was dressed and groomed as impeccably as ever, but he looked older. The job had a way of aging people from stress alone, but for an uncharitable couple of seconds Northrup couldn't help hoping it had given the fucker cancer, too.

"Daniel. Thanks for seeing me."

"Warwick." Northrup held the mask to his face for a breath. "Forgive me, I'm not much of a conversationalist now that I've got to keep sucking on the old aqualung." Another drag from the mask. "What's on fire?"

"Pardon?" McDermott pulled up a chair beside the bed.

"Things must be pretty bad if you've come for my help."

McDermott twisted a ring on his finger. Was that a Masonic insignia stamped into the gold? Northrup couldn't tell. "Sorry to disappoint, but the agency isn't burning down without you. In fact, we've made some progress with the tech you didn't want to touch. Just this morning I oversaw the testing of a plasma cannon. The next iteration should be quite powerful."

"Congratulations. What did you test it on; a frozen shank from one of the Dark Young?"

McDermott laughed. "Much better than that." He leaned forward to stage whisper: *"Lung Crawthok."*

Northrup's chest hitched and he sat up, seized by a coughing fit. He pressed the mask to his mouth and nose and it subsided. His eyes were watering when he was able to remove the mask and speak again. "You *summoned* it?"

"Not exactly, but for all intents and purposes, it's the same. We used a physical portal."

"What does that even mean?"

"I'm afraid that's classified."

"Like everything you've said to goad me since you sat down isn't."

McDermott shrugged. Northrup thought it might be the first time he'd ever seen the man enjoying himself.

"What do you want, Warwick? Can't you see I'm busy dying?"

McDermott withdrew a slim case from the inner pocket of his jacket. He turned it over in his hands, and his gaze turned inward. "Did you wear glasses as a child, Daniel?"

"No."

"I had my first pair before I was seven. They made you something of a target back then. But I was a bookworm, and they say reading causes myopia. Left to my own devices, I might have played outdoors and made more friends, but Mother rewarded learning and punished dirty fingernails. And I have her to thank for my achievements. Did you have someone like that? Someone who pushed you to excel when you only wanted to go fishing?"

Northrup grunted. "My grandfather."

"We may differ on methods, but we are members of the same elite group, you and I. Only strong-minded men can handle the truth of reality. And it is our duty to safeguard the sanity of simpler men by keeping their limited reality hermetically sealed."

"You came here to lecture me? Why? I'm irrelevant now."

McDermott, still fondling the case in his hands, grinned at a memory. "I used to sneak out and go fishing with one of the negro servants."

"How rebellious."

"I'm still repulsed by the taste, I throw them back. But I think it was the taboo that made it such a thrill. And soon, Daniel, I'm going to catch the biggest fish on Earth. The Priest of the Deep."

Northrup stared at the man with suffocating regret. He should never have let it come to this.

McDermott held the case up. "Destroy it all, you said. Don't study the tech, dismantle it. Grind the components to dust." He flipped the case open and presented it to Northrop. Inside were a pair of dark sunglasses with thick frames and a recessed button on one of the arms. McDermott stood, unfolded the glasses and placed them over Northrup's eyes.

"Behold," he said, and clicked the button.

A static charge swept over Northrup's skin. It occurred to him too late that a spark could ignite his oxygen flow. That didn't happen, though, and he relaxed, unaware that he would soon wish it had. The lenses, like night vision goggles, illuminated the dim room with an eerie lavender glow.

"What is it?" Northrup asked.

"One of my greatest accomplishments."

McDermott opened his briefcase and removed a pane of black glass the size of a hardcover book. Standing at the foot of the bed, he held it in front of his chest. At first sight, Northrup thought it was tinted, but on closer inspection, he saw it was clear glass, blackened by soot and oily residue. His body reacted to the knowledge of what it was before his mind caught up, tension contracting his muscles, his heart rate accelerating and breath slowing; the instinctive reactions of a trapped animal trying to make itself small and undetectable while priming its system for flight. He held the mask to his mouth and nose and kept it there.

"The goggles you're wearing contain a miniaturized Tillinghast Resonator. And this glass is from a window from…"

"The Wade House," Northrup said. "What's your game, Warwick?"

"What do you see, Daniel?"

Organisms that resembled marine/insect hybrids—centipedes with piranha faces—wriggled at the edges of the glass and bumped the barrier, testing its integrity.

"Are you acquainted with the *Bardo Thodol?*" McDermott asked.

"*The Tibetan Book of the Dead,*" Northrup said through his mask. The agitated creatures glared at him from their bulbous alien eyes.

Keeping the mask on his face was the only imperative he could hold onto. Taking the glasses off hadn't yet occurred to him.

"Yes," McDermott said. "Monks read it to each other when consciousness is departing the body at the moment of death, to guide the untethered mind toward enlightenment amid overwhelming visions of what they call the *peaceful and wrathful forms*. The angelic and demonic entities that would drag the dead off to realms of bliss or torment. Both of which would prevent liberation, according to the Asian worldview. They say the key is to recognize the illusory nature of these denizens of the beyond when one encounters them."

Northrup, drowning in dread, was having trouble focusing on McDermott's words and the sense of them, if there was any. He'd heard cultists go on tangents like this to reinforce their insane philosophies.

"But I imagine they look quite real to you now," McDermott continued, looking down at the glass in his hands as if he too could see the creatures.

Northrup dropped his oxygen mask and pulled the shades off his face. The windowpane was dark and empty again without them.

"Right," McDermott said. "Child's logic: If you can't see them, they can't see you. But do you know when they *can* see you again? When you shuffle off the flesh, with its rough senses, and slip between worlds. The monks are right about that. But they're wrong that it's an illusion. The shoal that was drawn to the glass, to this room, will linger here for a while. Because they can smell blood in the water."

Northrup swatted the shades from where they'd landed on the blanket to the floor. McDermott slid the glass pane back into his briefcase, then picked the shades up, switched them off, and returned them to their case, which he pocketed. Northrup wheezed into his mask again, glaring at McDermott. He removed the mask long enough to blurt, "You said we're on the same side."

"Are we, though?"

Northrup coughed, took a drag on the mask. "What are you, a *cultist*?"

"No, no. But Becca Philips might be. Did you aid her?"

Northrup shook his head.

"Did you steal a meteoric dagger from the archive before you left and give it to her?"

"No."

McDermott closed the door to the hall, and walked around the hospital bed to the oxygen tank where he rested his hand on the valve. "Who is the man she's with?"

"I don't know…who you mean…*wheeze*… Nurse… *Nurse!*"

"Who's helping her? Teaching her spells to sing? A man with a white beard." McDermott turned the valve.

"You're wrong about Becca," Northrup said. "She's…using…the voice…to fight back… If she has the blade and the book…she has a…*wheeze*…chance."

McDermott opened the valve and let some oxygen through. Northrup drank it deeply.

"She's been here. You admit it. What did she want from you?"

"Symphony… She wanted to destroy it. But you know we never had it."

"You said 'blade and book.' What book?" McDermott touched the valve again.

Northrup closed his eyes, drew a deep breath and removed the mask to speak. "You put your faith in *gadgets*, Warwick. Weapons over wisdom. You don't know…what you're fooling with…*wheeze*." Northrup clutched his chest, and McDermott placed the mask on his face.

"Stay with me, Daniel. Tell me what book and I'll go, and the critters will disperse. What book did you send her after?"

"*Voice of the Void*… DuQuette. It's a banishing manual." Northrup sucked on the mask. His arms and jaw were going numb. It felt like McDermott had placed a cinderblock on his chest. Was this what a heart attack felt like? The oxygen was flowing, but it didn't help. The mask fogged as he said, "Nurse. Get the nurse." But his voice was weak, and the room was dimming to a deep murk in which violet shapes wriggled toward the bed.

Chapter 17

DuQuette's cat greeted Django with a hiss before jumping over the couch and disappearing. The professor's university housing wasn't as spacious as Catherine's had been, but the clutter of books, papers, and shelves of trinkets made Becca feel right at home. He asked for her jacket and hung it on a rack already overburdened with various overcoats and fleece pullovers. Carrying her bag by the handle, Becca followed him through the maze of furniture. He had converted what would normally be a living room into a sprawling office space. There was no TV, but she counted one desktop computer, one laptop, and a large desk in the middle of the room that appeared to be reserved for working longhand with a stack of journals. Judging by the pipe rack, ashtray, and accumulation of dirty tea mugs, this had to be the desk where he did the majority of his work.

Django sniffed around the room, but thankfully, he didn't go looking for the cat. Becca only had to reprimand him once—for sticking his nose in one of the professor's boots. DuQuette gathered the mugs and, on his way to the kitchen with them, nodded at a powder blue love seat embroidered with peacocks in front of the main desk. Becca settled on it, and Django curled up on the rug at her feet with a sigh.

The sound of running water reached her from the kitchen as she took in the room. She was tempted to get up and examine some of the more intriguing objects more closely, but resisted the urge to stir Django, who would be restless if he thought there was a chance she might be leaving. The longer she absorbed the details of her surroundings, the more apparent it became that the knick-knacks were probably priceless artifacts, and the sofa, an antique.

A moment after the whistle of a kettle, DuQuette returned with two steaming mugs on a tray, along with milk, honey (in a plastic bear), and an assortment of teas. Becca chose a packet of green tea and a squirt from the bear. She took a pill case from her bag and downed two aspirin for her throbbing lacerations, along with the daily Zoloft she'd forgotten earlier. DuQuette didn't ask, allowing her to convalesce in silence until she was ready to talk. She was grateful for the space. Nor did he appear to mind her curious gaze lingering on the contents of the cluttered room, despite being the sort who entertained visitors seldom enough to have done away with his living room entirely.

Her gaze eventually settled on a scuffed violin case leaning against a bookshelf. He knew what she was looking at without turning his head. "Do you have it with you?" he asked.

Becca removed Luke's tattered and bulging notebook from her bag and placed it on the desk. DuQuette's hand hovered over the cover and she had the feeling that he was reluctant to open it for fear that it might disappoint him. He ran his thumb over the fringe of sheets protruding from the edges, scraps that Luke had taped or stapled into the book to supplement the work contained in the bound pages. Some of these were torn from pieces of brown paper bag while others were jotted on proper staff paper, cut to the size of the relevant fragment. Becca had poured over the notebook at Brooks' house, reveling in years' worth of her father's handwriting; but unable to read music, the book had yielded no secrets to her. She couldn't hear the notes in her head, only read the handwritten commentary, which may as well have been scrawled in Aramaic between the penmanship and the mystical content.

"He really did labor over it for years, by the looks of this," DuQuette said. He drummed his fingers on the cover, withdrew his pipe from the rack on the desk, and fingered the stem absentmindedly, his other hand reaching into a pouch of tobacco beside a green and gold banker's lamp. He was about to strike a match when he glanced up at her. "Do you mind? I won't get any ash on the paper of course."

Becca shrugged. "*He* sure did."

While the professor leafed through the notebook, Becca sipped her tea and scrolled through the photos of the birdbath on her camera. DuQuette's brow furrowed as he hunched over the notebook, a wreath of smoke gathering around his snowy head.

"Does your computer take SD cards?" Becca asked. "I'd like to see these on a bigger screen, if that's okay."

DuQuette nodded and reluctantly pried himself away from the notebook, rolling his leather chair over to the smaller desk with the laptop. He flipped the lid open, typed the password, and waved at the screen. "All yours, my dear."

He rolled back to the big desk and Becca took a seat at the computer, slotting her memory card into the reader. Within minutes, she was confirming the name of the docked cruise ship and typing it into a search engine. While she worked, DuQuette hummed to himself and occasionally grunted. Whether from agreement with Luke's notes or disdain, Becca couldn't tell. As the night wore on, he became more animated, pacing, lighting the gas fireplace, and finally placing his violin case on the desktop, popping the clasps, and rubbing rosin over the bow.

Becca slid her chair away from the computer, rubbed her eyes, and swiveled around to watch him as he tuned the instrument and played a long, pure note.

The cat reappeared and hopped up onto a stack of books. Django opened his eyes, but his snout remained on the rug between his paws.

DuQuette played through a few bars of one of Luke's inversions, then moved to a file cabinet with the violin tucked under his arm. He opened a drawer, walked his fingers through the file tabs, and pulled out a thick manila folder. He plucked a sheet from it, set it on his desk beside the notebook, and then played again. The music sounded similar, but subtly different. It was beautiful in the way that a lethal marvel of nature can be—a river of molten lava or a tidal wave.

Goosebumps broke out on Becca's arms in response to the music, but they were merely a surface level sign of a deeper reaction. Something fundamental moved in her, like the iron in her blood responding to a powerful magnet.

"He was so close," DuQuette said.

"To what?"

"I don't believe it's a stairway to heaven, as your father hoped it would be, but it feels like...a reconciliation."

"I don't understand," Becca said.

"Music is all about resonance. You've heard of how the right pitch can shatter a wine glass?"

"Sure."

"Maybe the right harmony can shatter the plane that our dimensions have in common, the great invisible *mirror*, if you will. I don't very well remember the young man your father was when I met him, but I regret now that I judged him prematurely. It appears he completed my work."

"Or you completed his," Becca said.

The professor smiled and scratched his beard. "If you still plan to step through and find the children, let me add one more arrow to your quiver first."

Becca bit her lip.

"You must learn to sing this melody," DuQuette said. "You must use the gift they've endowed you with against them."

"You can teach me?"

"Yes."

Becca held up a Post-it note between two fingers. "I found the cruise ship, the *Aegean Star*. It's docked in Zadar, Croatia. If you're right about all of this, that's where the children are."

"Zadar! Of course."

"Why there? Why would the pharaoh take them there?"

DuQuette tapped the ash out of his pipe onto the mantle. "There's a sea organ there."

"A what?"

"It's a giant set of tuned chambers built into the waterfront. The waves flow in, push air through the vents, and make music. It's an architectural sculpture. Part of the city's reconstruction, and not ancient in any way, but still...the music of the sea would have an attraction."

"Was the architect a member of the Starry Wisdom?"

DuQuette squinted at the flames in the hearth and set the violin on his shoulder. "Who knows? Perhaps. Or they may have simply found that it suited their purposes. Singing in harmony with the sea. Call and response..."

The old man was lost in his musings, thinking out loud. "It all amounts to the same thing, whether the mammoth instrument was built for the task or simply commandeered. A choir of Children of the Voice, an instrument played by the ocean... Their purpose is clear." He turned away from the fire, his eyes deadly serious.

"What?"

"They're going to raise Cthulhu."

* * *

Brooks stood in the bathroom doorway staring at the pillowcase on the floor. The mirror was exposed for the first time since Becca had moved in. Duct tape matted with dog hair still clung to the edges of the pillowcase. What had she done in here? Whatever it was, it probably paled in comparison to what she'd done at the asylum. But more alarming than the uncovered mirror was the lack of the zipper pouch with the Peruvian pattern on it; the one she kept her toothbrush and nail clippers in. She wasn't coming back.

"Shit," Brooks said, taking in the scene. He'd come to the bathroom first before reaching the guest bedroom, but he knew it would be equally empty of her possessions.

"What'd you find?" Merrit asked from the end of the hall near the stairs.

"Nothing. That's the problem. I don't know if she packed up her stuff before or after going to Allston, but she won't be back."

"Did you have a nanny cam or anything keeping an eye on her?"

"No."

Merrit had come to the bathroom. Brooks sidled past him and opened the guest room door. The bed was made. The novel she'd been reading still lay on the bedside table, but every other trace of her was gone.

"What's with this?" Merrit held up the pillowcase by one of its taped corners.

"I'll explain while we drive," Brooks said and started down the stairs.

They marched across the lawn to another black sedan parked on the street. Merrit lowered his head to the open passenger window. "We have any sightings of Frosty's car yet?"

"Not yet," Agent Kalley said. "They must have taken back roads."

Simultaneously, all four agents' wristwatches lit up. Brooks looked at his display:

CONFERENCE
DIRECTOR

He tapped the glass and McDermott's face appeared. "What do we have, gentlemen? Anything?"

The others looked at Brooks. It was his house. His hot seat. "Nothing. She's not here. Neither is her dog or her stuff."

"Did she leave a note?" McDermott asked.

"No. Not one that I've found anyway."

"Do you still think she's on our side, Brooks? Just too spooked to play well with others?"

"I do. Think about her history. She would never help raise the Great Old Ones. Whatever she's doing, she's doing it to stop them coming through."

"I'd like you to keep in mind that she may not be acting on her own volition," McDermott said. "Something's been pushing at her dreams, prying its way into her mind. Isn't that what you said?"

Brooks bobbed his head side to side, wanting to argue. "But she's strong. She was keeping it out."

"If she's so strong, why did she admit herself to a psychiatric hospital? I won't even get into your motives for signing her out and taking her home."

The young agent in the passenger seat, Kalley, was watching him for a reaction. Brooks took a deep breath and said, "I was trying to contain the situation. Trying to prevent civilian exposure to it. We've been over this."

"You did a pretty good job of preventing *agency* exposure to it, bud," Merrit said.

Brooks tilted his wristwatch screen away from his face and mouthed a *fuck you* to Merrit, who only grinned in reply.

"Did you explicitly tell her not to act alone?" McDermott asked.

Brooks sighed. "Honestly, sir, that would be like asking paint not to dry."

"She's not acting alone," Merrit said. "She's found someone she trusts more than Brooks. Frosty, in the silver Subaru."

"I have an ID," McDermott said.

The agents in the car sat up a little straighter. "His name is Anton DuQuette. He's a professor of Languages at Miskatonic, a known associate of Catherine Philips, and quite possibly a member of a secret society we've never been able to crack."

"Cultist?" Merrit asked.

"Undetermined," McDermott said. "He translated a rare book that was banned by the Starry Wisdom Church. At one point Reverend Proctor coordinated efforts to locate every copy and have them destroyed. We think he may have studied the book before tossing it on the fire, because he used mantras from it to banish entities during the Wade House operation. Brooks will recall that Proctor also used the dagger we saw Philips wielding in the asylum courtyard video. So maybe she still *is* on our side. *Maybe*. Regardless, we need to bring her in and find out what she knows. The professor's car was spotted on the Aylesbury Pike about 20 minutes ago. My money is on them hunkering down at his house tonight."

"Let me go," Brooks said. "If she sees anybody else, she'll run."

"Agreed," McDermott said. "Klinger and Kalley, I want you to keep a discreet eye on Brooks' house in case she returns. Brooks and Merrit will proceed to Arkham. I'm sending the professor's address to your watches. Merrit, you will hang back on arrival. Do not spook her. Brooks approaches first. If he fails to apprehend her with honey, you do it your way. Am I clear?"

"Crystal," Merrit said.

"We'll have air support in the area, should you need it. Bring them both in."

All four watches went dark.

* * *

"Again, from the top," DuQuette said. He looked tired. They had ordered out for Chinese and taken a short break from practicing the melody, but Becca could see that he was fading as the night wore on. He placed the violin under his chin and played through the melody slowly, watching her as she sang each note, and indicating with his eyebrows and the tilt of his head when she should go up or down. Becca followed along, her voice raspy as she tried to keep it from shifting into its more resonant mode. When he reached the end of the line, he tapped the tip of his bow against the floor and smiled. "That was better. You're getting it."

Becca closed her eyes and massaged her temples. The intensity of the day was catching up with her, and her practice was yielding diminishing returns. She felt like she'd never be able to sing it without him.

"Play it again for me, please," she said. "Let me just listen this time. I just need to hear it enough times."

DuQuette obliged her. Even he seemed to be trying to play the piece without any feeling, and not just because he was tired. Handling this music felt like mixing volatile chemical compounds near a flame. When he reached the end, he brushed his hair out of his eyes and said, "Together again," poising his bow for the first note and waiting for her to begin. When they reached the end, Becca tried again on her own, this time without error.

"That's it," DuQuette said. "You've got it."

"I just have to keep running it through my head."

"Cramming music in one session is never as good as practicing on successive days. It will come easier for you in the morning with just a little review. You'll see."

Becca stroked Django's head. The dog had retreated to another room when Becca bordered on slipping into her mutated voice.

Now he was back, sensing in her relaxed body language that they were done with infernal sounds for the time being.

"I can't stay the night," Becca said.

DuQuette looked up, with a raised eyebrow, from placing his violin in its case. "You brought all of your things. Where else would you go?"

Becca tilted her head in a way that said, *you know where.*

He absorbed the idea, wanting to protest, but seeing the wisdom in it. "Surely you'd be safe here for a night. They've no idea where you are."

"Would the children be safe? And I'm not so sure about SPECTRA having no idea. They're pretty good at finding people. I have the dagger, the mantras, and the melody. If I'm going, I should go."

"You don't know that they'll take you. Even if you sing the unaltered overture as an invitation, you don't know that he will lead you to the choir."

"There's only one way to find out."

DuQuette nodded and turned away, resting his eyes on the fireplace. Becca wondered if he was thinking of the same other hearth as she was, the one that concealed the door to a secret basement just a few miles from here.

"She'd never forgive me if she knew what I'm helping you to do."

"She might surprise you."

"Can I offer you something stronger than tea before you sing in your full voice?"

"What've you got?" Becca asked.

"Bourbon and wine."

"I'm not much of a drinker, but I'll take a shot of bourbon to numb my throat a little."

"Does it hurt?"

"Sometimes. It did after the chanting in the courtyard."

DuQuette opened a cabinet and produced a bottle and a pair of glasses. He poured them on his desk and offered one to Becca. "To Luke," he said, raising his glass. "For finding the key."

Becca clinked glasses with him and took a sip. The liquid burned her throat and she had to suppress a cough, but the buzz from it was almost immediate. She took another sip, this time appreciating the woody flavor and the spreading warmth. She sank into the love seat, gazing at the pulsing shadows the fire cast upon the ceiling. It was not a cold night, but the fire felt right. DuQuette, for all of his academic knowledge, was a man who understood the emotional value of fire. It mattered not that it was only a set of gas jets flickering through the gaps in a log that would never really burn. It was still a fire lit against the darkness. It was what you did before venturing forth to meet monsters.

The drink relaxed Becca, and she caught herself bobbing on the edge of sleep, Django's nose in her lap. The melody looped over and over in her head. She heard DuQuette pour himself another shot and light his pipe, and the sweet smell of raw tobacco reached her. It had been a long day, and the temptation to steal a few hours of sleep before crossing over grew stronger by the minute. She hummed the melody to focus her mind, faint at first, then stronger. The professor listened in silence, offering no corrections to her rendition.

Finally, she sat up and scratched Django's head. If she didn't go now, it would only get harder to find the will and make the leap. She was as unsure of her ability to confront the unknown as she had ever been—and that was exactly why she couldn't afford the luxury of lingering on the threshold, pondering her fitness for the task.

"Do you have a large mirror?" she asked. "Or do I have to go out looking for a pool?"

DuQuette drew a final puff and set his pipe in a notch on the ashtray. "Follow me."

He led her to a bedroom that was as neat as the front room was cluttered. Blue wallpaper and the buttery light cast by a Turkish lamp surrounded a queen sized bed with acorn finials on the posts. In the corner, beside the open doors of a walk-in closet filled with suits and sport coats, was a full-length oval mirror in an antique swivel frame. It reminded her of the one she'd seen on the second floor of the Wade House, and in her dreams.

"Perfect," Becca said, her stomach churning with anxiety. She went back to the living room for her bag, Django trailing her anxiously. She left her camera on the desk where she'd borrowed the laptop, and slid the dagger into a side pocket of the bag, handle up for easy access. She jotted a phone number on the Post-it pad and tore off the sheet. Returning to the bedroom, she found DuQuette slouched at the edge of his bed, hands clasped between his knees. He tried to smile at her, but he looked as nervous as she felt. She handed him the slip of paper.

"This is my friend Neil. If you don't mind keeping Django overnight, you can call him tomorrow. He'll take care of him while I'm away."

DuQuette nodded, took the paper and slipped it into his shirt pocket.

Django, whose head was cocked as they talked about him, twitched the other way suddenly and barked at the front of the house. Becca cupped her hand over the top of his nose and listened. She knew that particular bark. Someone was here.

Chapter 18

The brick house at 84 Garrison Street was set back from the road, a flagstone path winding between trees and a flower garden to the front door. A green copper lantern fixture illuminated the doorstep and an interior light shone through the drawn curtains. The car SPECTRA had tracked was parked in the driveway, a Subaru registered to Anton DuQuette. Merrit parked on the street and Brooks got out. He made sure to close the car door quietly, but halfway up the path, he heard a dog bark from within the house. The professor was not alone.

Brooks approached the side of the house, following a low hedge to where a plastic trash barrel stood beside another door, this one with windows in it. He looked in on an empty kitchen and tried the knob. It was locked. A quick circuit of the house turned up no ground level windows that he could see through to confirm Becca's presence, leaving him with two options: break in or knock. He decided to knock, but not at the front door. Any sign of complications in view of Merrit were likely to bring him running.

Brooks returned to the side door and knocked three times hard, eliciting a torrent of barks from Django. The dog lunged into the room, giving hell to the door. Brooks set his face in one of the small windows. "Django! It's me. Brooks. It's *Brooks*. You know me, buddy. Get Becca."

The shepherd pranced in circles, now whining between decidedly less aggressive barks.

A moment later, a heavyset man in corduroy pants and a blue button-down shirt ambled into the kitchen, taking his sweet time to get to the door. When he reached it, his white beard and swept-back mane of hair framed a face Brooks had seen on his wrist screen less than an hour ago: Professor DuQuette, his bright blue eyes appraising Brooks with a slant that suggested he had no intention of unlocking the door.

Brooks produced his ID wallet from his jacket pocket, opened the fold, and pressed it against the glass. "Mr. DuQuette, I'm Jason Brooks. I'm a friend of Becca. I know she's in there because you have Django. Let me in."

Enunciating each syllable clearly, so that Brooks could read his lips through the glass even though he was perfectly audible, DuQuette said, "Not without a warrant."

"Don't play it that way, Dumbledore. I'm the good cop. Open the fucking door."

DuQuette turned away and left the room. Brooks started counting to ten, deciding he would wait that long for Becca to appear before kicking the door in. But he only got to seven before a shimmering sound vibrated the glass, a high-pitched female voice buzzing through the door like a swarm of bees.

Brooks rammed his shoulder into the door, but it held. He backed down to the second of three concrete steps leading up to it and threw a kick, cracking the bolt through the frame and sending the door bouncing off a kitchen chair, causing Django to relapse into frenzied barking. Not a subtle entrance, but it didn't interrupt the ethereal song drilling into his ears and churning his stomach. Against every impulse of his body, he followed the sound through the house to the room it emanated from.

DuQuette, brandishing a golf club, blocked the bedroom doorframe. Beyond him, Becca stood with her back to Brooks, singing into a mirror. He could see her face reflected in the glass, as if in the surface of a wavering pool. Lost in the music, her eyes remained closed when Brooks drew his weapon, pointed it at the old man, and said, "Step aside."

To his credit, DuQuette did not look intimidated. Maybe he thought one of Becca's allies wouldn't shoot another. If so, he was wrong. Brooks still regretted not shooting John Proctor before he stepped through a shimmering portal. That moment came back to him now, bringing with it a wave of sweat and adrenaline as he stared down the professor. A voice in the back of his mind told him that he had to decide now whether or not he was willing to shoot Becca, that if he wasn't committed to that worst-case scenario, he would lose her to the other dimension, just as he had lost Proctor, and suffer the consequences. He glanced past DuQuette at Becca's legs, choosing a target of last resort. The possibility sickened him, but he didn't show it in his eyes when he fixed them on DuQuette again.

"Drop it," Brooks said.

DuQuette set the golf club on the floor slowly, stretching the time it took to complete the act; intent on giving Becca every last second he could to finish her song.

But she didn't finish it. She tapered off on a note that didn't sound like the resolution of anything, but what did Brooks know? It was strange, unsettling music. Still, he had the feeling that she'd stopped short of some climax.

"Three steps that way and down on your knees," Brooks said to DuQuette, who obeyed while Becca searched the glass for something. Brooks didn't think he could shoot out the mirror without risking hitting her. She was too close to it. Even if he missed her, she would end up with a face full of glass shards.

"Becca," Brooks said, "what are you doing? Are you awake?"

She raised her hand and touched the glass; it quivered and her reflection receded under the surface like a corpse claimed by the ocean. Shafts of green light frosted her hair and traced sine waves on the ceiling and walls.

Brooks lowered his gun and reached for Becca's shoulder. When his hand touched her, she spun around to face him, her placid brow furrowing with recognition, as if the song had put her in a trance that she was now emerging from. Brooks holstered his weapon and raised his right hand to touch her face. He didn't know what influence the old man had exerted on her, what trap he had laid, but it would all come out in the interrogation. For now, all that mattered was that Brooks had broken the spell in time, and he was taking her home.

"Brooks. I have to go." Becca said.

"You don't have to do anything," Brooks said. "It's okay. You're awake now. We're bringing him in."

"No. I have to go with him," Becca said. "The minstrel. He's come for me." She turned her head back to the mirror. The glass was gone, replaced by a tunnel of pointed arches receding to infinity. In the center, a figure in a crimson robe plucked the strings of a long-horned instrument, tongues of blue flame dripping from his slender fingers.

Becca put her hands on Brooks' chest. "It's for Noah," she said, and pushed off, sending each of them back a step—Brooks away from the mirror, and she through it. Brooks clawed at the empty air and watched her fall backward into the other world as the tunnel collapsed like a telescope, the minstrel closing the distance, as if to catch her. But the silvered glass rippled back into the frame before Brooks could witness their union, leaving him staring at his own stunned face.

* * *

"You helped her." Nico Merrit stared at Brooks down the barrel of his 9mm. "You let her go through. You could have stopped her but you let her go."

"I thought she was in a trance. I thought I broke it."

"Goddammit, Brooks! I don't know which of you to cuff first," Merrit said. He waved the gun at DuQuette. "Get up."

DuQuette's eyes ticked back and forth between them. "He says, 'get up,' you say, 'get down.' You guys should coordinate your routine."

"Fine, stay down. All the way down. Chest on the floor, hands behind your back."

Merrit knelt and cuffed the professor, then yanked him to his feet, cranking on the cuffs with enough force to torque the man's arms almost out of their sockets. Brooks wasn't a fan of the professor, but he winced at the excessive force. Merrit marched the man into his living room and pushed him onto the couch while Django slunk after the pair, growling.

"Oh, you want to start some shit with me, too, dog?" Merrit said.

"Leave the dog alone," Brooks said. "He's a hero."

"Right," Merrit said, wheeling on him, "Like your friend who colludes with cultists and jumps down the rabbit hole when things get hot."

"You threaten the dog again and we fight, *partner*," Brooks said.

Merrit scoffed and shook his head, pacing around the room. Brooks loosened his tie and shrugged his jacket off, throwing it over a chair. The room was overheated. It smelled like pipe smoke and cat piss.

"I'm not a cultist," DuQuette said.

"Shut up." Merrit picked at the items on the wide desktop, giving each of the books and papers a cursory glance. Brooks recognized the notebook that had belonged to Luke Philips. He picked it up and asked DuQuette, "What were you doing with this?"

DuQuette examined his fingernails.

Merrit rummaged through the desk drawers while Brooks moved to one of the smaller desks and nudged a mouse connected to a laptop. The screensaver gave way to a virtual desktop that was as cluttered as the one the machine was perched on. It would take the geeks at HQ time to comb through it all, but he started by pulling up the web browser and checking the recent history: the itinerary for a cruise ship.

"You thinking of taking a cruise, professor?"

The old man looked away.

"If you want to convince us you're not Starry Wisdom, tell me what she's doing," Brooks said. "Help us keep her safe."

DuQuette looked less defiant now and Brooks thought maybe he was reaching the guy. Back at HQ, methods would get vastly more persuasive, but they didn't have that kind of time. He saw the red robed musician closing in on Becca as the mirror world collapsed. It took effort to refrain from punching DuQuette in the face until some answers fell out of his bloody mouth along with his teeth.

No. He hadn't been that kind of cop and he wasn't that kind of agent, but when he thought about Becca in danger…

While Brooks riffled through the papers on the desk, Merrit swept the rest of the house for collaborators. He returned holstering his gun and tapping his watch. Brooks half listened to Merrit calling in a status report to the director, his gaze roving over the clutter until—in a cubbyhole at the back of the small desk—he spotted a Nikon camera with a familiar strap, and his heart rate jumped into a higher register. For a moment he was tempted to eject the memory card and pocket it while Merrit was distracted with his call. But that was a course of action he would be unable to retreat from if what he found on the card required the resources of the agency.

Torn between sheltering Becca from scrutiny and maybe locating her faster, he chose the latter and switched the camera on.

The photos loaded as a grid of thumbnails in the LCD. They had the eerie cast of infrared, the weeds and trees glowing stark white around the central object of focus: the birdbath at the Allston Asylum. It took Brooks a minute to figure out how to use the controls, but soon he was enlarging images, moving backward and forward through the sequence, and zooming in on details. He would need a bigger screen to make sure he wasn't missing anything, but unless she had done a double exposure trick, it looked like Becca had photographed images of a city in the water of the birdbath. The last photo was of a name on the back of a boat. Brooks felt a chill as he read the fuzzy letters, the same name he'd seen in the search history.

Beside him, Merrit spoke. "There's a team en route to scour this place for anything relevant, but we're expediting the professor back to HQ. Chopper's picking us up at the running track across the street at the university. What do you have there?"

"A photo. A cruise ship in Croatia. That's what she's interested in. I think that's where she went."

"I thought she went to the other side. To commune with her dark gods."

"You don't know her," Brooks said. "Whatever she's doing, it's to help those kids, to bring them back."

DuQuette had been watching the exchange and seemed to sense that he was witnessing a tipping point beyond which SPECTRA could take one of two approaches to pursuing Becca.

"He's right," DuQuette said. "She's risking herself to bring them back. She knows that her voice will grant her access to the children."

"How does she get from Massachusetts to Croatia without getting lost between worlds?" Merrit asked.

Brooks felt lightheaded as it dawned on him. He sat in the chair Becca had occupied and stared at DuQuette over a pair of empty whisky glasses on the desk between them. "She was fishing, wasn't she? With that song. She called the one who abducted the children, the avatar of Nyarlathotep. She called him to take her where he took Noah."

"Yes," DuQuette said. "A few miles on the Twilight Shore can take you halfway around the world."

"To Croatia?" Merrit said.

DuQuette nodded.

"Why there?" Brooks pleaded with the old man. He'd given them this much without pressure. Just a little more might prepare them.

"I'm not sure… There's a strange piece of architecture there, an organ played by the sea. I imagine they intend to use it as a setting for the ritual."

"What ritual?" Merrit demanded.

"When the stars are right, they will sing the spheres into permanent alignment. But not if she can stop it."

* * *

The helicopter soared over the Miskatonic River Valley toward Boston. Brooks scrolled through the photos on Becca's camera in the dark. She had been to the old textile mill on the Charles River. The mystic graffiti of Moe Ramirez—already documented by the agency in 2019—filled several frames. Even the older shots she'd taken on this card, things she'd photographed for her own amusement or artistic inclinations, were oddly enhanced by the infrared spectrum, lending familiar places and objects an aura of the sacred and profound: The facade of his house glowed against a dark daytime sky, the scraggly little patch of lawn transformed to a bed of snow-white grass; his nickel plated tea kettle perched above a propane flame that bloomed like a supernova; Django lay in a square of sunlight on a coil rug, his fur a shower of sparks.

The last one gave him a little shiver and made his thumb linger over the DELETE option: a perfectly composed portrait of his own sleeping face, ethereal in the glow of the alarm clock, as if painted in oils by an old master.

Chapter 19

Becca followed the Crimson Minstrel across the Twilight Shore. The black sand burned her feet and the mustard gas sky made her head throb in rhythm with the expansion and contraction of the swirling clouds that seemed to breathe. There was something at the center of the maelstrom above, but she couldn't force herself to look up at it, certain it would unravel her sanity as it had done to Mark Burns, the biologist on the Wade House expedition.

Her guide plucked the strings of his instrument as he walked, his robes rippling in the wind. The notes reached her in gusts, between the poundings of the distant surf—the breakers crashing about a mile to the east, assuming they were walking north. As a New Englander, she thought of the ocean as lying to the east out of habit. But terrestrial geography meant nothing in this in-between place.

They crested a ridge from which she could see where the black water met the black sand by a lace of foam. Descending into the sheltering hollow of the dunes, a closer sound than the boom of the waves reached her ears: a mixture of clacking percussion and a droning chant.

Memories of what Mark had described after passing through this place scratched at the locked doors of her mind. He had been broken and scrambled like an egg by a few hours here. Towering marble columns floated into view above the line of the dunes. This had to be the temple of the Twilight Choir—a circle of black cloaked, eyeless singers who listened for celestial currents of song, then amplified and harmonized them for transmission to the dream realm, where they would reverberate in the minds of sleeping sensitives.

It was coming back to her now, everything he had explained. Everything that had sounded like lunacy at the time. Did her own nightmares pass through here each night, gathered in the neural nets of singers who boosted the signal with tongues marinated in cephalopod ink, through mouths ringed with shark teeth?

Becca shivered as she passed their shadowy forms, keeping her eyes on her boots and watching for the faces of northern stargazer fish concealed by the sand, poised to administer their electrified bite to the unwary traveler.

The minstrel's clawed hands quickened their pace on the strings, tangling his own music with that of the robed figures in a syncopated conversation. The choir chittered as he passed, and Becca—imagining that they sensed her even without eyes—picked up her pace.

The temple behind them, her guide cut a course for the ocean. Becca scanned the horizon for structures, but finding none, returned her gaze to her scuffed boots kicking up jet-black grains, and the featureless footprints of the one she followed.

With proximity to the water came a scent on the air—spicy and sweet. Becca's headache thrummed in her ears, ringing her skull like a bell. She needed out of here, and soon. But there was no going back. The framed mirror had vanished a mile or more behind her, swept away by a curtain of mist, as if the atmosphere of the realm was capable of devouring the materials of her dimension like an acid bath.

The only way was forward.

The minstrel had walked ahead of her from the moment she had emerged into this world, confident that she would follow, not turning to glance back at her even once as they crossed the desolate plain. And the longer he didn't, the more she dreaded what she would see in the hood of his cloak if he did. Now, as they approached the rolling surf, he slowed his pace, allowing the waves to soak the bottom of his robes.

Becca clutched at the canvas bag slung over her shoulder. She could feel the hard contours of the dagger she had placed hilt up in the side pocket and was tempted to draw it, to stab the bipedal beast between his shoulder blades with a howling mantra to accompany the blow. Finish him here between worlds before he could ever set foot on terra firma again, before he could return to the children he had assembled to serve as an earthly analog to the choir they had just passed, another watchtower to receive and transmit the signal fire that would burn the world.

But if she murdered her guide—if that was even possible in this realm—she would never find her way back.

For a woman who had spent years suffering under the weight of depression, it was an odd awakening to realize that somewhere along the way, she had put suicide into a category of last resorts. She wanted to live. She wanted to grow old and put the monster years behind her. She wanted to see her dog again, see Brazil again, and maybe even find love again. But first she wanted to see Noah Petrie and return him to his parents.

And so she stood paralyzed in a wash of realizations, her thumb caressing the spine of the dagger through the damp canvas, when the shadow of a great wave fell upon her. There was just time to suck in a deep breath before the crash.

*　*　*

Someone was playing an organ underwater. The music conjured images of creaking playground equipment—seesaws and swings, rusty chains, even before she saw the children in the water. When the bubbles cleared, they were soaring through shafts of light in the dark water, tumbling and somersaulting. They wore bathing suits and swim shirts and had gills curling behind their ears, running along their jawlines. They were beautiful until they sang their joyful songs in dark harmony with the moaning organ and then they were terrible, their eyes lit with blue phosphorescence.

Becca was falling away from them, to where the shafts of light thinned. Her clothes, bag, and boots dragged her down to the darkness, and she was drowning. She ran a numbing finger along her jaw, but found no slit for breathing seawater. She kicked and clawed her way upward, but soon lost her sense of direction. What she'd thought was the direction of daylight was now murky. She thrashed in the water and spun herself around, searching for light.

Or was it her consciousness that was dimming? The children were gone. She was alone, exhaling her air, a cloud of silver bubbles in the black.

* * *

Becca woke in a hospital bed. She could tell by the equipment, the blood on the floor, and the woman in the next bed groaning through what might have been a miscarriage. She couldn't be sure—both the woman and the nurses were speaking a different language—but the emotional content was unmistakably agony and grief. The urgency of the scene snapped her from sleep to high alert.

She coughed and her lungs burned. One of the nurses in black scrubs stepped away from the hemorrhaging woman and approached Becca's bedside, setting a hand on the railing.

"I kako se sada osjecate?" the nurse asked.

"I don't understand," Becca said.

"How do you feel now?"

"I'm okay. How long have I been here?"

"Dr. Novak will see you in a minute."

Becca tried to sit up but was wracked with a coughing fit. The nurse put a hand on her shoulder and eased her back to the pillow. Her nametag read: Petra.

"Petra, how long?"

"Rest," the nurse said, and turned back to the other patient.

Becca felt her chest. The golden scarab was gone. She sat up and threw the sheet off. They had dressed her in a hospital gown. Scanning the room, she saw her own clothes dried and folded on a chair beside the bed. Her army bag hung from the strap slung over the chair back. The nurse was coming at her again with a look of alarm on her face. The other patient continued to moan, but it sounded like the worst of her suffering had passed.

"You need rest," Petra said.

Becca ignored her, digging in her bag for the dagger. She felt it right away, cold and metallic, then her probing hand touched something soggy: the small leather-bound book of mantras that had taken a swim with her. She was afraid to look, but she pulled the swollen and warped volume out and pried it open. The ink had blurred and the pages stuck together. Well, if she didn't have the mantras memorized by now, it was too late for study anyway.

"Miss, you need to lie down."

Becca turned toward the new, more authoritative voice and found a petite brunette with wrinkles at the corners of her mouth and eyes. She wore a white jacket over her scrubs and a nametag with a caduceus beside the name: Anja Novak M.D.

"What's your name?" the doctor asked. "Are you Canadian?"

"American. I had a necklace," Becca said, still rummaging through the damp bag. These people had probably saved her life, and a part of her knew she should be grateful, but it was a small part, buried deep in her throbbing, clouded head. Mostly, she felt her mood veering off toward a white-hot rage the longer she was awake. She felt violated and thrown off track, her quest threatened, her possessions picked through, her clothes removed while she was out cold. "Where is it?"

The doctor took a step back, reading the intensity on Becca's face, but before she could answer, Becca's fingers touched the chain. She withdrew the scarab from the bag and clutched it in her fist, her hoarse breathing settling down to a normal rate, her heart still pounding. The talisman had no magic left in it without the red gem between the beetle's pinchers, and yet losing it to the ocean or a thief was unthinkable.

Dr. Novak touched Becca's elbow gently. "We couldn't find any identification. No passport. Did you fall out of a boat?"

Becca thought about it for a second, then nodded her head. "My friends will be worried. Where am I?"

"The Opća Bolnica," Dr. Novak said. "You need to lie down. You almost drowned."

"Is this Zadar?"

"Yes, the hospital in Zadar. Please, back to bed."

"My friends will be worried," Becca said again, picking through her folded clothes for her underwear. She stepped into them and then pulled her pants on under the hospital gown.

"You can't leave. We need to run tests to make sure you didn't suffer brain damage."

Slipping her bra on and then the gown off, Becca said, "Thank you, but no. I have to go."

"Slow down. We don't even know your name."

The doctor visibly relaxed as Becca sat down on the edge of the bed, but it was only to put her socks and boots on.

"They're almost dry," Becca said. "How long was I out for?"

"We put them in the sun for a few hours. A jogger found you washed up on the sea organ steps at dawn. He called an ambulance when he couldn't resuscitate you. He's worried. He left a phone number." She took a slip of paper from her jacket pocket and passed it to Becca, who dropped it in her bag, pulled her T-shirt over her head, and slung the bag over her shoulder.

The nurses had pulled a curtain around the woman in the other bed. Over the top of the metal railing, a wall clock read 1:10. Becca didn't know exactly what time the sun rose here, but if days hadn't passed on the Twilight Shore or in the hospital, she'd been out for something like… "He pulled me out of the water at sunrise? So I was out for six or seven hours?"

"Yes. You regained consciousness briefly, after you were resuscitated, but then you slept hard. We need to at least check your lungs now that you're awake."

"I have to go."

"Your larynx looked inflamed on the scans. There may be damage. Honestly, I'm surprised you can even speak. I've called a colleague, a specialist. I want him to see you before…"

But Becca was already staggering into the corridor, searching for a staircase or an elevator. She'd glimpsed a red tile rooftop from the window. She needed to reach the ground floor, the exit, the street, and the waterfront. A nurse yelled after her, and she ran.

* * *

Nico Merrit had not risen swiftly through the SPECTRA ranks or secured lead status on sensitive operations by questioning Warwick McDermott's wisdom to the man's face. But in the nascent hours of April 30th, he had pushed back hard against the little video representation of the director's face on his wristwatch in a bathroom stall at Pease International Trade Port in Portsmouth, New Hampshire, where the helicopter had been redirected en route to Boston.

Merrit objected to taking Brooks on the flight to Zadar. He was too emotional when it came to Becca Philips, too personally involved to think clearly and act decisively. The events at DuQuette's house in Arkham proved that once and for all. But McDermott stood by the decision, citing Brooks' EDEP. He could see things others couldn't, and maybe not just monsters. Maybe, the director had suggested, Brooks could see things in Philips that no other agent could. Like where her loyalties lay. Merrit wasn't so sure about that. Love blinded people. You saw that in the news every time some nut mowed down a classroom with an assault rifle. The people closest to the killer were always in denial. Brooks might see something, but if he did, would he say something?

Now, at the end of an eight-hour nonstop flight on a SPECTRA jet, there was nothing left to do but prep his own rifle while the Navy SEALS loaded the Zodiac with gear. The boat was a 24-foot rigid hull raft with twin outboard engines and a plasma cannon mounted to a swivel base on the nose. It could hold fourteen people, but their crew was only eight: five SEALS, including the captain of the craft, plus Merrit, Brooks, and Kalley, who had received a crash course in the operation of the plasma cannon before flying out. Merrit didn't understand the power source for that bit of Elder tech, but he'd seen how low its weight dropped the boat in the water. Merrit had used boats like this one in the Mediterranean while patrolling the Syrian coast with the Navy in 2017. They'd schlepped a lot of gear back then, too, but he'd never seen a Zodiac of this size dip so low without personnel.

It seemed a shame to overburden the craft with something so tenuously useful. He'd seen what the cannon could and couldn't do at the quarry in New Hampshire. McDermott claimed the modified operator gloves would make the difference, but Merrit was grateful to be riding out with his sniper rifle. The gun had never let him down when he was deployed, and he knew this game wasn't going to be won by hurling plasma balls at gods. If it came to that, they were all fucked.

One of the SEALS sauntered over to Merrit, bobbing his head to music only he could hear. He tugged a pair of wireless headphones off his ears to dangle around his neck, where they leaked thin strains of the Beatles' "Helter Skelter." The SEAL tipped his chin at Merrit's weapon and slapped him on the back. "Nightforce scope?"

Merrit nodded.

"Good choice, but are you sure you don't want to leave the shooting to us, Agent Merrit?"

On the jet, it had been just the three agents. They'd met the SEALS upon landing at LD57, the abandoned Sepurtine training base that now served only as an airfield. It was an ideal touchdown point, close to the water and just a little way up the coast from the sea organ pavilion. There hadn't been time yet to sort out the pissing contest of rank.

Merrit scowled at the man. "You will follow my lead on when to shoot. Is that clear, sailor?"

"Yessir. I thought Agent Brooks had command of the operation, sir. They told us in the briefing he's the only one who can see the entities."

"That's not true," Merrit said. He took a slim metal case from his vest, opened it, and placed a pair of Tillinghast shades over his eyes. The SEAL shrank away from him when he powered them on, spilling violet light over his cheekbones and neatly trimmed black goatee.

"If you and your men have infrared goggles, I advise you use them. Not just for night vision. They're not as good as these, but they just might save your life."

The grunt worked his jaw, reappraising Merrit, or gathering the nerve to ask a question. "Are they really gods, or is that bullshit?"

"That's a question for the philosophers," Merrit said. "I am not a philosopher. I've been a soldier and a sailor, and now I'm a spook. But what I've *always* been is a hunter. To me, they are predators. Reality itself has been their camouflage. And it's been a thin skin of armor for us. These children are trying to change that. Don't forget it."

The SEAL nodded, put the cans over his ears again, and walked back to his own gear with less bounce in his stride, despite the fight song.

Brooks approached next. He had a sheet of yellow paper in his hand, the edges torn where they weren't covered in packing tape.

"What's this?" Merrit asked.

Brooks held up the paper, a flyer torn from a telephone pole or a streetlamp.

The Crimson Minstrel Presents:
THE DIVINE PROVIDENCE CHILDREN'S CHOIR
Performing a Selection From
The Music of the Spheres
A Cosmic Chorale
In Harmony with the Zadar Sea Organ
At the Monument to the Sun
ONE NIGHT ONLY!
May Eve 2025

* * *

Becca stood in the middle of a narrow cobblestone street, staring at the poster, mouth agape, as passing tourists jostled her with their shopping bags. After hours of walking the waterfront, combing the city for signs of the children with a slow blooming sense of despair, here at last was confirmation that she wasn't too late. They would be singing tonight. And yet, with the relief came a new kind of dread fluttering in her stomach. The pharaoh, or minstrel, the monster clothed as a man, was *promoting* what they were about to do, making a spectacle of it and inviting an audience. It showed a brazen confidence that she found unnerving. What was his purpose in gathering a crowd? To shatter their minds and expose them to harmonics that would initiate them into the perception of predatory gods? After what she'd witnessed in Boston, that felt right.

There was no time listed on the flyer, but Becca would wait at the sea organ all night if she had to. She took her pocketknife from her bag and sliced through the packing tape holding the flyer to the pole. Then she strode across the alley to a shop with a display window facing the place where the flyer had been posted.

Entering the little boutique, Becca gave a cursory glance to the wares on display—blown glass sculpture and jewelry. A woman with short gray hair and fashionably colorful glasses looked up from a display case upon which a tabloid lay open. There were no customers in the shop, and the woman, whose glasses looked like she'd chosen them to echo her stained glass merchandise, gave Becca an appraising look without bothering to flip her magazine closed, as if she could tell at a glance that the girl in the weather-stained clothes with the wild hair wasn't buying.

"How may I help you?" she asked without enthusiasm.

Becca held up the faded flyer. "This was posted across the street. I wondered if you saw who put it up."

Having confirmed that she wasn't dealing with a customer, the shopkeeper slid a cigarette out of a pack tucked under the tabloid and lit it. When she'd taken a drag and exhaled, she said, "He's kind of hard to forget."

"How so?"

"Attractive man." She shrugged. "Tall, dark, young. Helping sick kids. Playing that strange guitar with his long fingers, like he just stepped out of the Middle Ages or something." She leaned forward, elbows on the glass case, and tilted her head, gazing mischievously up into Becca's eyes. "Are you a smitten kitten? Is that why you're looking for him?"

"No."

The woman smiled. "It's okay, you can be honest. I know he's too young for me. But a free-spirited hostel girl like you... American? You should go for it. He will find you exotic just for your accent."

"He's Croatian, this man?"

"I think so. We only talked for a moment." She waved her cigarette at a neat bulletin board at the back of the shop where another copy of the same flyer, this one less sun faded, was tacked between ads for Yoga on the Waterfront and beach house rentals.

"What did you say about sick kids?" Becca asked.

"Honestly, I didn't catch all of it, what with his eyes and everything. He said something about touring with his children's choir. I think they're terminally ill. He had one of them with him, poor little sunken-eyed thing. I think they do religious music." She waved her hand dismissively, knocking ash to the counter, which she chased away with a puff of breath. "The show is tonight, if you really want to find him."

"Have you seen other children besides the one that came with him to post the flyers?"

The woman nodded. "Sometimes you spot him by the sea organ, playing his guitar while the kids swim."

"Did you get his name?"

"Tristan," she said with a wistful smile. She took another drag and squinted at Becca through tendrils of smoke.

Becca left the shop and did another pass of the waterfront. The sun was beginning its descent toward the water and the foot traffic on the pavilion was picking up. Gentle waves rolled in, lapping at the concrete steps amid the perpetual music of the sea organ. Her stomach groaned with hunger and her feet ached from walking all day, but her head felt clearer than it had in days and her throat no longer burned. She knew she would be in the right place at the right time. It was just a matter of waiting for the children to gather. She sensed that wouldn't happen until nightfall or later, and risked a short walk through the Old Town again, in search of something to eat that she could buy with the few crumpled American dollars she had in her pocket, stiff from soaking and drying, or the credit card in her bag—assuming the chip still worked after a trip across the Twilight Shore.

Leaving the disquieting moans of the sea organ fading behind her, she thought of how the sound would continue to haunt this place for centuries, even if humans were exterminated. Barring a bomb or an asteroid shattering the pavilion, this place would sound the same in a post-apocalyptic world. Making her way to the nearest pizzeria, she couldn't decide if the notion was a comfort or a horror.

* * *

When Becca returned to the pavilion with the inverted melody looping in her mind, dusk was falling over the city, the setting sun gilding the languid waves, the notes of a guitar flitting in and out of the spaces between the organ's deep breaths.

A tingle passed down the nape of her neck beneath her ponytail, and she touched the dagger through the bag at her hip.

A silhouette came into view as she turned her head toward the music. A musician sitting on a step, facing the lowering sun that enflamed his hair and gleamed off of the tuning keys of his exotic instrument, blazing violet trails on Becca's eyes that followed her gaze as she blinked. Could this really be him? As she approached, she thought she'd made a mistake. The shopkeeper had caught her off guard with her description of him. Becca had only interacted with what she thought of as his true form in the space between worlds. But even that form was likely only one emanation of a being that could manifest in myriad guises. Catherine had been fascinated with Nyarlathotep, and had told Becca stories about some of those forms. At the monstrous end of the spectrum was the Crawling Chaos; at the human end was the Black Pharaoh. But this earthy avatar of the god had to be a body he'd chosen to inhabit for its charm and musical dexterity. She walked around him, shielding her eyes from the sun with her hand, positioning herself between the musician and the water, where she could see his face—it was a face a child could trust.

"I thought we'd lost you," he said. His voice was husky and kind. His fingers continued roving the fret board between the instrument's long, curved horns.

"I almost drowned for following you," Becca said. "That was you, wasn't it? Without this mask."

He laughed. "You've never seen me without a mask. And I don't think you'd like to. Not yet."

"Why not?"

"You're not ready."

"Where are the children?" Becca asked. She tried to keep her tone light and curious, but could hear the tremor in it.

"Somewhere safe," he said.

"I saw them. Breathing underwater."

"You might too, someday. They were born with all of their gifts. Yours are growing on you." He strummed a minor chord and resolved it, as if to say that her deficiency was a sad state that could be rectified.

"I've heard a song in my dreams," Becca said. "I can't get it out of my head, and...maybe I don't want to anymore."

Something flashed in the depths of his storm-gray eyes. "Do you tire of holding a door closed that should be opened?"

Becca sat on the step beside him and looked out over the water, the gold light of the setting sun falling across her face and neck doing nothing to reduce the chill she felt in the presence of this creature in the guise of a man. "I do."

"Do you see the folly of driving a wedge between worlds that were meant to be joined?"

Careful of appearing too eager, she said, "Everything human in me resists it. My mind...can't accept what I want to do."

"What do you want to do? In your heart."

"I want to stop fighting what I'm becoming. I want to sing the song I hear in my dreams. I feel like I'll die if I don't."

The minstrel raked the fingers of his right hand over the strings, then reached out with them and brushed a stray lock of hair away from Becca's eyes. "You should listen to that voice," he said.

"But won't everything human in me, in the *world*, die if I give in to it?"

He looked away and played his strange instrument, and for a second, the bustling pavilion appeared empty to her, as if the centuries had already passed, her race already fallen into extinction, the forms of the tourists around her mere ghosts, their desires and fears reduced to ephemeral whispers of no consequence amid the eternal lament of the ocean in the organ. And then he played the music in reverse, and the sun raced west to east across the sky, and the days and nights strobed backward from that tranquil moment to a day when the setting sun over Rome was replaced with an incandescent mushroom cloud, and she knew that he was answering her without words, showing her what mankind would bring to the earth she treasured: the melting of the polar ice caps, the death of the oceans, nuclear winter. He was showing her what she'd always known but had kept hidden from herself in moments of greatest crisis—that mankind was not the arbiter of rationality or the ultimate steward of the earth. *Man* was a force of chaos, driven by tempests of whim and violent emotion. And all life on Earth would suffer the consequences if he were not exterminated by the Great Old Ones who had once flourished in primeval peace, and would again when the children of man sang them home.

Becca buckled forward, the breath knocked out of her. The sky cleared, the sun came to rest in its proper place at dusk on Walpurgis Night, and the white noise of the crowd swelled up around her over the drone of the organ.

She turned toward the minstrel, but he was gone, if he'd ever been there in the flesh in the first place. A chill wind blew in off the water. Becca shivered, pulled her jacket close around her, and reached into her bag to grasp the hilt of the silver dagger, as if it might warm her cold blood.

* * *

The children came at nightfall, dressed in black. They gathered at the Monument to the Sun, four boys and four girls, each taking a position on the photo luminescent disk of a planet, all facing the giant disk of the sun, upon which other children and parents and lovers gathered as they did every night to watch the play of colored light beneath their feet. The disks, relative in size to the planets they represented, were small in relation to the sun disk. A faint orange light flickered between the feet of a blonde haired girl standing over Venus, while pink light encircled a hollow-eyed boy poised to sing at the center of Jupiter. Becca walked the steps of the sea organ, observing from a distance, as if afraid she might be swept into their orbit if she got too close. Was that Noah, motionless in the blue glow of Neptune? And where was the minstrel, Tristan?

Did she catch a glimpse of him, a flash of crimson in the gloom, wending his way through the crowd, roving the outer reaches of the pavilion, a dark uncharted planet?

A low hum, barely audible, spread over the pavilion. At first, it was almost impossible to differentiate the sound from the sea organ itself. As it swelled slowly, Becca realized she was hearing a droning unison note from the children's throats, buzzing like a downed power cable or a hornet's nest. A cascade of icy guitar notes rained down around the crowd, and the chatter thinned out to a patchwork of whispers. Now she could see Tristan in his red robe, circling the sun disk. Parents pulled their children away from him, off of the illuminated ground.

Becca, despite her fear, found herself following in Tristan's footsteps, walking toward the sun disk as the crowd parted around her, a song rising in her throat, the dagger she'd tucked into the waistband of her pants and covered with her shirt entirely forgotten.

Chapter 20

The Zodiac raft approached the pavilion from the north under cover of darkness, moving fast. It hugged the coast until clear of the cruise ship dock, then, after passing the *Aegean Star*, cut a wide circle to the west for a direct approach. Brooks felt a wave of *déjà vu* reading the name off the back of the ship. He checked his holster for the third time and adjusted the fit of his Kevlar vest. Colored lights pulsed on the concrete pavilion ahead, throwing black silhouettes. A crowd was gathered around the largest colored disk, in a crescent formation, open on the ocean side. He'd known there would be civilians, but the sight of them was still unsettling; there were so many, and some were children. But then, most of their targets were children.

McDermott had emphasized the directive to take the kids alive, and Becca as well, but Brooks didn't trust Merrit to comply. He needed to be first out of the boat when they landed, to put himself between the SEALS and Noah—at *least* Noah, if he couldn't do better. The thought of looking Tom and Susan in the eyes when he got back to Boston weighed heavy on him as the growl of the twin engines was overtaken by a louder drone.

Light flared around the boat. For a second, Brooks thought Agent Kalley had fired the plasma cannon, but then he saw that the sea was illuminated from below, as if a blue star were rising from the deep. The light was so bright that the silhouettes of fish and rays could be seen roving above it. Were they fleeing its approach?

The crowd around the monument where the choir sang had also noticed the glowing ocean. Some broke away and descended the steps of the sea organ for a closer look, probably marveling over what special effect the minstrel had employed to extend the light show from the pavilion to the water.

Brooks could see that figure now, orbiting the largest lighted disk in a red robe, blue sparks flitting about his head like a crown, his face a patch of blackness darker than night. The sound of his guitar carried over the water, a skeletal structure supporting the flesh and blood formed by the mingling of the choir voices with those of the sea organ.

The music was causing something to manifest around the star rising in the water. It bloomed in the deep, unfurling tendrils and limbs of twining fire. Brooks felt an overwhelming urge to urinate at the sight of it. He had seen this entity, this phenomenon before. Azothoth, the book breakers called it. It had been unleashed by Darius Marlowe's sonic bomb on the Red Line subway in 2019 and had ascended the sky to a zenith from which it endowed other entities with the power to manifest; a puppet master dripping strings of black oil over Boston. Becca's scarab had fractured this god of chaos, blasted it into fragments that had snowed black flakes on the region, swirling around the Wade House until its chimneys sucked them back into the deity's native dimension. But here it was, about to breach, about to be born anew. And this time, the talisman capable of shattering it was itself shattered; the gem of power lost to that other world.

Brooks scanned the pavilion. He had passed over the night vision goggles while gearing up, choosing instead to rely on his EDEP.

The Children of the Voice glowed with a greenish aura like swamp gas, while the minstrel burned a bright red that seemed to gather intensity from the music's crescendo. Another adult (Becca?), standing at the center of the largest lighted disk, was wrapped in a shifting veil of yellow and violet. He could hear his shipmates exclaiming about the star rising beneath the boat—even they could perceive that burgeoning manifestation, but he doubted they would see the choir in the same way he did if they removed their goggles. Whatever was flourishing in Becca and the children was not yet fully formed in this dimension.

Not yet… Not yet… Not yet.

As the boat passed over the glowing water, a school of giant jellyfish broke the surface and rose into the air like helium balloons of billowing tissue, flickering with electricity in their cores. The crowd let out a sigh of awe as the boat sped away from the floating creatures, away from the light, and ate up the remaining yards to the concrete shore.

And then, the time for nervous anticipation had passed. The captain cut the engines and two of the SEALS tilted them out of the water to keep the props from grinding on the steps. The nose of the Zodiac bounced, and Brooks was out, running up the sea organ steps toward the crowd and the choir.

Facing the water, Becca looked past Brooks, or through him, her gaze fixed on the rising jellyfish creatures and the surfacing star. The minstrel was nowhere to be seen. He had melted into the shadows of the crowd again, the sound of his instrument fading, as the sound of the choir surged. The song sent waves of pain rippling through Brooks' head, patterns of violet stars speckling his field of vision. He struggled against the compressed air, as if he were running into the water rather than away from it, his momentum thwarted by the sonic surf.

The heads of the children seemed to float in the darkness, their black clothes blending with the shadows, their faces wavering in the shifting light cast by the disks and the glowing sea, as the rising creature's aura covered the final stretch of water and touched the bottom step of the monument.

Becca, like the children, looked hypnotized, enraptured. What had they done to her to make her sing?

The crowd was dispersing, losing interest in the choir. Some walked toward the jellyfish creatures hovering in the air at the water's edge, flashing like heat lightning, trailing tendrils of some viscous substance. Others focused on the men with the guns, goggles, and armored vests jumping out of the raft behind Brooks. Some froze in place, paralyzed. Only a few retreated, knocking into each other, casting around for something that would make sense of the scene. But no one that Brooks could see was doing the sane thing—running away from the waterfront into the shelter of the town. They might know that the soldiers represented danger, might sense that the physics-defying creatures represented worse, but in most of them, denial was winning out over self-preservation. Denial and curiosity. The deep-seated belief that the unfolding spectacle would soon be unmasked and resolved as an entertainment. And then he noticed that the ones closest to the water, who had gravitated toward the danger, were holding their devices up, framing shots and recording video, secure in the feeling that their lenses and screens offered some kind of immunity by placing them in the category of witness rather than victim.

One of the SEALS was shouting at the spectators, waving the muzzle of his rifle, telling them in his best American drill sergeant holler to, "Get out the way! Get down or *get the fuck outta the way!*"

When almost no one responded, the first weapon discharged, shearing the night with the sound of lethal reality crashing in on the hypnotic fantasia. Brooks didn't know who fired at the sky, but it had the desired effect. People hit the ground or scattered. Parents swept up children in their arms and sheltered them, but Becca didn't even flinch. She kept singing and staring at the sea. Brooks had almost reached her when another shot rang out, a single crack, followed by a moan. He whipped his head around as one of the children crumpled to the ground, a boy on one of the larger disks.

Dear God, was it Noah?

Brooks' own weapon was in his hand now, though he didn't remember drawing it. It was only a handgun, but it dispersed the crowd around him. Brooks watched in horror as the child squirmed on the plate of pulsing light, a dark pool of blood spreading like a shadow growing from his neck.

It was Phineas Malik. For a flash, Brooks was back in the child's bedroom in Sedona, seeing his scattered Legos and the mirror he had crawled through, seeing the fear on his mother's face.

The killing shot broke the spell. The song faltered and the other children wandered from their stations, not fleeing like the bystanders now were, but wandering toward the water, like kids lost in a mall, scanning the crowd for their parents.

Brooks turned to the water, searching for which of his companions had fired the shot, but he knew even before his gaze landed on Merrit, poised on the third step of the organ, sweeping his rifle over the remaining children, tracking them through the scope. Beyond Merrit, the SEAL team was divided: some aiming their weapons at the flaming orb god rising from the water, others hauling the Zodiac around to point toward the water so that Kalley—manning the plasma cannon with those weird gloves—could get a fix on it. It wouldn't be difficult; the thing was fucking huge.

A woman's scream cut the air. A large man in a floral shirt and swim trunks had been seized by one of the mammoth jellyfish, his upper half vanishing into its cloudy flesh, his legs bicycling wildly as it lifted him into the air. Blood poured over his exposed belly from the monster's convulsing maw and dripped from his sandals, pattering on the white stone. One sandal fell off and bounced, leaving a red mark; the only sign he had ever been there when the rest of him was sucked into the billowing pink tresses.

A SEAL fired at the jellyfish as it floated out over the sea, but if the bullets pierced it, they had no effect.

Brooks looked at Merrit. He was staring through his scope at the body of Phineas Malik, his lower lip trembling, his one open eye glistening with an unshed tear. He blinked, swallowed, and trained the rifle on another target. Brooks followed his aim and saw that Becca was next in his sights. He stepped into the line of fire, shielding her as the children ran past him to the water.

A crackling ball of light erupted from the cannon mounted on the nose of the Zodiac and soared over the water. Azothoth rose into the air like an eclipsed star, a heart of darkness sprouting roots of black light through a white corona, ascending among the retinue of jellyfish. But before the plasma ball from the cannon made contact, the creatures faded to transparency, and Brooks knew that Kalley's shot wasn't responsible—Merrit's was. In taking down a member of the choir, he had shattered the song, depriving the god of the energy drawing it into the world.

It was over. There was no need for Merrit to take Becca, too. Standing in front of her, Brooks raised his gun and aimed it at Merrit's face. "Leave her be," Brooks said. "Find the minstrel."

"Step aside, Brooks," Merrit said.

"She was hypnotized. They all were. We take them in alive."

A swath of red fabric, like a matador's cape, flashed at the waterline, south of the team gathered around the boat. Brooks pivoted and fired at it and Merrit flinched. The robe seemed to ripple like a pool of paint, the man wearing it gliding down the wide steps into the waves. Caught by the wind, the cloak flapped up, unfurling like a giant flag, revealing the Children of the Voice. They flocked behind their leader, splashing into the dark water under the canopy of his billowing cloak.

Then Becca was running after them, past Brooks. He snatched at her arm but only felt the sleeve of her jacket slipping through his fingers. He ran after her, reaching the water just behind her. The crimson cloak floated on the surface a few yards out. The sea had gone dark again in the wake of the god's withdrawal. Bullets plunked in the water from Merrit's rifle. Brooks paid them no heed, flying down the stairs amid the unceasing moans of the organ.

Becca walked down the steps into the water, following the vanishing cloak until only her hair trailed behind her on the surface. Then she was gone.

Brooks took a deep breath and dived in after her.

Chapter 21

Becca vomited brine onto stone. Daylight blazed in her eyes and made her head pound while her stomach spasmed and convulsed. The sound of surf reached her ears, but all she could focus on was the cold, wet stone beneath her hands. There was something wrong with it. It wasn't the flat concrete of the sea organ steps. And where was the breath of the organ, those long ambiguous chords lingering between major and minor?

She wasn't in Zadar anymore.

She had swum into darkness with the children. She had followed a ribbon of red through the gloom. It was coming back to her now. She had almost drowned again for the second time in twenty-four hours.

She put a hand to her jawline, felt a flap of flesh, a *gill*, and recoiled from the touch.

A hand on her shoulder, small and gentle. She looked up into Noah Petrie's big green eyes. Becca drew a ragged breath and managed to exhale without retching again. The boy smiled at her. She shifted to a sitting position and seized him in her arms, pulling him into a wet embrace. Noah squirmed and struggled, causing Becca to let go. He took a few steps back and smiled at her.

Her voice was hoarse when she spoke. "Are you okay, Noah?"

He nodded. "I thought you drowned," he said.

Becca coughed, clenched her fist in front of her mouth, then stood up, carefully. She wondered if the tide had battered her against the rocks. Every muscle ached, every bone throbbed. The shrieks of children reached her ears, filtered through wind and surf. Playful shrieks of wild abandon.

"Where are we?" Becca asked.

"Tristan says it's Easter Island," Noah said. "But we can't find any eggs. Anyway, Easter already happened."

Easter Island? Had they walked the Twilight Shore again? A memory flashed into her mind—or was it a nightmare? She and the children riding on the back of a giant white sea serpent through tide pools and coastal rivers.

"Where is Tristan?" Becca asked, looking around the shore, her hair fluttering in her face. She spotted two of the children playing in the tall grass where the cliff sloped down to a beach, but no sign of the one who had brought them here.

"He went to the cave, to get the treasure," Noah said.

"It's a lava tube," a girl's voice said. She had come up the beach to stand beside them. Her black dress was stiff with salt, trimmed with white sand. In her blonde hair, strands of red seaweed were tangled like ribbons. "Tristan says the caves were made from lava. They used to hide in them and travel underground like in a subway."

"Who?" Becca asked.

"The cannibals," the girl said with a tone of impatience. "The first folk of the Starry Wisdom. The ones who made those."

Becca followed the girl's pointing finger to a ridge where a line of cyclopean heads carved from dark stone ranged across the horizon. She had seen pictures of these icons growing up. Occasionally on TV, but mostly in Catherine's books. Her mind reeled at the sight. After all of the weirdness she had experienced in the past few years, the past few days, it suddenly seemed that the most impossible fact confronting her was that she should be here, on Rapa Nui, looking at an *ahu* platform on which a line of *moai* stood sentinel, gazing across the ocean. Across the centuries.

"Come, Noah," the girl said. "We're making a sand castle of the citadel."

Noah gave Becca a look of concern, then followed after the girl, who spun around to face Becca again as something occurred to her. "Are you going to help us?" she asked. "Since Phineas is dead, will *you* sing Saturn when we raise R'lyeh?"

Becca touched the hilt of the dagger—still tucked into the waistband of her cargo pants—through her damp shirt. "I hope so," she said. "If Tristan wants me to. Where is the cave? I need to find him."

* * *

She found him by the sound of his instrument. He sat cross-legged like a sitar player atop a stone outcropping overlooking the ocean, the cave mouth at his back half-obscured by a curtain of ferns and vines. He wore no cloak, only a black T-shirt and jeans. He was barefoot, his skin pale, his hair a nest of tangled curls.

Eyes closed and face placid, he breathed in the sea air, and breathed out with the lazy phrases of an exotic minuet ringing from the sound hole of the lyre guitar between his thighs. Golden spruce and abalone gleamed in the sunlight.

A low cloudbank was smeared with pink along the horizon.

Becca tried to stay focused on the cold dagger pressed into the hollow of her pelvis as she approached Tristan, the carved hilt rubbing against her belly to the rhythm of her stride, the syllables of the mantra of destruction circling in her mind. But with each step, the mantra grew more muddled, and the dagger warmed from the friction of her flesh.

She climbed a grassy slope and reached the minstrel's perch. He kept his eyes closed until she was beside him. As the last chord faded and his eyelids drifted open, he gazed out over the ocean and spoke. "You've gained the second gift," he said. "You can breathe in the water now, like the children."

Becca's hand drifted up, away from the dagger, to touch the gill on her neck. It seemed to have closed up since she'd regained consciousness at the waterline, but she could still feel a ridge, like scar tissue. She examined Tristan's stubbled jawline and neck for the same, but found nothing.

"Why here?" Becca said, her voice cracking. "Why did you bring us here?"

Tristan set the guitar down in the grass and leaned it against the rock on which he sat. He shuffled off of his perch, held up a finger to signal that she should wait for him, then jogged up the slope to the cave. He disappeared through the fringe of ferns, into the blackness. A moment later, he returned with a gourd in his hands, ambled down the slope, and offered it to Becca. "Drink," he said. "You need to restore your voice. We sing again tonight."

Becca held the gourd up to her nose and sniffed.

"It's only water," Tristan said. "From a spring."

The liquid was clear and odorless. Becca took a tentative sip and thought she had never tasted such purity in her life. She drank deeper, spilling some out the sides and down her neck. When she'd quenched her thirst, she wiped the back of her hand across her chin and set the gourd down in the grass beside the guitar.

"How do you swim with it?" she asked, indicating the instrument.

"I don't need to. It's a part of me. Like my robe. It manifests when I have need of it. It answers my call, just as the Priest of the Deep will answer us tonight."

"Priest of the Deep?"

"Cthulhu."

Becca felt a thrill ripple through her body, a wave of goose flesh, followed by an immediate aftertaste of shame that whatever was growing inside her should override her revulsion at the mention of the monstrous god.

"Was that him, rising from the water at Zadar?"

"No. We almost raised the Blind Lord of Chaos. But the loss of a child broke the spell." Tristan's gaze was far away, on the ocean again, but she sensed that the horizon was just a placeholder now, that he was turned inward, toward the memory. Was that *grief* etched in the corners of his eyes? Was a creature such as he capable of it?

"They killed him," Becca said. "A boy. A little boy."

"Yes. I'm sorry you had to see that."

"What was his name?"

"Phineas. His mother's name is Demi. She's not much older than you. His father has been in and out of consciousness in a concrete box for the past week. Tortured by white devils for his faith."

"SPECTRA," Becca said.

Tristan nodded. "Sometimes, in meditation, I visit him when he blacks out. He's a man, not a mutant like his son. The waterboarding and electricity haven't broken him…but this will."

Becca's breath hitched in her chest. She couldn't help it, and she teetered there on the brink of hot tears for a moment. She hadn't known the child, but he was like Noah, could have *been* Noah. Tristan placed a hand on the small of her back, and for an instant, she reeled at the prospect of him feeling the dagger through her shirt. It was lucky that she'd tucked it in front…but what did she plan to do with it anyway? Kill this man, this demigod, the only one capable of protecting those children down on the beach?

Becca looked into the minstrel's eyes—so deep, gray flecked with gold, the pupils like obsidian. Was she falling under his spell? And if she was, when had the enchantment begun? In Zadar? On the Twilight Shore? Or had the process begun months ago, in her dreams, and only a thin film of rationality on the surface of her mind had ever resisted it?

"In the city," he said, "when we met… I knew you weren't one of us then. You were playing at it. But now, twice baptized, I believe you are awakening. I'm glad you joined us, Becca. Your voice last night was an adornment of our song, but tonight it will be the foundation. Will you take Phineas' place? Will you honor us, honor *him*, in a song to raise R'lyeh?"

"The sunken island…"

"Where our lord lies dreaming. It will rise again, held aloft by the music of the spheres. And what we nearly accomplished in Zadar will be accomplished here—the union of worlds, forevermore. And arrogant humanity will be cast from the throne."

"I thought the time when that could happen passed last night."

"In Zadar, the time has passed, yes. But we've raced the sun, in and out of time. Here, on Rapa Nui, it's still Walpurgis. And night is yet to fall. I can see now that it was meant to be this way. I thought we needed the organ because He first answered my call through its pipes. But here, so close to where He sleeps… I brought the children here to protect them, but we were *meant* to come here. To sing here."

She'd been looking at the ocean. Now she looked into his eyes again. "What happens to us after He comes?"

Tristan brushed a strand of Becca's hair away from her temple with a long, cold finger. His hand flashed black when it touched her skin, his eyes emerald. "We inherit the Earth."

Chapter 22

In the afternoon, the children splashed in the shallows and dived down the shelf where the sea floor dropped off into darkness. They grinned in shafts of green light, their teeth shining like pearl shards. They laughed bubbles and caught fish in their mouths and ate until their hunger was sated, rolling through red clouds in the water.

They emerged from the surf, refreshed and revived, and warmed their pale bodies at the bonfire that Tristan built in the lavender evening. And when the first stars appeared, the minstrel led his appointed priestess into the cave with a flaming torch from the fire to light the way, his guitar slung over his back. The children followed, tromping naked through the grass, as if they'd been born on the island and had never known civilization.

The cave was cold and damp. Slimy water dripped from a chalky ceiling free of stalactites, pooling around piles of stones assembled by the ancients. A draft howled from some deep fissure beyond the reach of the torchlight. Eventually, they came to a place where a great round stone had been rolled aside to reveal a low cavity in the rock wall. Beyond the stone, a body lay on the ground, wrapped in a shroud.

Tristan swept the torch down beside the mouth of the little cave within a cave, vanquishing the shrouded body to the shadows. He called Noah and Sarah forward, then instructed them to crawl in and recover the treasures.

The children looked frightened for the first time Becca could recall in the hours she'd spent with them on the island, but each taking courage from the other's company, they stooped and entered the low passage. Their voices and actions echoed incoherently, and they emerged a moment later bearing dusty burlap sacks tied with fraying twine.

Tristan patted Sarah on the back of her blonde head, and she beamed up at him. Noah, clutching his sack to his chest, stared expectantly into the deeper darkness beyond the reach of the torchlight, where the body lay unmoving.

Tristan handed Becca the torch and slid the guitar around from where it hung on his back. His brow furrowed in concentration, he coaxed a gentle, yearning melody from the strings, cocking his head to listen as the last note hung in the humid air.

Something slithered along the floor, winding out of the shadows toward the light.

Instinctively, Becca took a step back and touched the scarab pendant through her shirt.

A creature emerged, roughly delineated by the wavering yellow light. It resembled a trio of octopi fused together, the glistening mottled flesh forming a chain of tentacles, bulbs, and eyes. Becca held her breath as she watched it shamble out of the darkness and wrap its limbs around the shrouded body behind the stone.

With alien grace, the creature lifted the body and carried it toward the mouth of the cave, limbs heaving in such a way that it looked as if the shrouded form were floating on gentle waves of black oil.

* * *

The children hummed a mournful hymn as they followed the monstrous pallbearer in a solemn procession to the place on the beach where the bonfire still raged. There, it laid the body on a megalithic slab of pitted volcanic rock, and then withdrew from the heat of the fire. The departing dusk dragged its vestments slowly across the sky. Tristan tossed more driftwood on the fire, sending a shower of sparks up toward the cold heavens. The children gathered in a crescent around the slab.

Tristan gestured at Noah and Sarah, and the children untied the sacks at their feet, tossing aside the twine, and removing items that sparkled in the fire light: a white-gold diadem and necklace adorned with iridescent seashells and fiery opals. The metal was exquisitely carved with lines reminiscent of marine and amphibian anatomy.

The children's humming had tapered off when they took their positions around the slab. Tristan plucked his guitar and they started up again, a song of howling alien vowels with no words.

The sinewy octopoid creature poured itself over the sand like a waterfall of congealing black paint to reach the pair of jewel-bearing children. As the light leached from the sky, Becca could tell even less where the monster's limbs began and ended. Two of the tentacles curled up and received the artifacts from the children. Next the creature glided to Becca. At its approach, a faint voice, sequestered behind a locked door in her mind, urged her to do something—to lash out with the blade she carried—but that voice was dim and distant, drowned out by the dawning sense of awe overwhelming her.

The creature moved like a thing breaking apart and reconstituting itself, and before her eyes could make sense of the motion, it was behind her, its languid limbs sliding up under her shirt and slipping the damp fabric over her head with a delicacy that belied their size and strength, revealing the silver hilt of the dagger jutting out of the waistline of her sea-stained cargo pants.

Becca looked down at the exposed weapon against her pale skin, almost surprised to find it there. She had a vague notion that the sight of it should alarm her, that she should do something to defend herself against the roving tentacles and the minstrel who orchestrated their motions with commands conveyed in the language of the chords and phases he played. But that was *old* thinking; claustrophobic, paranoid, *human* thinking, from a lower limb of the evolutionary tree. A diseased, withering limb.

The tentacles wound around Becca's torso. One caressed the hilt of the dagger where its own form was mimicked in metal; another lifted her hair from the back of her neck, while yet another broke the chain holding the scarab. It fell to the ground at Becca's feet, followed by her bra.

Undulating tentacles placed the sprawling necklace and diadem on her chest and head. Looking down at the dagger, Becca saw that it completed the trinity of power objects, and was in its proper place after all.

The music ceased and the sound of the waves rolled in to fill the void. The black silhouettes of the colossal heads watching from the ridge seemed to melt into the molten sky. Above, the icy light of dead stars was scattered like shattered diamonds cast across black velvet.

The Crimson Minstrel passed behind the slab, gazed at the choir over the shrouded body, and struck the opening chord of the third movement of *The Invisible Symphony.*

The children sang. Their harmony churned the air in waves deep and majestic. It seemed impossible that children could make such a sound. The fire leapt. The mottled tentacles climbed the black slab, and unwrapped the shrouded body that lay upon it.

Tristan's fingers roved the fret board of the lyre guitar, weaving trails of phosphorescence between the strings, sparks leaping from the nails of his right hand swept into a vortex churning in the half-moon sound hole. He looked up, and Becca, turning to follow the direction of his gaze, saw that the maelstrom in the guitar was mirrored by another gathering on the horizon. The bruised clouds cast a noxious light over the sea. Veils of rain parted below them, and it was as if the swirling clouds and rain formed the crown and vestments of a colossal king. It lumbered toward the island, feet thundering on the sea floor, setting tectonic plates trembling at its approach, tidal waves swelling to herald its coming. Slouching toward Rapa Nui, where it was worshipped of old, to be reborn.

* * *

In Boston, musk spread like a toxin through Copley Square, and the Goat Mother moved in the mirrors of the Hancock Tower, flanked by her dark young.

At the quarry in Berlin, New Hampshire, something broke the surface of the water without the aid of a door. It struck its claws into the granite, sending out a spray of rock shards, and climbed from the pit, its scorpion tail swaying behind it, its shadows cast in triplicate beneath the arc lamps as it approached the SPECTRA huts where sensors pinged and klaxons blared.

In a derelict textile mill on the Charles River, and in a stagnant bird bath at an abandoned asylum, and in a meadow in Concord, Massachusetts—where all that remained of the support beams of the Wade House was a fine dust of charcoal on the poisoned weeds and the rubble of foundation stones fractured by jackhammers—in all of these places where the membrane was thin, the denizens of another world stirred and tasted the air, and listened for the reverberations of distant music.

And in the basement of the JFK building at Government Center in Boston, Warwick McDermott gazed through violet-lit shades and bulletproof glass at a soot-smudged mirror in a tarnished antique frame. It was a room he visited often; at least once every three days since Engineering had perfected the shades. He would stand behind the glass and search the mirror's surface for a glimpse of what lurked in its depths.

The mirror, removed from the Wade House before it burned, was the most precious artifact in the agency's collection—a perfect portal. He had dared not risk its use in tests like the one at the Manchester quarry. The stakes would have been too great. Only a minor deity haunted the region beyond the door they'd employed for that experiment. This mirror, however, had revealed to him the presence of another lurker at the threshold since its installation at Government Center, a threat of a far greater order. The bulletproof glass would do nothing to restrain such an entity, but then, the glass was there to protect the mirror from overzealous or paranoid agents. Agents who might harbor sympathies for the Northrup doctrine of destroying such objects. McDermott liked to think he had routed out all personnel of that persuasion, but one could never be certain. Agent Brooks might have been the last of them, and he had apparently drowned in Zadar, although no body had yet been recovered.

Today, as McDermott stared into the mirror, he was not alone. He approached the glass flanked by agents. Behind him, a plasma cannon cycled through power modes, manned by an agent fitted with one of two enhanced pairs of gloves. The other pair was on a SPECTRA jet over the Atlantic, returning home with Agents Kalley and Merrit.

While the bulletproof glass may have offered no protection to the director and the men surrounding him, there were other defenses in place. The legs of the mirror's frame rested on beeswax disks graven with the *Sigillum Dei Aemeth* (the Seal of the Truth of God), an elaborate mandala of angelic names devised by the Elizabethan sorcerer, Dr. John Dee. The metal floor beneath the disks and mirror was laser engraved with additional protective wards, sigils, and divine names in a series of concentric circles dusted with consecrated powders. The agency's think tank of occult scholars had spent a year cross-referencing grimoires seized in Starry Wisdom raids to arrive at the combination most likely to constrain a major manifestation, and McDermott had high confidence in their untested conclusions.

But he had more confidence in the weapon he had refined over the past week. He had seen the video beamed back from Croatia and believed the cannon would have worked, if the ceremony hadn't been interrupted.

So why wasn't he eager to test it?

The choir had vanished into the ocean in Croatia, their ritual incomplete and one voice silenced. But McDermott wasn't naive enough to think the crisis was averted. The apocalypse had only been delayed. Merrit confirmed that Becca Philips was present at the event and working *with*, not against, the choir, in defiance of Brooks' misplaced trust. The music required eight voices, and she could fill the role of the fallen child. It was only a matter of time before the minstrel tried again. And when he did, would weapons like the cannon make any difference? Would this mirror, a kind of canary in a coalmine, reveal that the moment had come by releasing the entity McDermott had glimpsed prowling its depths?

Someone was talking, requesting his attention, but he couldn't seem to pry his gaze from the mirror in which he already saw the greatest horror: an abject failure standing among those who would soon realize it, in front of the pea shooter he'd placed his faith in.

"Sir?" A female voice. "We have a signal from Agent Brooks' wrist unit."

"Brooks?"

"Yes, sir. We have GPS coordinates from his device. He's moving. That is…if he's still alive and wearing it."

McDermott looked away from his glare-clouded reflection, at the agent beside him with the tablet. Stratford. He squinted at her, seething skepticism. What did it matter if they found Brooks' body at this point? "Cadavers do tend to move in ocean currents, Agent Stratford."

"Not this far."

"Where?"

She passed him the tablet, which displayed a tracking icon at roughly -27 degrees South, -109 West. Easter Island. The icon flashed on land, near the coast, less than three miles outside of the remote island's only town, Hanga Roa. McDermott handed the tablet back before Stratford could see it trembling in his hand.

"Do we have anyone in Santiago?" he asked.

"No. That was the first place I checked. The nearest agents are in Mexico City, and even on a light jet, it's at least eight hours from there."

"How long for a fully-equipped team from Houston or L.A.?"

"Ten hours with time for gearing up."

"Too long." His eyes flicked back to the mirror. Had something moved in it? "Other options?" he asked.

Stratford frowned. "Only a precision strike on the island from an F-35 or a Predator. We're moving a satellite into place for imagery as we speak. With respect, sir, we should get you to the command center." She tipped her chin toward the mirror beyond the glass. "There's nothing you can do here if something comes through. Let your men handle it."

A ripple of agitation passed through the small assembly. Something black and viscous bubbled out of the mirror onto the floor of the sealed room. Stratford turned her head and gasped. McDermott took the Tillinghast shades off.

It was still there.

"It's too late," he said.

Stratford dropped the tablet on the floor and stepped away from the director, reaching into her jacket for the service weapon in her shoulder holster.

"Director McDermott, step aside, sir!" the agent at the cannon shouted.

McDermott walked backward, out of the line of fire, keeping his naked eyes on the manifestation the entire time. The entity poured into the glass cell, a pool of iridescence spreading in rivulets toward the walls. A pattern swirled on the surface of the oily material like ten thousand eyes roving in synchronous motion. Some of these expanded into spheres and broke away from the main mass, floating toward the ceiling. Others popped and spattered oil at the glass. McDermott was near the front of the crowd, and a spray of black droplets landed on the back of his hand and the cuff of his shirt, where they smoldered and sent up curling ribbons of white smoke. He cried out and wrapped a flap of his jacket around the burning hand. It came away smeared with blood where the oil had eaten through his flesh like acid. The glass had offered no barrier, was no deterrent for this alien state of matter.

The soup of dark rainbow spheres spread across the floor beyond the glass cell, sending the agents fleeing to the back wall of the room before the substance could touch their shoes and eat through the leather. As the crowd parted around the cannon tripod, they left a channel immediately exploited by the entity. It surged forward, overtaking the cannon, and melting it in seconds. The gunner shook the flipper gloves from his hands as if they were oven mitts that had caught fire. He stumbled and fell, sizzling and liquefying, leaving only a swirl of blood, marrow, and burning hair on the surface of the encroaching pool.

The entity froze in place. All at once, the floating orbs and iridescent eyes swiveled, fixing their unified gaze on the terrified humans huddled against the wall.

It happened quickly after that. Yog Sothoth, Lord of Time and Space, collapsed time in that place.

McDermott could not look away, could not break eye contact with the sphere that scrutinized him. But he felt the effects, saw the symptoms manifest in his flesh and that of the agents around him as their agonized and astonished moans filled the ozone-tinged air.

His skin shriveled, contracted and thinned. His spine compressed and bowed. His hand before his face wrinkled and contorted into a claw, the fingernails growing in yellowing spirals. Tumors sprouted in his bowels; his hair receded and drifted to the floor in white strands; his hearing and eyesight mercifully dimmed as his sinuses filled with the overwhelming odors of putrefaction. His knees gave out and he crumbled to the floor, withering to a desiccated husk, a shriveled mummy curled like a fetus at the edge of the pulsing pool.

* * *

The first fighter jet to reach Easter Island from the *USS Theodore Roosevelt* was an F-15E Strike Eagle. It thundered over the scattered lights of Hanga Roa, leaving the island behind in a flash, then circled around the storm for a southerly approach to the lumbering monster. Captain Glen Datlow eased the throttles two percent as the monster emerged from the weather, causing his stomach to drop like a bunker buster. "Jesus. It's as big as a fucking building," he said to his Weapons Systems Officer over the intercom. "You getting this on the thermographic, Naf?"

In the seat behind him, Lieutenant Nafpliotis pulled up options on a target that was impossible to miss. "I've got it," he said, sending the infrared image from the LANTIRN system to Datlow's HUD. "I tagged the head in two places. That's a head, right?"

"Fuck if I know…" Datlow scanned the screen. Watching the thing move in green pixels was easier than trying to interpret it with his naked eyes through the cockpit glass. At least, it made his eyes ache less. "Yeah…between the bat wings. Gotta be." He switched the red button on the control stick from the video recorder to weapons release mode and let a sidewinder fly.

The missile flared away and vanished into an expanse of what looked like elephant hide covering the dome of the titan's tentacle-fringed skull. A cloud of orange fire bloomed in the dark and Datlow pulled away. By the time they came around for another pass, the thing was reconstituting itself, fragments of amorphous flesh raining inward like a meteor shower, regaining the shape it had held before the strike.

The jet buzzed the creature's congealing head, strafing one of its shoulders with gunfire. A golden eye as large as the aircraft, rolled behind a gelatinous membrane, tracking them as they passed, and Datlow felt his mind shatter under the weight of its baleful gaze.

He laughed into his mask, his voice distorting as it cackled through the intercom.

"Captain, are you all right?" Naf sounded panicked. "*Captain.* Give me control!"

Datlow laughed harder, unclipped his oxygen mask from his helmet and tore it away from his face. Wild-eyed and whooping, he floored the control stick, plunging them into the heart of the abomination.

Chapter 23

Becca sang at the center of a vortex of song. Jewels and precious metals dripped from her breasts, climbed like interwoven vines from her temples toward the stars. She sang and rose up on an escalating wave of ecstasy, every nerve aflame with newly-awakened power.

The Crimson Minstrel led the choir with his instrument, his face a howling abyss of emptiness in the hood of his cloak. Becca could not take her eyes off the permutations of his fingers, the arcane alphabet of chords pulsing signals to the choir—cues of pitch and vibrato, of lull and crescendo. As she watched and listened enraptured, the music guided not only her voice, but her body as well, instructing her in the secrets of how to dance and gesture with the silver dagger, how to carve mandalas in the air with its gleaming blade, how to raise it to its zenith above the sacrificial offering to He who moved between sea and storm, blotting out the southern stars with His shadow.

The other creature, the one she now thought of as her attendant, cradled the sacrificial victim in its tentacles and spun it on its axis, unspooling the dirty white shroud, then laying the bound and gagged body down again on the volcanic stone slab.

The song faltered on the priestess's lips, the dagger poised above the man's bare chest. The tentacles withdrew, and the creature cascaded sideways out of the path of the blade.

She knew this man. He stared up at her in terror and awe. His gun belt and vest had been discarded with his shirt. He was barefoot, clad only in black field pants, his pale freckled skin crusted with salt and sand. He was, in a way, her mirror image, but while she wore white metal wrought in the likeness of kelp, his wrists, ankles, and mouth were wrapped in strips of the real thing. Where she embodied primeval power, he writhed under the knife, arching his back, his bright blue eyes pleading with her.

She knew this man. And she knew something else, something she had forgotten… A melody. A *different* melody. One that would irreparably alter the dark harmony swirling around her, resonating around the globe.

His name was Brooks. She saw him sitting awake at her bedside; saw him carrying a spider rescued from a kitchen sink, throwing a ball for her dog. He was a soldier of sorts, a protector. He was kind. And that was something the Great Old Ones would never be, no matter how many aeons passed on Earth.

The minstrel approached the altar, focusing his cold consciousness on her, willing her to finish the song, to spice the air with infernal harmonics and the scent of hot blood.

Becca released an incoherent cry and brought the dagger down, sweeping the blade across Tristan's throat, releasing a jet of black blood and a gurgling howl. The children, their eyes closed, continued swaying to the rhythm of their song, lost in its currents, even as the blood splashed their faces. Becca pivoted and brought the blade up, retracing the path of its downward arc and severing the strings of the guitar before plunging the tip through the minstrel's chest, a mantra vibrating on her lips.

The crimson robe folded in on itself, collapsing like a ball of crumpled paper at the heart of a fire, a cloud of black specs swarming out of it and scattering on the rising wind. The choral music staggered and lurched, dragging part of her mind along in its wake. Without a conductor or an instrument to guide it, the song stumbled onward, the children shaken but too fevered to stop.

Becca drew a deep breath and added her voice to theirs, guiding the harmony into a new region with the force of her inverted melody. She had forgotten it for a time, but it returned to her now, and as she sang, she twirled, lashing out with the blade, clearing the air around Brooks, hacking the probing tentacles off the creature circling the slab.

Black blood soaked the sand. Forked lightning struck the sea from the roiling clouds. And Great Cthulhu, unfurling vast, tattered wings, tilted his elephantine head and roared in agony at the shattering sky.

The children collapsed, and in the fading echo of the falling beast, a species of silence prevailed in the spaces between wind and waves.

* * *

Brooks carried a torch along the shoreline beneath a river of stars like spilled milk. The storm had lost its energy and scattered to the west, and the waves that had battered the south shore of the island for hours had finally subsided. Becca had cut his bonds with the dagger that now stuck out of the sand beside her where she slept on the beach, the last thing she'd done before passing out among the children. Brooks, seized by fear that the song had killed them, had scampered around the bodies checking for pulses. When he'd verified they were all alive, he rebuilt the faltering fire, lit the discarded torch, and hiked to the cave to retrieve the clothes and gear that had been stripped from him when he'd washed up unconscious at the minstrel's feet.

His watch was waterproof, but he was still surprised when it indicated a satellite link and displayed the local time, as well as a log of attempted calls from Nico Merrit. Brooks called HQ from the mouth of the cave and Merrit answered immediately.

"Brooks. What's happening on the island?"

"It's over," Brooks said. "Why are you answering the director's line? Put him on."

"McDermott's dead. Assistant Director Spiegal, too. And Bill Klinger, Irene Stratford… Jesus, Brooks, it was a massacre. You got me because I'm acting director. I got back after it happened."

Brooks felt the urge to vomit. He held the watch away from his face and took a few slow breaths until the feeling passed.

"You there, Brooks?"

"Yeah. How?"

"Something came through a mirror just after 21:30. They didn't have a chance. It *aged* them to death."

"I don't understand."

"No one does. But it vanished as fast as it manifested. We had sensors pinging at all of the known hotspots at the same time, but it all stopped at once."

"It was Becca," Brooks said. "She put an end to it…did something to the music to knock the spheres out of alignment. How soon can you get us home?"

"There's a team on the way already. Give it six or seven hours."

"Okay."

"Brooks…" On the screen, Merrit held a fist to his lips. Brooks let his finger hover over the watch, let the silence spread between them while Merrit gathered his thoughts. "What I did in Zadar…was the last thing I wanted."

Brooks nodded. He ended the call and walked back to the beach, scanning the sky where satellites roved among the stars. Somewhere over the Pacific was an unmanned vehicle, veering away from a trajectory that had placed it within striking distance. Or maybe it was an aircraft carrier that had been redirected from patrolling the Chilean coast. Something that no longer needed to decimate a children's choir at a World Heritage site.

*   *   *

On the beach, something gleamed amid the crab grass. Brooks swept the torch over the ground until it caught his eye again; Becca's golden scarab. He picked it up by the chain and put it in his pocket. The tiara had fallen from her head in the melee, and he kicked it away from where she slept. The elaborate necklace she wore could wait for morning. For now, he shook the sand out of her discarded shirt, placed it over her slumbering body, and lay down beside her.

For a while he watched the fire burn down, then rolled onto his back and gazed up at the stars and the fissures of darkness between them. Eventually he dozed off, but woke out of habit at the hour when his biological clock was trained to be vigilant. He checked his watch for Boston time: 3:33.

Becca, with no protective wards etched in the drift of sand that served as her pillow, did not sing in her sleep. Neither did she moan in fear or distress. Brooks shone the cold light of his watch on her face. Her eyelids were still, her breathing deep. He was not a religious man, but he said a silent prayer that she and the children would wake in the morning, and then surrendered to sleep.

When he woke again, to sunlight on his face, he could hear the children playing on the beach and feel Becca's limbs wrapped around him. He squinted at the shoreline, and for a second thought he might be dreaming. Noah Petrie was petting a dog, a friendly local mutt with shepherd traits. "Django!" the boy cried, with enough delight in his voice to reassure Brooks that he would be okay after all.

Becca stirred and opened her eyes.

Acknowledgements

I first read H.P. Lovecraft in junior high when I picked up a paperback with a lurid cover, probably as part of a haul that included Stephen King, Peter Straub, and Clive Barker. It felt kind of like finally checking out the bluesman who influenced your favorite rock guitarists. The licks weren't as slick and refined as the modern stuff, but the feeling was there and you could see where it had crept into everything that followed.

I've had a lot of fun riffing on Lovecraft's themes over the course of the SPECTRA Files trilogy. I've tried to expand the Mythos in my own way and highlight where it resonates with contemporary fears. For better or worse, Lovecraft's unique concoction of anxieties and cosmic conceptions is as relevant today as it was in the 1930s, maybe more so.

There are plenty of writers smarter than me contributing to a dialog around the intersection of Lovecraft's work and the problematic views underlying it. By and large, it's a surprisingly diverse and supportive community, and I feel lucky to have found a place in it. I owe a debt to H.P. Lovecraft, not only for the Mythos, but also for the friendships that in some measure I can trace back to picking up that paperback when I was fifteen.

I would also like to thank the following friends, writers, readers, and publishing folks who supported and inspired me over the past three years while I wrote the series: Chuck Killorin, Nick Nafpliotis, Jill Sweeney-Bosa, Jeff Miller, Mike Davis, Pete Rawlik, Chris Kalley, Frank Michaels Errington, Charlene Cocrane, Christopher Golden, Laird Barron, Neils Hobbs, Daniel Braum, Irene Gallo, Christopher C. Payne, and Vincenzo Bilof.

I found invaluable resources along the way in the works of Leslie Klinger, S.T. Joshi, Alan Moore, Daniel Harms, and Michael Bukowski.

As always, my deepest gratitude to Jen and River for constant love and support.

Photo by Jon Colt

DOUGLAS WYNNE is the author of five novels, including *The Devil of Echo Lake, Steel Breeze,* and the SPECTRA Files trilogy. He lives in Massachusetts with his wife and son and a houseful of animals. You can find him on the web at www.dougwynne.com

RED EQUINOX

DOUGLAS WYNNE

31901062615200

CPSIA information can be obtained
at www.ICGtesting.com
Printed in the USA
FFOW03n0327310318
46082897-47041FF

9 781945 373916